THE LEAGUE OF BEASTLY DREADFULS

The Dastardly Deed

WARNING

This book is chock-full of DREADFULS things (Secrets! Danger! Stinky Cheese!) and is NOT suitable for Nice Little Boys and Girls.
READ AT YOUR OWN RISK!

The League of Beastly Dreadfuls

#1 *The League of Beastly Dreadfuls*

#2 *The League of Beastly Dreadfuls: The Dastardly Deed*

#3 *The League of Beastly Dreadfuls: The Witch's Glass*
(Coming Soon!)

THE LEAGUE OF BEASTLY DREADFULS

The Dastardly Deed

· BOOK 2 ·

HOLLY GRANT

pictures by

JOSIE PORTILLO

A Yearling Book

 Published in the United States by Yearling, an imprint of Random House Children's Books, a division of Penguin Random House LLC, New York. Originally published in hardcover in the United States by Random House Children's Books, New York, in 2016.

Yearling and the jumping horse design are registered trademarks of Penguin Random House LLC.

Visit us on the Web! randomhousekids.com

Educators and librarians, for a variety of teaching tools, visit us at RHTeachersLibrarians.com

The Library of Congress has cataloged the hardcover edition of this work as follows:
Grant, Holly.
The dastardly deed : the League of Beastly Dreadfuls, book 2 / Holly Grant ; illustrated by Josie Portillo. — First edition.
pages cm
Summary: Anastasia has barely managed to escape the nefarious clutches of CRUD when they are brought to the underground Cavelands, where she finds out she is Caveland royalty and her family figures into a centuries-old scandal that began with the disappearance of her grandfather.
ISBN 978-0-385-37025-7 (trade) — ISBN 978-0-385-37026-4 (lib. bdg.) — ISBN 978-0-385-37027-1 (ebook)
[1. Orphans—Fiction. 2. Secrets—Fiction. 3. Kidnapping—Fiction. 4. Princesses—Fiction. 5. Humorous stories.] I. Portillo, Josie, illustrator. II. Title.
PZ7.G766757Das 2016 [Fic]—dc23 2015009492

ISBN 978-0-385-37028-8 (pbk.)

Printed in the United States of America
10 9 8 7 6 5 4 3 2 1
First Yearling Edition 2017

Random House Children's Books supports the First Amendment and celebrates the right to read.

CONTENTS

THE LEAGUE OF BEASTLY DREADFULS

The Dastardly Deed

1

S'mores

ALL GREAT ESCAPES require pluck, brains, and courage. If you're lucky, you may also enjoy the convenience of a reliable getaway vehicle.

In this respect, Anastasia McCrumpet was *very* lucky. You might even say that she had won the *jackpot* of escape rides: an all-expenses-paid cruise in a hot-air balloon. And not just *any* hot-air balloon, mind you! The HMB *Flying Fox* was a *chameleonic craft*! This means, dear Reader, that—like a clever chameleon—this balloon transformed to blend in with its surroundings. At the moment in which we join Anastasia, the *Flying Fox* was a superbly stealthy, almost black blue, scintillating with hundreds of starry twinkles and practically invisible against the night sky.

Two other passengers crouched in the wicker balloon basket with Anastasia:

MISS PENELOPE APPLE, librarian extraordinaire and (she had revealed not five minutes earlier) Anastasia's secret aunt;

And the dashing, mustachioed *BALDWIN*, an ally in Anastasia's escape from a fate most terrible. This wonderfully bewhiskered gent was, Anastasia had just discovered, Miss Apple's brother. And that made him Anastasia's secret uncle.

It was a night for learning secrets.

Anastasia itched to learn the biggest secret of all: why had Primrose and Prudence Snodgrass, two celebrated kidnappers of children deemed potentially dangerous, nabbed an absolutely average almost-eleven-year-old from the humble town of Mooselick? Why had two nefarious agents of CRUD (Committee for Rubbing-out Unnatural Dreadfuls) snatched Anastasia from her humdrum life and locked her up in a soggy former lunatic asylum? "Why," she asked, "did Prim and Prude bother with *me*?"

Miss Apple and Baldwin exchanged a Serious Look.

"It's a long story," Baldwin finally said. "And chock-full of scandal and shockers. Real jaw-droppers. Are you sure you want to find out?"

"Tell mc," Anastasia urged. "I want to know."

"Brave girl." Baldwin nodded his approval. "First of all, we're going to need s'mores."

Miss Apple rummaged in the picnic basket she had packed for their balloon voyage.

"Secrets of this caliber," Baldwin explained, "are best revealed under the stars, around a fire, whilst eating s'mores."

"Really?" Anastasia raised her eyebrows.

"I'm utterly serious," her uncle said, and he was. "Why do you think so many children whisper stories around a campfire? There's a proper way to do everything, and you should be particularly methodical whilst revealing whopping great secrets."

"Baldwin's right, dear." Miss Apple tore open a plastic packet of jumbo marshmallows and handed one to Anastasia.

"Too bad Ollie and Quentin aren't here," Anastasia said. "Ollie loves sweets."

Besides, Oliver and Quentin Drybread had plenty of s'mores-worthy secrets of their own. First and foremost, they were *Shadowboys;* that is to say, they possessed a peculiar talent for shifting into shadows. And second, they belonged to a completely confidential, wholly hugger-mugger, so-hush-hush-and-mum's-the-word-only-three-people-in-the-world-knew-about-it, pinky-sworn-to-secrecy league. But we'll get to that later.

Anastasia consoled herself with the hope that they would all gobble plenty of future s'mores around future campfires. Following their daring skedaddle from St. Agony's Asylum, Quentin had promised they would see each other again soon, somewhere at the end of the balloon journey.

"You've seen a great many new things this past month, child," Miss Apple said, passing out sticks. "Boys who turn into shadows! An auntie who transforms into a mischief of mice!"

"An uncle who transmogrifies into a majestic wolf," Baldwin added, spearing his marshmallow.

"Oh, Baldy," Miss Apple said. "You are *so* vain."

"I'm not vain at all." Baldwin poked his marshmallow into the flame of the balloon burner. "I'm simply stating a fact. And by the way, I think *you* make rather a majestic mischief of mice, Penny."

"Me too," Anastasia agreed, remembering the swarm of acrobatic squeakers (all Miss Apple, it had turned out) dancing and leaping and somersaulting through St. Agony's Asylum not one day earlier.

"So you already know," Miss Apple went on, "that there are people who can transform into other creatures."

"Metamorphose," Baldwin said. He pulled his marshmallow from the flame and examined it.

"People who morph," Miss Apple said. "And those people are called . . . *Morfolk*."

"I'm a Morfo," Baldwin said. "Penny's a Morfo."

"And so," Miss Apple added, "is your father."

Anastasia's mouth popped open. Drab little Mr. McCrumpet—a vacuum cleaner salesman who wore orthopedic shoes—was a Morfo? Preposterous! However, she reflected, her father had vanished on the day of her kidnapping. No one knew where he was, but Baldwin and Miss Apple seemed to suspect that CRUD—the villainous ring with whom Prim and Prude worked—had something to do with his disappearance. Clearly there was more to Fred McCrumpet than met the eye.

"Fred morphs into a guinea pig," Miss Apple said.

"A guinea pig?" Anastasia gasped.

"A *magnificent* guinea pig," Baldwin assured her.

Anastasia mulled this over. It explained her dad's special relationship with Muffy, the McCrumpets' pet guinea pig. She recalled how Muffy would squeak to Fred McCrumpet and he would solemnly nod, as though he understood every peep. Speaking of Muffy—

"Where's Muffy?" Anastasia asked.

"She's with Miss Jenkins, dear," Miss Apple said. Miss Jenkins was Anastasia's former fifth-grade teacher. "That woman *adores* rodents. She'll take excellent care of her."

"But Muffy's one of my best friends," Anastasia protested. "Even if she's cranky. Even if she revenge-poops in my shoes."

"I know," Miss Apple said softly. "But we had to leave Muffy in Mooselick. We couldn't involve her in your great escape from St. Agony's."

"And we can't go back to get her now," Baldwin mumbled through a gob of marshmallow and chocolate. "The minions of CRUD will be hunting everywhere for you, and that means they'll be watching all your known associates in Mooselick, including Muffy."

Anastasia blinked to keep tears from spilling onto her cheeks. She couldn't return to Mooselick to hunt for the missing Mr. McCrumpet. She couldn't return to fetch Muffy. She was, dear Reader, at a dizzying Point of No Return, some three thousand feet above the Earth. Anastasia wondered if she would ever see home, or Muffy, or Mr. McCrumpet, again.

"I'm sorry, child." Miss Apple squeezed Anastasia's shoulder. "This is part of the hardship we Morfolk face—Baldwin and your father and I . . . and you, too."

"Me?" Anastasia whispered.

"You've got Morfolk blood, missy," Baldwin said. "You're a Morfo, too."

Anastasia stared at him.

"That's why Prim and Prude kidnapped you. They suspected you were a very dangerous, very beastly Morfo."

"CRUD is a group of people devoted to scouring the world for Morfolk," Miss Apple explained. They take adults—children—"

"There's a special group of lady kidnappers who work to snatch the Morflings," Baldwin said. "Morflings like *you.*"

"But I can't change into a wolf, or a pack of mice, or even a guinea pig!" Anastasia insisted. "I can't even do a cartwheel, for crumb's sake!"

"Most Morfolk children start to shift when they're about eleven years old," Miss Apple said. "So it makes sense that you haven't yet transformed."

"*I* was a late bloomer," Baldwin admitted. "Didn't start morphing until I was nearly *fifteen,* and then I was constantly shifting into a wolf at the most embarrassing times! Ripping through my clothes at the dinner table, and the school dance, and in the middle of math exams! And when you morph back . . . *you're in your birthday suit.*"

Miss Apple nodded. "It's hard to control your morphs when you're just growing into them," she said. "I once morphed during a piano recital."

"But you pulled it off," Baldwin said. "You pulled it off

beautifully! After a moment of stunned silence, Anastasia, your aunt here started hopping up and down on the piano keys and finished 'Flight of the Bumblebee' to a standing ovation!"

Miss Apple shrugged modestly, but a pleased blush crept into her cheeks. "The trills were difficult, but I managed."

"Thank goodness you didn't morph in front of Prim and Prude," Baldwin said to Anastasia. "They would have snuffed you on the spot."

"But why did they wait?" Anastasia asked. "I was stuck in the asylum for over a month. They had plenty of opportunities to—to—"

"It isn't that simple," Miss Apple said. "CRUD kidnappers can't kill anyone until they make a positive Dreadful identification."

"Tons of paperwork," Baldwin said. "They have to document all sorts of things."

"Especially with children," Miss Apple said. "They have to be certain. And as we told you, most Morflings don't start to manifest their Morfolkiness until they're about eleven years old."

"So the kidnappers grab them, and then they wait and watch," Baldwin added gloomily.

"Morfolkiness?" Anastasia asked.

"Shifting, for one," Miss Apple said. "And developing a silver allergy. Once you have the sensitivity, just *touching* silver can make you break out in welts. And if silver enters your bloodstream, you can get a terrible infection. You can die from it."

"Silver is poisonous." Baldwin shuddered. "It's toxic. It's venom. That's how they'll get you: with silver knives—"

"Or silver buckshot." Miss Apple frowned at Baldwin's bullet-grazed ear, bloodied during the daring asylum break-out.

"Or silver teeth." Anastasia thought of the Snodgrass sisters' weird dentures.

"The first rule of being a Morfo: avoid silver like the plague," Baldwin told Anastasia. "Silver is *worse* than plague! Do you understand?"

"Sure," Anastasia said. "But I'm not a Morfo."

"Just give the idea some time, Anastasia," Miss Apple said quietly. "I know it will take a while for you to believe it. And if you don't believe it right away, that's fine. But *do* stay away from silver."

"I guess I should get rid of this silver necklace, then." Anastasia crooked her thumb under her collar and yanked out the chain. "I don't even like it. Prim and Prude gave it to me."

"To check you for silver allergies, no doubt!" Baldwin growled. "Throw that poisonous trinket overboard!"

Anastasia undid the clasp, and then she stood and leaned over the edge of the balloon basket, dangling the necklace out into the starry night. The heart charm swung at the end of its silver strand, its tiny ruby glaring. Anastasia opened her fingers, and the necklace streaked like a tiny shooting star down into the carpet of clouds below them.

"Well," Baldwin said with satisfaction, "that's that!"

Anastasia's mouth stretched into a jaw-crackling yawn. "Are we going to land soon? Where are we going, anyway?"

"To Switzerland!" Baldwin declared. "To jolly, lovely, fantabulous Switzerland! Oh, how I adore Switzerland. I love the rolling green hills. I love the chocolate. I love," he rhapsodized, "the cuckoo clocks. I collect them, you know. I own over two hundred cuckoos."

"*You're* cuckoo," Miss Apple said fondly. "We're going to Switzerland, Anastasia, so you can meet the rest of our family."

"Our family lives in Switzerland?"

"Near a town named Dinkledorf," Miss Apple said.

"Dinkledorf is the quaintest village under sun or stars," Baldwin enthused. "It's *lousy* with charm. There's a master glassblower there who makes the prettiest snow globes you can imagine. . . ."

But Anastasia's exhausted brain box was past imagining pretty snow globes. She had already slipped into moon-colored dreams, and she dreamt them as the HMB *Flying Fox* drifted ever onward into the night, ever closer to her secret family waiting across the sea.

Following Stars

ANASTASIA, PEEPING THROUGH the layers of scarves bundling her face, gazed down at the Atlantic Ocean glimmering far below.

"Whale ho!" Baldwin trumpeted. He jammed a telescope to his eye and leaned dangerously over the edge of the basket. "Whale at three o'clock!"

Anastasia focused her own spyglass just in time to glimpse a tip of fin and the crash of white foam. "Sighted!"

"Cookie at twelve o'clock!" Baldwin yelled. "Mmm. Snickerdoodle. My favorite whale-watching cookies! Thanks, Penny."

Anastasia lowered her telescope. Miss Apple had pulled a tin of cookies from her picnic basket that, like Mary

Poppins's magical carpetbag, burped forth an incredible and endless succession of treasures. "Here you go, dear."

Anastasia munched her snickerdoodle. She had quashed her initial bouts of balloon sickness and was now enjoying hovering above the sea, watching for whales and islands. They had even spotted a cruise ship swarming with what looked like a conga line of ants dancing across its top deck. Of course, the ants were really humans vacationing off the coast of Nova Scotia.

Sipping cocoa from a mug, Anastasia brooded on the previous night's fantastical conversation. "What will *I* change into?" she asked. "Am I going to turn into a guinea pig, like Dad?"

"Aha!" Baldwin grinned. "It sounds like you might just believe that you are, in fact, *One of Us.*"

"Well," Anastasia hedged, "I'm just not saying *I'm Not One of You.*"

"We don't know how you'll shift, my darling," Miss Apple said. "We won't know until it happens. Most Morfolk change into bats. But then there are wolves and mice and shadows and other things."

"Like guinea pigs," Anastasia said.

"Your father is very special, dear. He's the only Morfo I've ever met who transmogrifies into *Cavia porcellus.*" Miss Apple brushed cookie crumbs from Anastasia's collar.

Anastasia fell silent, thinking about Mr. McCrumpet.

Where was he? Had he run away, or had CRUD snatched him? There was, she thought, a chance that her dad was alive somewhere, but she knew this chance was very slim indeed. Anastasia could not imagine her timid father escaping the deadly silver weapons of CRUD's determined agents. Particularly not, she ruminated, if his only defense was changing into a guinea pig.

"Besides," Baldwin said, "you're *half* Morfo, so you're even less predictable."

"It might take you a little longer to start shifting," Miss Apple mused. "And there is a chance you might not shift at all."

"Half Morfo?" Anastasia asked. "So my mom wasn't a Morfo?"

"No, dear. And I'm afraid that's really all we know about her," Miss Apple said. "We never got the chance to meet her. Fred wasn't talking to us at that time, you see."

"But why not?"

"There was a big family fight," Miss Apple said awkwardly. "Fred moved to Mooselick, which is a long way from Switzerland. It took Baldy and me ages to track him down, and by that time . . . your mother was gone."

Anastasia stared into her cocoa.

Secrets, as you may have already discovered, dear Reader, can be many things: delightful, or exciting, or shocking, or awful. One of the secrets Anastasia had learned in the hot-air balloon was shocking *and* awful. Trixie McCrumpet, the woman Anastasia had called *Mom* for almost eleven years, wasn't actually her mom at all. Trixie was Anastasia's stepmother, and she had run away with a podiatrist (foot doctor, that is) a few weeks earlier. Anastasia's real mother had died when she was just a baby.

"Fred was in a sort of daze," Baldwin said. "He just cut himself off from everyone in the family."

"I think he didn't want to be a Morfo anymore," Miss Apple pondered. "He didn't want to remember our—er—our special kind of trouble."

"But even if Fred didn't want to be a Morfo, he *was,*" Baldwin said. "Even if he convinced himself that he was no more than a boring vacuum cleaner salesman. And Morfolk can't just wander around defenseless, you realize. Not with CRUD stalking us."

"That's when Baldwin and I went undercover," Miss Apple said. "I got that librarian position at Mooselick Elementary so I could watch you at school."

"And *I* got a job twisting pretzels at the Mooselick Mall," Baldwin said. "Employee of the Month seven times. Seven!"

"So," Anastasia said, "tell me about this family we're going to meet."

"Your grandmother Wiggy is very excited to meet you," Miss Apple said.

"Wiggy?"

"Short for Wigfreda. It's an old-fashioned name. And speaking of names"—Miss Apple hesitated—"your last name isn't really McCrumpet. It's Merrymoon."

"Merrymoon?"

"That's right. Fred changed his name when he moved to Mooselick. But you're a Merrymoon, dear."

Anastasia Merrymoon? Anastasia squirmed, trying the name on. It didn't fit properly, not quite; it was like wearing someone else's shoes.

"And I'm not actually an Apple. That was my undercover librarian alias," her aunt went on. "I'm a Merrymoon, too."

Anastasia blinked at her. "So . . . should I call you Aunt Penny?"

"You can call me whatever you like."

"Aunt Penny." Anastasia tested the new title. She smiled. "That sounds nice."

"It sounds *beautiful.*" Penny hugged her.

"And you have another aunt," Baldwin sighed, "but once you meet her, you'll wish you didn't."

"Baldwin!" Penny chided.

"Admit it, Penny: Ludowiga's a stinker." Baldwin chomped another snickerdoodle. "Hard to believe she's Fred's twin."

"Twin!" Anastasia exclaimed. "My dad has a twin sister?"

"Yep. But you wouldn't know it just to meet her. She's shaped like a stick insect and has a personality to match."

"Baldwin, that isn't fair," Penny protested. "Stick insects are perfectly pleasant creatures."

Baldwin hooted.

"Ludowiga's daughter is just six months older than you," Penny told Anastasia. "Her name is Saskia."

Anastasia perked up. "So she's my cousin? What's she like?"

Penny shrugged. "We haven't seen her since she was very little. Remember, we haven't been back to Switzerland since *you* were a baby."

"Ah, Switzerland!" Baldwin cried. "I can't wait to go home!"

The balloon trip across the Atlantic was going to take them, Penny estimated, about a week. Luckily the basket was large enough that they weren't *too* cramped. There was even enough room for two people to lie down, snuggled into the plaid flannel sleeping bags Penny had packed for just that purpose. It worked out splendidly, because Penny and Baldwin had to take turns sleeping and piloting the balloon. They used a compass and all kinds of fancy golden gadgets to make sure they were on course, but Baldwin's favorite method, as Anastasia would learn over the next few nights, was the stars.

"The stars are better than any of these man-made trinkets," he whispered to her. "They've been twinkling up there for ages, for longer than any of us has been alive. Find your star and follow it, Anastasia. Trust your star over anybody else's idea of where you should go."

The only disagreeable aspect of the balloon journey was the dilemma of using the bathroom. There *wasn't* a bathroom. Uncomfortable as it was, the passengers aboard the HMB *Flying Fox* had to perch on the edge of the basket and do as nature intended over the side, buttocks exposed to bracing wind and the impolite gaze of curious seagulls. Although Penny had erected a Japanese printed screen to create as much privacy as was possible aboard a hot-air balloon, Anastasia found herself wishing that she had packed her chamber pot from St. Agony's Asylum.

It was all rather like camping, but in the sky. Anastasia snuggled in her sleeping bag with Mr. Bunster, the stuffed bunny she had rescued from the asylum. Baldwin sang funny old sea shanties. Penny studied her maps and compasses. They toasted s'mores and drank cocoa, and at night they followed their stars.

"Land ho!" Baldwin gripped his telescope. "There it is, ladies! Europe!"

He sounded relieved. He had suffered balloon sickness all afternoon, spending several hours on the private side of the Japanese screen and making a painful ruckus that Penny and Anastasia pretended not to hear.

"We're over Newquay, on the coast of Cornwall," Penny said, consulting her diagrams. "We should be in Switzerland in just under two days!"

"Let's take her down a bit, Penny," Baldwin suggested. "We can show Anastasia England from above."

"No-oooo." Penny hesitated. "Too risky."

"Oh come on," Baldwin cajoled. "When are we going to fly over England again? Let's have a little fun."

"Fun!" Penny said. "You won't think it's fun when we're being shot out of the sky!"

"Just for ten minutes," Baldwin pleaded. "CRUD won't spot us in ten minutes. Live a little, Penny! Please? Pretty please?"

"Pretty, pretty please, Aunt Penny?" Anastasia joined in.

"Baldwin, you're a bad influence." Penny yanked a cord on the silk envelope and the HMB *Flying Fox* dipped down toward the Earth.

Anastasia lifted her telescope. Through its superb lens, cars crept against the dark ground like queues of fireflies, and windows twinkled like faraway birthday candles. As they swooped lower, she could even make out strings of colored lights blinking in trees and on the eaves of houses. She thought—although she probably just imagined it—that she could hear, very faint and far away, the sweet, high voices of children singing.

"It's Christmastime," she said slowly. "I'd forgotten all about Christmas."

Baldwin pulled a pocket watch from his coat and peered at it. "By gum, it's *Christmas Eve.* Time certainly flies when you're evading murderous minions."

"Look how lovely Newquay is," Penny said. "Isn't it lovely, Anastasia?"

Anastasia nodded, thinking of the shabby little McCrumpet house. There wouldn't be any Christmas lights blinking upon its roof, because Fred McCrumpet had always been the one to string them up. He had never done a very good job—usually half the bulbs fizzled off and on, and the other half never lit up at all—but he always let Anastasia plug them in the first time, and he had always said in a solemn, proud way, *"Magic!"*

She wiped her nose on the back of her sleeve.

Baldwin looped his arm around Anastasia's shoulders. "Let's have a toast," he said, handing her a thermos of hot chocolate. "To your first Christmas in a hot-air balloon."

Penny raised her mug toward the moon. "And to your first Christmas with Baldy and me."

Baldwin lifted his flask. "And to many, many more."

"Descent in twenty minutes!" Penny rustled a map. "Prepare for landing!"

Through her spyglass, Anastasia followed the balloon's shadow as it glided across the white-peaked mountains and pale hills swelling below. The green and flowered Switzerland that Baldwin had described was, for now, slumbering beneath a blanket of snow.

"My goodness," Penny said. "My glasses are icing over!" She removed her spectacles and blew on the rimed lenses.

Anastasia lowered her telescope, flashing on a peculiar phenomenon from the asylum. "Aunt Penny, do Morfolk—um—breathe frost?"

Penny paused. "No, dear. Why would you ask that?"

"Well . . . *I* do. I breathe frost."

Baldwin grinned. "It's so nippy today we can all see our breath." He demonstrated by huffing a little cloud.

Anastasia shook her head. "At St. Agony's, whenever I breathed on a piece of glass—a window or a picture, and Prim's glasses—it turned into frost."

A Grown-up Glance ricocheted between Penny and Baldwin.

"The asylum was pretty cold, Anastasia," Baldwin said. "No wonder you saw patches of ice! I'm surprised the entire blasted shack wasn't frosted inside like the guts of a crusty old freezer."

"But it made *pictures*," Anastasia insisted. "And words."

"Anastasia," Penny said gently, "you have a marvelous imagination. And it's entirely understandable that your imagination may have—er—invented some fun and fanciful things to help you endure your ordeal at the asylum."

"No harm in it," Baldwin declared. "Why, I made an imaginary friend to help me get through seventh grade! Cuthbert Haberdash. Ah, he was a wonderful chap. His feet smelled, though."

"But I *didn't* imagine it. Watch." Anastasia twirled her telescope and puffed on the lens. As the fog evaporated from the glass, so, too, did her conviction fade. Perhaps her rattled brain *had* embroidered her weeks at St. Agony's. She bit her lip, sheepish.

"Don't feel bad, dear. Imagination is the jewel of intellect." Penny planted a kiss on Anastasia's forehead. "Be thankful yours is rich and bright. Now, we'd better don our alpine gear." She pulled a jumble of padded ski overalls from one of her trunks.

The balloon dipped, inch by inch, toward the tips of the snowcapped trees. Cows tromped in the rolling pastureland, mooing in low cow voices. It was so quiet and still that Anastasia could hear the bells jingling on their collars.

"That's Dinkledorf!" Baldwin pointed at a cluster of houses huddled in a dell. From the balloon, Dinkledorf looked no bigger than the miniature porcelain villages that nestle beneath a Christmas tree.

"We'll land in the fields beyond that grove of pines, and then we'll snowshoe into town," Penny said. "We can't exactly thump down in the middle of Dinkledorf."

"Do you think we'll make it to the cuckoo clock shop before it closes?" Baldwin wheedled. "I'm just itching to buy one of Franz's new cuckoos."

"For all your interest in timepieces, you keep forgetting that we're on a tight schedule." Penny fiddled with a gadget on the burner. "Wiggy is expecting us."

"Franz has marvelous cuckoos," Baldwin told Anastasia. "He descends from the original cuckoosmiths of the German Black Forest, you know."

"Yes," Anastasia said. "I know." Baldwin had already mentioned Franz's cuckoo-clocking forebears several times that afternoon.

"Almost all the cuckoos in my collection are his work," Baldwin went on. "His latest design is *brilliant.* I saw it on his website, cuckooforyou.com. Instead of a bird popping out the door every hour, it's a tiny opera singer, and she belts out the aria from *The Magic Tuba.*"

"Have you ever heard an opera, Anastasia?" Penny asked.

Anastasia had once heard a few seconds of warbly singing on the radio, but her stepmother had shouted, "Turn that ruckus off! If you want to listen to cats fighting, go find an alley!" She didn't mention this to Penny, however. She just shook her head.

"Then we're taking you to one in January," Baldwin announced. "There's going to be a performance of *The Flinging Fledermaus.* Bellagorgon Wata, the world's greatest soprano, stars in a tale of star-crossed lovers and premature death. It's divine. You'll adore it." He flung his scarf over his shoulder.

Anastasia leaned forward and stood on tiptoe to scrutinize her uncle's lapel. "Baldy, I think you have dandruff."

"Dandruff!" Baldwin twisted his chin to peer at the white flakes spangling his jacket. "What the deuce!"

"It's not dandruff!" Penny said. "It's snow!"

And lickety-split, the vanguard of dainty crystals ushered in a squadron of huge kamikaze snowflakes.

"By Zeus's Zamboni, it's coming down fast!" Baldwin exclaimed.

The swollen snow bombs pummeled the silk balloon, slopping slush into the basket below. Baldwin swiped a row of tiny icicles from his mustache. "Should we take her back above the clouds?"

Penny removed her frosted glasses and blinked up at the sky. "No. We need to land soon or we'll blow completely off course."

"We're blowing off course *now*!" Baldwin pointed out.

"Crumbs!" Anastasia's galoshes skidded as the basket pitched and she thumped to her bottom. "What just happened?"

"The basket scraped against a tree!" Penny shouted over the shrilling wind. "We're descending too quickly! All this snow is weighing us down!"

"I say we go back above the clouds and wait for the storm to pass," Baldwin yelled. "It might take an extra day or two—"

"We don't have the fuel! We're almost out!"

At this moment, two alarming things happened. First: the yellow glow of the balloon's flame disappeared entirely. Second: the wicker basket smashed into something with a sickening crunch.

"Hang on to your rumps!" Baldwin hollered. "We're going down!"

3

The Cheesemonger's Secret

OBSERVANT READER, HAVE you ever beheld through the round window of an industrial washing machine the cataclysm of its spin cycle? Anastasia had, and she felt like a sweater churning through the belly of a particularly zesty washer as the world around her kaleidoscoped with scarves and boots and snow as they all went cartwheeling helter-skelter from the basket and down to the ground below.

"We've landed," Penny groaned. "Are you all right?"

"I broke the Japanese screen." Anastasia pulled her head from the smashed panel that had, not one minute before, been a lovely scene of a stork wading through a lily pond. "But I'm okay. Just dizzy." Her stomach lurched as she staggered to her feet, and she wondered where the HMB *Flying Fox* Official Vomit Receptacle might be. She could dimly discern the basket smashed in the snow several yards away.

"Does anyone know where the compass is?" Penny asked.

"The balloon's over there," Baldwin piped up from a nearby snowdrift. Penny waded to the wreck of wicker splinters and began digging through the snow with the intensity of a squirrel seeking its favorite nut.

"Ruff! Ruff!"

"Baldy, is that you?" Anastasia asked.

"No," he said, "but I hear it, too."

Fear surged through Anastasia. As an aspiring detective-veterinarian-artist, she normally loved all beasts of the animal kingdom. However, as the old saying goes, *Once bitten, twice shy,* and while Prim and Prude's vicious poodle platoon hadn't actually managed to chomp Anastasia, they had tried. She hugged herself, shivering. "Do you think it's a guard dog?"

The barking grew louder.

"What if it's a poodle?" Baldwin quavered, wallowing through the snow to Anastasia's side. "You know I'm poodleophobic."

"That's not a poodle!" Penny leapt up. "Würfel! Würfel!"

"Fur . . . full?" Anastasia asked.

"No. *Würfel.* He's—"

Before Penny could properly reply, a shaggy torpedo of doggy smell knocked Anastasia back to the ground.

Something wet and warm rasped against her cheek. She opened her eyes just in time to observe a large glob of slobber splash down to her chin from the grinning jaws of an enormous Saint Bernard. A small barrel with a faucet was riveted to his collar.

"Würfel!" Penny danced a jig of delight.

"You know this dog?" Anastasia croaked as Würfel slopped her face with another canine smooch.

"Indeed we do!" Baldwin said. "Ah, Würfel, you're wearing your barrel. Fine fellow!" He patted Würfel's fluffy pate. "Man's best friend. Penny," he called, "be a dear and find the brandy snifters, won't you?"

Würfel bounded out of sight into the whirling snowflakes, announcing the felled balloonists' arrival with a volley of barks.

Anastasia wiped her face with the back of her mitten. "Do I have any freckles left?"

Baldwin stooped and peered solemnly at her cheeks. "Yes. Quite a few."

"Look!" Anastasia pointed at a golden glow bobbing toward them.

"That must be Rolf," Penny said.

"Who's Rolf?"

"A Morfolk farmer," Baldwin said. "He and Penny have been friends for ages. We were supposed to land in his field, and it appears that we have. What fabulous navigation!"

The light brightened until they could see the silhouette of a man approaching through the bumbling snowflakes, Würfel trotting by his side. "Penelope? Baldwin?"

"Rolf! *Guten Tag!*" Penny yelled, staggering over to him.

"*Guten* what?" Anastasia echoed.

"She's speaking German," Baldwin chuckled. "We've landed in the German-speaking part of Switzerland, girl. A nip of brandy to celebrate!" He plucked Anastasia's cocoa mug from a nearby cushion of snow. "Yoo-hoo! Würfel! Here, boy!"

Penny finished explaining something to Rolf in German and then beamed over at Anastasia. "This," she said, "is our niece."

"Anastasia!" A smile twitched Rolf's blond beard. "*Guten Tag,* little one! It's an honor to meet you. An honor!"

"Thanks," Anastasia said. "It's an—um—honor to meet you, too."

"Want a sip, Penny?" Baldwin asked, pushing the mug beneath Würfel's barrel and twisting the nozzle. "Lovely stuff, brandy. Warms the entrails."

"My entrails are just fine, thank you," Penny sniffed.

"I wouldn't have found you if it weren't for Würfel," Rolf said. "The visibility is awful."

"Do you think we can still snowshoe to the village?" Penny asked.

"Not a chance," Rolf replied. "The drifts are already too high. It's supposed to storm like this for days—you should probably stay at my house until it clears up. And," he added, grinning at Penny, "I have a delicious fondue planned for dinner—enough cheese for an *army* of mice!"

"Fondue?" Penny nibbled her lower lip. "Oh dear. That *is* tempting . . . but Wiggy is waiting for us, and she'll worry if we don't show up. Isn't there some other way into town? I thought you had a dogsled in your barn."

"You'd be welcome to it, except all my huskies are down with a flu," Rolf apologized. "I've got them tucked into bed right now, poor fellows. And Würfel never pulls the sled. Arthritis."

"A dogsled, you say?" Slugging back the last of his brandy, Baldwin lurched through the drifts to hunker on the opposite side of the mangled Japanese screen. His hat whizzed over the top. Then his scarf sailed over, and next his jacket and snowsuit and sweater and pants and even—Anastasia gasped—a pair of red long johns.

"Baldwin, what are you doing?" Penny protested. "You'll freeze to death!"

"Naooot at aoool!" Baldwin howled, galloping from behind the screen. But he was no longer a strapping six-foot-tall specimen of manly manhood; he was, as you have perhaps already guessed, in the form of a big ginger wolf. Würfel grumbled and charged, and he and Baldwin somersaulted through the snow, yodeling and yelping and catching snowflakes on their long pink tongues. It looked like a lot of fun. Anastasia's heart pattered with new, strange stirrings of hope that she, too, one day would metamorphose into a wolf.

"Genius!" Penny said. She collected Baldwin's clothes (minus the long johns) and shoved them into a suitcase. "Let's get you harnessed up, Baldy. Anastasia, do you have everything?"

Anastasia squinted. Spotting the strap of her satchel, she yanked it from a snowdrift and slung it over her shoulder. "Yep."

"My barn's this way." Rolf lifted his lantern and turned to trudge back whence he came. They tramped after him. Well, to be accurate, Anastasia and Penny slogged behind Rolf, and Baldwin and Würfel loped and leapt in joyous doggy fashion. Within a few minutes the shadowy blur of a barn appeared through the flurrying flakes.

"Beware of cow pies," Penny warned Anastasia as they struggled through the door into a musty shed smelling of hay and animals and manure. A few cows eyeballed them grumpily as Penny and Rolf dragged a dogsled from a nearby stall.

"Moo," Anastasia said.

The cows stared at her, steam puffing from their damp nostrils.

Soon Anastasia and Penny were swaddled in heavy blankets, huddled together in the dogsled as Rolf adjusted a harness around Baldwin's furry torso. Anastasia trembled and edged closer to her aunt. Her hands and feet were numb, and she still felt a little wobbly from the balloon's crash landing.

"There." Rolf snugged a leather strap through the final buckle. The bells on the harness jangled softly. "Just leave the sled once you get there," he said, swinging the barn door open. "I'll go fetch it after the storm." He held out the lantern, and Baldwin grasped its handle between his wolfy jaws.

"Thanks ever so much, Rolf," Penny said. "We'll have to meet for a game of Scrabble soon. I still remember your triumph of '97. *Quirked.* Twenty-one points."

"That *was* a good word." Rolf chuckled. "And I have some others up my sleeve. I'll get you with *zincify* next time."

"I'll zincify *you.*" Penny tugged the pompon on Rolf's long knit hat. "All right, we're off! *Auf Wiedersehen!*"

Baldwin galloped forth, the lantern swinging from his muzzle.

"Bye, Würfel!" Anastasia called.

Würfel's barks chased them into the snow and darkness until they grew fainter and fainter and finally petered out completely.

"The village isn't far," Penny said. "Perhaps fifteen minutes. Thank goodness our destination is on the tippy edge of town. I doubt many Dinkledorfers will be out in this storm, but we wouldn't want anyone to see us arrive in a wolf-drawn sleigh."

Snowflakes blurred the outlines of pine trees. Anastasia's head lolled. She closed her eyes and listened to the chiming sleigh bells: *jingle, jingle, jingle, jingle . . .*

"Wake up, dear," Penny murmured. "We're here."

"I think my eyelashes froze together." Anastasia blinked. A narrow cottage appeared through the snow, nestled amongst the pines. Wooden lace trimmed its snowcapped roof, and white Christmas lights twinkled around its frosted windows. It looked just like an oversized gingerbread house. It looked, Anastasia thought, just as a grandmother's house *should* look: snug and sweet and straight out of a storybook.

Penny hopped from the sleigh and tromped to Baldwin's side, peeling off her mittens and setting to the task of unfastening the harness. "Anastasia, dear, can you grab the suitcase?"

Leaving the sled cached in the pine grove of shadow and snow, the trio galumphed through the drifts to the gingerbread-y chalet. Wolfy paws whirling, Baldwin scrabbled a path up the steps to the front door. Penny produced a key from her pocket and coaxed the lock open. "In you go."

The floorboards creaked beneath Anastasia's galoshes. Baldwin padded in behind her, nudging the lantern into her hand. She held it aloft, illuminating the darkened cabin.

Cheese! Slabs of cheese the size of dictionaries! Cheese wheels large as tractor tires! Lumps of luminous white cheese glowing beneath the curved lid of a glass case! Cheese stacked from the wooden countertops to the rafters; cheese crammed in every nook and cranny! Beauteous, splendiferous, magnificent *cheese*!

"Ahhh!" Penny gazed about with all the awe of Aladdin beholding a treasure trove. "Heaven!"

Anastasia crinkled her brow. "*This* is Grandma Wiggy's house? Is she a sometime-mouse, too?"

"No, dear." Penny smiled. "Didn't you see the sign out

front? . . . Oh, it must have been iced over. This is Die Munter Maus."

"Dee . . . what?"

"The Merry Mouse. It's a cheese shop."

"Dinkledo-oo-owoorf is kno-ooown for three things," Baldwin said. "S'moo-oo-res. Snoowoo globes. And cheese."

"This cheese is some of the finest in the world." Penny stroked a nearby wheel as though it were a beloved pet Persian. "See this, Anastasia? Merry Mouse Gruyère. Oh, it's delicious! I would trade all the cheddar in Mooselick for a gram of Merry Mouse. The milk comes fresh from Rolf's cows, you know."

"Does Rolf own this shop?"

Penny shook her head. "No. The Dinkles do. They're a family of master cheesemongers. In fact, Dinkledorf is named after them! This store was founded in the eighteenth century by Klaus Dinkle, history's greatest cheesemonger." Penny's cheeks, already pink with cold, turned even pinker. "He used to send me boxes of lovely cheese balls. So delicious! And he was such a good dancer. Oh, how that man could clog-stomp. Better than anyone for miles."

"But, Aunt Penny . . . ," Anastasia puzzled. "If Klaus Dinkle lived three hundred years ago, how could he have sent you cheese balls?"

"Morfolk live long lives," Penny said. "Most of us live centuries."

Anastasia goggled. "How old are *you*?"

"Two hundred and seventy-six."

"Crumbs! You're *ancient*!"

"Your father is even older than me, dear," Penny chuckled. "By four years."

"I'm the baby oow-oof the family," Baldwin piped up, padding behind an enormous barrel brimming with cheese balls. "I'm awooonly two hundred and seventy-three. Penny, I'll take my clo-oothes now."

Penny fished his gear from her suitcase and tossed it to him.

"Avert yoo-oour eyes, ladies."

"One of the—er—trickier aspects of metamorphosing is that your clothing doesn't change with you," Penny explained.

"I had high hopes with the invention of spandex," Baldwin called. "I thought maybe a Morfolk tailor could design a suit that would fit both my human and wolf forms. But we conceded defeat after I ripped through five prototypes." He eased from behind the wooden cask, fully dressed. "Hmm. Maybe we should take a cheese ball for the road."

"When you say human form," Anastasia said slowly, "do you mean you're *not* a human?"

Penny hesitated. "We do have many human qualities . . . but no, we're not exactly human."

"I guess you *couldn't* be," Anastasia pondered. "Not if you live for hundreds of years!"

Penny sighed. "I'm sure it must seem very strange to you, Anastasia, but all creatures have different life spans. Butterflies only live a few weeks, and tortoises can live over a century."

"How long will *I* live?" Anastasia asked.

There was another uncomfortable pause.

"We don't really know," Penny finally answered, squeezing Anastasia's shoulder. "You're the only half Morfo we've met."

"The most important thing about life," Baldwin said softly, "is the *quality,* not the quantity."

Penny nodded. "In that respect, life is very like cheese." She patted one of Anastasia's braids. "Now come with me, dear. We have something interesting to show you." She weaved through the cramped aisles to a little door at the back of the shop. She opened the door and started down a staircase, and Anastasia and Baldwin followed her to a long room with a rocky ceiling and rocky walls. Wooden racks lined this cellar, their shelves sagging beneath great hulking wheels of cheese.

"Is this—a cave?" Anastasia cricked her neck to peer around the peculiar bunker.

"Indeed it is!" Penny said. "A *cheese* cave."

"Cheese needs to ripen and age," Baldwin said. "And this cave is chock-full of splendid minerals and bacteria just right for flavoring the cheese."

"And it's just the right temperature," Penny said.

"It's *cold,*" Anastasia chattered.

"People have been cave-aging cheese for thousands of years," Penny thrilled.

"Switzerland is laced with these wonderful caves," Baldwin said. "These hills and mountains are just like Swiss cheese: full of holes."

"That's interesting," Anastasia said politely. "But why are we here, exactly? Are we getting a snack before going to Wiggy's?"

Baldwin's eyes twinkled. "There's more in these caves than cheese, my dear girl. See this rack?"

"Ye-es," Anastasia said.

"It looks just like all the other racks in this cellar, doesn't it? But it's different. It's more than just a rack of cheese." He pushed on the second and third shelves, and the entire case shifted inward an inch or so. Then he released his hands, and the case pivoted to reveal a fissure in the cave wall. *"It's also a secret door."*

The secret door was more of a *hole,* really. It was rather like an enormous mouse hole. However, for Anastasia, an aspiring detective-veterinarian-artist, the curious cranny triggered all sorts of snoopy gumshoe instincts. She knew from reading Francie Dewdrop mysteries that hidden portals opened onto mysterious and magical places. In *The Case of the Buccaneer's Cipher,* for example, Francie discovered an intriguing hallway behind a bookcase, and that hallway led to a chamber full of stolen Aztec gold.

"Take a look," Baldwin said.

Anastasia crouched to poke the lantern closer, letting its pale lamplight spill out onto a spiral of stone steps.

"Where does this go?" she breathed.

"That," Baldwin said, "is the way to Grandmother's house."

4

Stardust Cavern

BEFORE ANASTASIA COULD ask "Why is there a secret stairwell in the Merry Mouse cheese cave?" or "Why would Grandma Wiggy be down there, wherever there is?" or even "When are we going to take a bathroom break?" Penny stooped to scramble into the hole. "Come along, dear!"

Anastasia waffled just one heartbeat, and then she shifted her satchel between her shoulder blades and climbed into the stairwell. Baldwin squeezed in after her, reaching back to pull the cheese case snugly behind them.

"This staircase has exactly ninety-nine steps," Penny said. "And they're narrow and steep, so please be careful."

"My friend Basil once fell down the whole shebang," Baldwin said. "Ah, what a night that was! We had some wonderful fun at the Dinkledorf pub before he broke his arm."

There wasn't a railing, so Anastasia steadied herself by sliding one palm along the stairwell's clammy, curving inner wall. Down, down, down they went. *Zither, whoosh, swizzle,* hummed their snow pants. The air was cold and damp and left a strange, gritty taste on Anastasia's tongue.

"Where are we going, exactly?" she asked.

"Nowhere Special," Penny said.

"It must be a *little* special if we have to take a secret staircase to get there," Anastasia reasoned.

"No, dear. Nowhere Special. It's the name of the city we're going to," Penny said. "We'll be safe from CRUD there."

"An underground city?" Anastasia squeaked.

"A *secret* underground city," Baldwin corrected her. "It's a shame we don't have s'mores and a campfire, because the history of Nowhere Special is long and fascinating and just *dripping* with delectable secrets."

"It's dripping, all right," Anastasia observed as a chilly droplet fell from the rocky ceiling and splashed on her nose.

"We're coming to the bottom," Penny said. "Ninety-eight . . . ninety-nine . . ."

The stairwell yawned into a low, craggy cavern. In this cavern was a man, sitting on a little chair and examining his fingernails by the glow of a lantern perched on his knee.

When he saw them, he jumped up and clicked his heels. "Salutations!"

"Hello, Belfry!" Baldwin called. "How have you been this past decade?"

"Very well, Your Most Excellent," Belfry said. He was wearing a tri-corner hat, a stiff black suit with trousers that ended just below his knees, and white hose, and his long hair was arranged in sausagey white curls tied back in a black bow. He looked, Anastasia thought, rather like paintings she had seen of George Washington.

"Presenting our Most Excellent Niece, Anastasia!" Baldwin said, clapping her shoulder. Belfry bowed at the waist. Then he turned and pressed his lantern into the darkness, illuminating a boat bobbing in a canal behind his chair. The boat was long and black. It was just wide enough for two people to squeeze in side by side, provided neither one had a very large bottom.

"Last one in is a rotten egg!" Baldwin crowed, taking a long-legged leap into the craft and nearly capsizing it in the process. "Here, Anastasia; alley-oop!"

"Keep your hands and feet inside the gondola," Belfry intoned as she squished in next to Baldwin. "The eels have been particularly active tonight."

"Eels?" Anastasia yawped.

"*Electric* eels," Belfry added somberly.

Penny hopped to the seat in front of them, and Belfry

followed, hanging his lantern on a hook curling from the boat's prow. "Virgil!"

A dark shape detached itself from the shadows and fluttered to land on the tip of Belfry's hat, swinging to dangle upside down.

"Is that a *bat*?" Anastasia gasped.

"There are lots of bats down here," Penny said. "I'm glad you like animals so much!"

Belfry untethered the boat and grabbed the handle of a long oar, and they glided into the gloom.

"Your Most Excellent?" Anastasia whispered to Baldwin. "Is that how people say *sir* down here?"

Baldwin shrugged and smiled.

"Mind your heads," Belfry cautioned as the gondola slid into a tunnel.

"There are tunnels all over the Cavelands," Penny said. "Some of them link to the aqueduct system, and some of them are dry."

Faint greenish light gleamed ahead, and it grew brighter and brighter until the channel blurted them into another cavern, and Belfry bellowed, much like a trolley conductor announcing stops, "Bacon Grotto."

Big rock formations bristled from Bacon Grotto's vault. "Those are stalactites," Baldwin said. "They take thousands of years to form. They're even older than your aunt here, Anastasia!"

“Oh, Baldwin!” Penny rolled her eyes. “But it’s true that they’re old.”

“They start with just a bitty drop of water on the ceiling,” Baldwin said.

“There’s a little bit of mineral mixed in,” Penny explained. “Each drip leaves behind a smidgen of limestone, and over time the limestone builds up to form those spikes.”

“What about those?” Anastasia asked as they passed some crags steepling from a stone ledge.

“Stalagmites,” Penny said. “When the stalactite dribbles onto the cave floor, it splashes and leaves some limestone behind. Eventually the drops grow upward into a stalagmite.”

“Sometimes the stalactite grows so long and the stalagmite grows so tall that they meet in the middle and kiss!” Baldwin said, winking.

"What's that glowing green stuff?" Anastasia asked. "It looks like nuclear mold."

"It's phosphorescent moss," Baldwin said. "And those blinky little lights up there? Twinkle beetles. They blink like that to attract their girlfriends, randy fellows!"

"Prrrrp! Squee!" Belfry piped up. Anastasia boggled as Virgil screaked in return, then rustled his wings and zoomed out of view.

"Virgil is a courier, you see," Penny said.

"Sort of like a singing telegram," Baldwin added. "We don't have telephones down here."

"Or electricity," Penny said. "Everything is lit by lamps and candles, and we have to do things the old-fashioned way. And we use bats to send messages.

Virgil just flew ahead to tell Wiggy we're almost home."

"Belfry *talked* to that bat? And told him all that?" Anastasia said. "And Virgil is going to—to *squeak* the message to Grandma?"

"Precisely," Baldwin said. "They were speaking Echolalia, the ancient bat tongue."

Belfry churned his oar, propelling the gondola from Bacon Grotto and down another dark conduit. The lantern swung to and fro, its reflection warping on the rippling water.

"Look!" Baldwin tugged one of Anastasia's braids, tilting her gaze up to the stalactites. A platoon of enormous bats, their wings spread to reveal steel-tinseled torsos, hung from the scraggy dripstone.

"What are they wearing?" Anastasia squinted at the creatures' strange vests.

"Chain-mail armor," Baldwin said. "They're Royal Guard Bats."

"They're called flying foxes, but of course they aren't foxes at all," Penny said. "They're fruit bats."

"Just try to make a Royal Guard Bat laugh," Baldwin said. "You can't! You can't even make them *smile* when they're on duty. These bats are very professional. Highly trained! Just watch!"

"Oh, bother. Anastasia, brace yourself for some very bad jokes," Penny warned.

"Here's a bit of fruit-themed humor for you boys," Baldwin called. "What do you call a shoe made from a banana?"

"A flip-flop?" Anastasia guessed.

"Good try, but no cigar," Baldwin said. "The correct response is: a *slipper*!"

"Baldwin, that was pathetic," Penny chided. "Did you make that up yourself?"

The bats didn't react at all. They were still as stone, their eyes glittering in the lamplight.

"See?" Baldwin said. "Not a smile! Not a snicker! These bats are stoic as heck."

"We're not smiling, either," Penny said, even though she was.

Belfry cleared his throat. "Next stop: Stardust Cavern."

Reader, have you ever—perhaps in a great cathedral, or observatory, or state capitol building—beheld a super-colossal vault? Stardust Cavern outsized any such man-made rotunda, and still its splendor surpassed its scope: every inch of it was splendiferous. Anastasia fancied they'd sailed into the belly of a star. Aglitter with snowy-white minerals, a-twinkle with thousands of candles, the luminous wonderland doubled in the silver lagoon carpeting its depths like a wall-to-wall mirror. From the center of this lagoon rose a castle, and a most phantasmagorical castle it was. Its domes puffed like the crowns of soft-serve ice cream cones, and its towers swirled like jet streams tootled by daring stunt planes.

"What *is* that place?" Anastasia breathed.

"Cavepearl Palace," Penny said.

"Home," Baldwin added. "Not too shabby, eh?"

"Home?" Anastasia exclaimed. "*Our* home?"

"Yes, dear." Penny's lips twitched in a silent librarian

giggle. "You see, your grandmother Wiggy is queen of the Cavelands. And that makes Baldy a prince, and me a princess."

"And you're a princess, too, Anastasia," Baldwin said.

"Biscuit crumbs! A *princess*? *Me*?"

Her head reeled. Freckled, tragically flatulent Anastasia McCrumpet (or Merrymoon), *royalty*? Absurd! Codswallop! Dottier, even, than the notion that she might one day turn into a mouse or bat or guinea pig!

"We didn't tell you earlier," Penny apologized, "because we didn't want to overwhelm you with everything all at once."

"And my dad is—"

"A prince," Penny said.

"Gosh, it's nice to be home," Baldwin said. "We've been abovecaves for ten years, Penny. Think of that."

A low sob rippled through the cavern.

Anastasia patted Baldwin's arm. "It's okay to cry. I know what it's like to be homesick, too."

"I'm *not* crying," Baldwin insisted. "Look at my eyes. See? Dry as a desert."

Boohoo. Boooohooooboooo.

Anastasia turned. "Was that you, Aunt Penny?"

"No, dear."

"You're merely hearing the lagoon, Princess," Belfry said.

"Ah! I'd almost forgotten," Baldwin exclaimed. "This is the Gloomy Lagoon, Anastasia. It's always moping and weeping. Sometimes it actually *bawls,* which is very unpleasant." A wail rose from the silvery water. "Oh, stop your blubbering."

"But how can *water* be sad?" Anastasia quizzed.

"Mystery of nature." Baldwin shrugged.

A fleet of black gondolas bobbed beside a dock stretching, like a snowy lane, from the palace entrance. Belfry eased his craft alongside this dark flotilla. "Your Excellencies."

"Thanks ever so much for the ride, Belfry," Penny said.

The royals trod the pier to an arch flanked by two Royal Guard Bats and passed through this into a shadowy corridor. Candles guttered in nooks in the rippling rock walls, and crystal spikes bristled from the ceiling. Penny drew her face close to Anastasia's ear. "You mustn't be nervous," she murmured. "Wiggy is very serious, but she's also kind."

"And don't let her eyes frighten you," Baldwin cautioned.

"Why would her *eyes* frighten me?" Anastasia asked, but Penny put her index finger to her pursed lips.

"Look," she whispered. "There she is."

5

The Crystal Crown

ANASTASIA'S GALOSHES SQUEAKED as she edged into a forest of twisted stalagmites and shadows and golden candelabra the size of small trees. At the far end of this weird throne room glittered a quartz-studded crevice, and inside this crevice sat a silent figure dressed all in white, surrounded by bats. A crown of tall crystalline spikes crested her white-gold head, and a lace collar puffed around her neck like an enormous snowflake. Anastasia gaped at this mysterious lady: the smooth, solemn face unlike the face of any grandmother she had ever imagined; the queenly dress, voluminous skirts ballooning a good three feet from each hip.

The queen studied Anastasia, too. Her unblinking mirror-colored eyes fastened upon our young heroine, and there they stayed, flaring every few moments with strange light. Anastasia's skin began to prickle. Was the queen counting her freckles? She shifted her weight and her snow pants made an embarrassing noise.

Finally the queen spoke: "Granddaughter."

Anastasia tiptoed forth.

Wiggy reached out and gently lifted Anastasia's chin. "So this," she said thoughtfully, "is Anastasia." The name *Anastasia* sounded utterly lovely strumming from the queen's regal vocal cords, as though it were the title of a dainty princess living in a fairy tale castle of mists and snow, and not some fifth grader with mousy-brown hair and tragic flatulence.

The queen's attention shifted to Penny and Baldwin. "My children. You've been gone so very long, and you've traveled so very far."

Penny knelt to kiss the gobstopper-big opal curiously aglimmer on the queen's forefinger, and then Baldwin did the same. It seemed, to Anastasia, an awfully strange way to greet one's mother, especially after ten years away from home. Maybe the queen didn't want people crumpling her fancy collar with hugs. Or maybe, Anastasia reflected, the queen just wasn't the hugging type.

"How does the evening find you?" Wiggy asked.

"Famished." Baldwin clutched his stomach.

"Of course." Wiggy rose with a whisper of white silk, and the cortege of bats rustled from the alcove. "Nourishment at the end of a long journey. At ease, Ugo."

Anastasia jumped as a man sidled into view. He was half-hidden in the gloom, for he was garbed in gloom-colored finery, but he smiled and she caught the glint of sharp teeth.

"Your Wigginess," this man said, bowing low. "I am, eternally, in your service."

And he withdrew into the darkness.

"That was Lord Monkfish," Penny told Anastasia as they followed Wiggy and her bats from the throne room. "He's Wiggy's top adviser."

"And he's also a real downer," Baldwin muttered. "If you ever want someone to poop on your parade, just summon old Ugo."

The queen led them to a dining hall, where her cloud of bats flitted to roost from a chandelier illuminating a glass table long as an ice-rimed river. Wiggy glided to its head, and a white-wigged fellow scrambled to pull out her chair. Three more servants slid out three more chairs for the rest of the royal diners, and Anastasia took a cautious seat. She sneaked a sideways glance at the queen. How in blue blazes could this fanciful figure be Fred McCrumpet's mother?

"What would you like to eat, Anastasia?" Wiggy asked. "The cooks can prepare almost anything. Lobster thermidor? Caviar? Escargot?"

"Fish eggs," Baldwin translated. "Snails."

"Snails?" Anastasia gasped. "Why would anyone eat *snails*? Could we—could we just have pizza?"

"Three pizzas, Rawlins," Wiggy told the footman by her elbow. "What toppings?"

"Pepperoni and pineapple," Anastasia said. "And ham. And honey for the crusts." Remembering her manners, she added a princessy "If you please."

"And my usual veggie deluxe," Baldwin said.

Wiggy waved her hand and Rawlins spun on his heel and strode from the room.

The queen turned to Penny and Baldwin. "How were your travels?"

Baldwin cleared his throat. "We got caught in a blizzard, Your Mommyness. It was pretty bumpy for a few minutes, but we landed right on course. Nothing broken. Except for the balloon."

"So you weren't injured?"

"CRUD got Baldy in the ear with silver buckshot," Penny piped up, and Baldwin shot her a scowl. The scowl said: *tattletale.*

"How bad is it?"

Baldwin grumbled and tucked his hair back from his face.

"Baldy!" Penny cried. "It's gotten *much* worse! Why, your earlobe is simply *festering*!"

"We'll send for the doctor." Wiggy chirruped, and one of the bats dangling from the chandelier whizzed off with the message. "He'll salve your ear tonight."

"But I don't like Dr. Lungwort!" Baldwin quibbled. "And silver salve *stings*!"

"No arguments, Baldwin," Wiggy said. "You don't want to lose your ear, do you?"

"I have *two* of them, don't I?"

"Ah! Dinner!" Wiggy announced as a line of attendants filed into the hall, each one bearing a domed platter. White-gloved hands whirred root beer floats and piping-hot pizzas to the table. It was Anastasia's first real, sit-down-at-a-table meal in months, and she forgot all about the balloon crash, and the Cavelands, and even the slightly frightening queen sitting not two yards away. It was all pizza and root beer and bliss. Then, sitting back with a hiccup, she glimpsed a small black bat alight on Wiggy's lace collar. The bat peeped, and the queen's eyes flashed.

"Bring them in."

The bat zipped away.

"Anastasia, your cousin Saskia Loondorfer has just

returned from Paris, where she has been studying art for the last school term," Wiggy said. "I'm pleased that you two will meet tonight."

"She likes art?" Anastasia said. "So do I."

"I haven't seen Saskia since she was a baby," Baldwin said. "Tell me, Your Mommyness, is she still very fond of clawing?"

"Clawing?" Anastasia echoed.

"Like a velociraptor," Baldwin warned. "If she goes for your throat, don't hesitate to defend yourself. Use your fork."

"Well, well," hissed a voice at the end of the dining hall. "The mouse and wolf return."

Baldwin rolled his eyes at Anastasia, and then he twisted in his chair to grin at the froufrou-gowned woman at the threshold. She was very tall, and the white wig towering from her head made her seem even taller. Anastasia had never seen such a wig. It was at least three feet high, and a dozen small bats rustled amongst the curls.

"Greetings, Loodie!" Baldwin hallooed. "How we've missed you, lo these ten years!"

Ludowiga sniffed. Then she sailed into the dining room, trailing in her wake a blond girl in a satin dress.

"Your Mommyness." Ludowiga curtsied.

Saskia curtsied, too. "Your Grandwigginess." But her gaze was fixed on Anastasia, and Anastasia gawped back. Her cousin's pale hair cascaded down her back like a fall of moonshine, and her eyelashes were long as pine needles.

"You look just like a princess," Anastasia blurted. "Like a princess in a storybook."

"I *am* a princess." Saskia burst into tinkly laughter. It sounded like someone had rammed a music box behind her tonsils.

"So this is the little Anastasia we've all been so curious about," Ludowiga said. "Welcome, my dear." Her mouth pressed into a smile so thin it was a slit.

Saskia turned to her mother. "I thought you said she was my age."

"She is," Penny said, putting her hand on Anastasia's shoulder. "She'll be turning eleven in a couple of months."

"So, cousin," Saskia drawled, "can you metamorphose yet?"

Anastasia's voice lumped, like a piece of super-sticky taffy, somewhere behind her molars. She shook her head.

"You can't turn into a bat or a shadow or"—Saskia's scrutiny traveled from Anastasia's mussed hair to her dripping galoshes and back up again—"a rat?"

"There's nothing wrong with rats," Penny said crisply. "Or any rodent, for that matter."

"Oh, of *course* not," Ludowiga said. "Why, our own brother Fred shifts into a guinea pig! It's a marvelous shape. So . . . *nonthreatening.*"

"I metamorphosed in Paris. Madame Legrand says I shift like a fourteen-year-old." Saskia tossed her hair to reveal a dainty bat clinging to her collar.

"You've always been advanced for your age," Ludowiga said.

"Indeed you have," Baldwin said. "I remember you scratched me like a full-grown Siberian tiger when you were only four months old."

"Remember, Saskia," Ludowiga said, ignoring him, "Anastasia is a Halfling, and as such she won't develop at the same rate as you. Why, she may never metamorphose at all."

"Isn't that funny, Mother?" Saskia asked. "A *Halfling* princess."

"Very funny." But Ludowiga wasn't smiling.

"In terms of Anastasia's *development,*" Wiggy spoke up, "I am hoping, Ludowiga, that you will tutor her in matters of Cavelands dress and decorum."

"Your Mommyness," Penny protested, "Ludowiga is not . . . that is to say . . . I'm sure that Baldy and I could help Anastasia acclimate."

"And so you shall," Wiggy replied. "But Anastasia has much to learn, and Ludowiga is particularly well versed in ceremony. Let us not forget, Anastasia is completely unschooled in courtly manners."

"*I'm* mannerly," Baldwin complained. "And so is Penny."

"Nonsense, Baldwin. Neither of you has ever taken an interest in politesse." Ludowiga smirked. "Worry not, Your Mommyness. I shall take the burden of the princess's finishing lessons upon myself."

"Excellent," Wiggy said. Anastasia sank a little lower in her seat.

"Speaking of dress," Ludowiga said, "what an unusual coat you have, Anastasia."

"Oh." Anastasia finally found her voice. "I actually hate fur coats, because I love animals. I think it's wrong to—"

Ludowiga swooped down, her pointed nose inches from the collar. She sniffed.

"Um." Anastasia froze. Perhaps smelling one another was a Morfolk courtesy? Maybe her etiquette lessons were starting already.

"What kind of fur is this?" Ludowiga demanded.

"I—I don't really know. I found it in a wardrobe at the asylum—"

Ludowiga's thin nostrils shrilled. "This coat is *Morfolk.*"

"What?" Penny cried.

"You're wearing a Morfolk coat." Ludowiga glared at

Anastasia. "That's the fur of a Morfo skinned when he was in wolf form."

"Disgusting!" Saskia said.

"A Morfolk coat?" Anastasia leapt from her chair in a panic, tearing back the furry lapels.

"Coats like that are illegal," Ludowiga spat. "Where did you say you got it? From those humans with whom you've been hobnobbing?"

"You know full well that Anastasia wasn't *hobnobbing* with anyone," Penny objected. "She was abducted and held captive."

"Those old crab apples practically starved her to death, and she had to use a *chamber pot,*" Baldwin bristled.

The coat slithered to the floor. "I—I didn't know," Anastasia stammered, tears prickling her eyes.

"It's all right, dear." Penny hopped up and hugged her tightly. "I didn't know, either."

"Well," Ludowiga snapped, "in the future, Princess, I trust you will avoid wearing the fur of our dead fellows. We wouldn't want the public to question your loyalties." Her eyes narrowed. "After all, we've never had a Halfling in the palace before."

"Nobody's going to question Anastasia's loyalties," Baldwin scoffed.

Ludowiga patted her wig. "Saskia, we're going to be late for the Duchess of Dunlop's banquet."

“It’s a welcome-back party,” Saskia simpered. “Sorry I can’t chitchat more with you tonight, Anastasia, but I’m the guest of honor.”

The Loondorfers both curtsied to Wiggy, and then they swept from the dining hall with nary a backward glance.

“Anastasia,” Penny said, “you mustn’t feel bad about wearing that coat.”

“But I *do*,” Anastasia quavered. “I’ve been wearing it for almost two whole months.”

“And it kept you warm and cozy. I’m sure that the Morfo who lost it would be glad to know this coat helped a victim of CRUD,” Baldwin said.

“Binkley, remove this coat,” Wiggy said softly, and a footman darted forward to whisk away the fur. The queen turned her strange eyes to Anastasia. “You must be tired, my child. Let’s summon your bat-in-waiting, and she can show you to your cavern.” She whistled. “Your bat-in-waiting, Anastasia, will henceforth accompany you everywhere.”

“Is she like a pet?” Anastasia, lover of all creatures great and small, perked up.

“No; your bat-in-waiting is your *companion*. Your *lady*. These bats are *my* ladies.” She indicated the fuzzy brood hanging from the chandelier.

“Were the bats in Ludowiga’s wig her—um—ladies?”

Wiggy nodded. “The bats-in-waiting descend from the Great Bat of North Cave, a noble line renowned for dignity and grace—*good heavens!*" She broke off as a brown puff catapulted over her crown and crash-landed in the middle of her plate. "Gracious. Anastasia, allow me to present your bat-in-waiting, Pippistrella."

Pippistrella rustled her wings. "Squeak!"

The princess studied her scruffy lady in mute admiration. She reminded Anastasia, somehow, of Muffy. Was Pippistrella prone to revenge pooping, too? Were bats-in-waiting *allowed* to revenge-poop? Anastasia's heart warmed as Pippistrella capsized a goblet, splashing root beer across the tabletop. A *clumsy* damsel! In that respect, they were two peas in a pod.

Anastasia smiled.

"Pippistrella will guide you to your chamber. It's your father's old room." Wiggy rustled in the folds of her skirt and withdrew a key, which she pressed into Anastasia's palm. It was heavy and gold and capped with a large purple crystal.

"While Pippistrella understands English, she obviously can't speak it," Wiggy went on. "You'll begin Echolalia lessons soon, but in the meantime you'll just have to work out some form of communication."

Anastasia turned the key over in her hand. Keen as she

was to see the room that this glorious key would unlock, she did not relish the prospect of wandering through a spooky underground palace. "Well . . . good night." She hugged Penny, and then she hugged Baldwin. After a moment's hesitation, she aimed a curtsy in Wiggy's direction.

Pippistrella peeled herself from the queen's plate and flapped from the dining hall, and Anastasia hurried after her into a grand hallway chockablock with glass globes. They were snow globes, Anastasia saw. She drew her nose close to one, peering at the tiny drowned world: a Japanese pagoda clasped between miniature cherry trees. The next one: a dinky village of houses no bigger than thimbles. Was it Dinkledorf? Beneath her gaze, the artificial snowflakes began to quiver and flurry, and then they whirled. She twisted to behold the other globes and saw that they, too, churned with their individual blizzards. Magical!

As she watched the swirling twinkles, Anastasia's memory spun back to the frosty pictures she had puffed—or fancied she had puffed—upon panes of glass at St. Agony's Asylum. Penny and Baldwin reckoned Anastasia's addled noodle had projected the delicate designs upon her shadowy prison. Her brow crinkled. Was her imagination *really* so dextrous, so nimble?

"I didn't want to discuss Fred in front of Anastasia." Wiggy's murmur floated from the dining room. "Have you heard anything? Found anything?"

Hark! All of Anastasia's fine eavesdropper instincts galvanized. Holding her breath, she rotated her ear toward the hushed voices.

"No, Your Mommyness," Baldwin said. "He just disappeared."

"Is there a hope—the faintest hope—that he's alive?" Wiggy asked.

Anastasia's pulse pummeled her ribs. The snow globes quaked, their Lilliputian tempests building.

"There is a chance," Penny finally said. "We have our top agents hunting for him, but you already know that."

"If only Nicodemus were here!" Wiggy lamented. "*He* could find Fred. His blood-and-ink compass never fails; *never.* Of course," she added sadly, "the chance of finding Nicodemus is even slimmer than that of finding Fred."

The globe by Anastasia's elbow rattled dangerously near the edge of its pedestal. She swooped it to her chest, straining her eardrums for any last dribble of secret conversation. But it seemed Dr. Lungwort had arrived, and the discussion turned to medicine and pus. Crumbs! She fumbled the snow globe back to its ledge and turned to follow Pippistrella.

They zigzagged down a maze of craggy hallways, passing doorways to candlelit galleries of statues, parlors populated with humpbacked harps, and salons abloom with phosphorescent moss. Pippistrella kept a brisk pace, so these wonders flashed by in dreamlike glimpses until they reached a heavy wooden door hinged with gold. "PEEP."

"Is this it?"

"Squeak!"

Anastasia removed the golden key from her pocket. "Well, let's see my dad's—I mean, *our*—room."

The chamber included everything needed for the comfort of a Cavelands royal:

One cavern, its walls freckled with crystals: check.

One merry fire blazing in an amethyst-encrusted cranny: check.

Two plush rugs to protect genteel toes from chilly marble floors: check.

One wardrobe, extra-large: check.

One four-poster bed, canopied with thick curtains: check.

One pair of flannel pajamas (pink plaid), folded on the pillow: check!

Anastasia scrounged her imagination for an image of her father spending his boyhood days in the baroque cavern, but she came up blank. Her shoulders slumped. It was impossible to envision Mr. McCrumpet as a child, let alone a princeling lolling on a velveteen mattress. "Well, I guess I'll unpack."

She upturned her satchel, spilling out Mr. Bunster and her tattered sketchbook and a few marble eyeballs pilfered from the asylum's taxidermied menagerie. A silver timepiece slithered into the jumble: a pocket watch purloined from a hatbox once belonging to Prim and Prude's great-aunt Viola.

Anastasia closed her fingers around the watch, waiting for a telltale tingle: an itch, a rash, some welter of silver allergy. Nothing happened. She shoved the clock back into her bag. Would she never manifest her Morfolkiness? Ludowiga's barb niggled her memory: "Anastasia is a *Halfling*."

Sighing, she grabbed Mr. Bunster. Too weary to shuck off her muddy snowsuit, she ignored the pink pj's and crawled into her canopy bed. "Good night, Pippistrella."

"Crrr-peep." Her bat-in-waiting zipped around the cavern, squeaking out candles with huffy little bat breaths, one by one by one.

Anastasia's limbs sank leadenly into the squishy mattress, but questions flurried her mind as fast and wild as the wintry flakes whirring Wiggy's snow globes. Who was Nicodemus? What was a *blood-and-ink compass*? And why was *he* missing? Had CRUD snatched *him*, too?

And could he really find her dad?

6

The Royal Toilette

DING DING DING *ding ding!*

Anastasia burrowed her nose into her duvet, sleep fuzzing her thoughts. *Dingalingaling!* What was that noise? Quentin sometimes wore a bell; the kidnappers had attached one to him at the asylum, in much the same way one links a chime to a cat's collar. Quentin and Ollie! She cracked her eyelids, expecting to find herself in St. Agony's; expecting to find her two best friends.

Instead, a blur of strange faces stared down at her.

Anastasia jozzled awake, remembering in a rush that she was in Cavepearl Palace. "Who are you?" She recoiled from the gang of women silently crouched around her bed. "What are you doing in my room?" Had the nefarious agents of CRUD tracked her to the Cavelands to snatch her anew?

She leapt to her feet and flung Mr. Bunster at the nearest assassin.

"Eeeek!" the woman wailed. "My wig!"

"Princess," snapped a figure near the fireplace, "these are your Royal Maids."

Anastasia peered across the cavern to Ludowiga, perched on one of the chairs and fluttering a lacy fan.

"Maids?" she echoed.

"But of course. You're a princess, and a princess needs maids."

Anastasia stared. The intruders, she fathomed, were not crouching for attack. They were curtsying.

"I'm Lady Lumpkin, Maid of the Royal Morning Alarm," proclaimed a maiden in a pink wig, brandishing a little bell. *Tingalingaling!* "Time to get up! Rise and shine!"

"They're here to help with your toilette," Ludowiga said.

"My toilet? They're plumbers, too?"

"Your morning toilette, you ignoramus," Ludowiga said. "They're here to bathe and dress you."

"But I don't *need* help."

Ludowiga shook her head. "Wiggy entrusted me with the arduous duty of making you as presentable as possible. It's your first day in the Cavelands, and you'll be going out as a princess and therefore as a face of the royal family. A *freckled* face, unfortunately, but that isn't my fault."

"We have a nice bath drawn for you, Princess," chirped the victim of Anastasia's catapulted bunny. "I'm Lady Vowels, Maid of the Royal Sponge. *WHEELBARROW!*" she hollered, and two more bewigged women bustled into Anastasia's chamber, rolling forth a bathtub on wheels. Foamy water sloshed over the edge.

"Um." Anastasia scratched her elbow. "Thanks. You can go now."

"But, Princess!" cried Lady Vowels. "How will you scrub the back of your neck? It's ever so difficult to reach! Surely you need help with that."

"No, I don't!"

"Clearly you do, Princess. Your hygiene is atrocious," Ludowiga said. "When was the last time you bathed?"

Anastasia scrunched her face, thinking hard. "I guess October."

Lady Vowels clutched at her chest. "This isn't the fifteenth century, Princess!"

"I don't want you to see me in my birthday suit," Anastasia stammered.

"Ugh!" Ludowiga said. "Only peasants bathe in the altogether. You'll wear this bathing gown, of course!" She held up an old-fashioned cotton nightie.

"Why on earth would I wear clothes to take a bath?" Anastasia objected. "That's seems silly."

"You're the one being silly," Ludowiga retorted. "You don't want your maids to see you au naturel, correct?"

"Come along, Princess," coaxed Lady Vowels. "And your bat needs a bath, too."

Anastasia sighed and poked the snoring puffball nested in the canopy's swag. "Wake up, sleepyhead."

Pippistrella rustled and stretched her wings.

"We're supposed to get baths," Anastasia informed her.

Pippistrella squeaked in dismay.

"Um, Ludowiga?" Anastasia asked, clambering from her bed. "Where is the—er—chamber pot?"

Ludowiga grimaced and pointed to a narrow gap in the wall, and to this gap Anastasia pranced a little I-have-to-go-to-the-bathroom jig. She froze, eyeing the tiny nook. Her latrine was smaller than a broom closet, lit by one candle stumped on a jag of cave bacon. A gurgling gray bump swelled from the floor. There was an opening in the top, and wisps of fog wafted from this opening. It resembled the model of a volcano Anastasia had once made for the Mooselick Elementary School science fair.

"Is this volcano thing supposed to be a toilet?" she called.

"Yes! Hurry up and go!"

After a clammy experience indeed, Anastasia donned her bathing gown and hopped into the tub. The maids launched their attack.

They scoured her armpits!

They savaged her head with perfumed glop!

The Maid of the Royal Nose plunged Anastasia's nostrils with a tiny brush. "*Stop!* That tickles!"

Pippistrella screaked angrily as a maid assaulted her with shampoo. "But, Lady Bat, don't you want your fur to smell of roses?"

"On to Phase Two," Ludowiga barked.

"Phase Two?" Anastasia exclaimed, galumphing from the tub and into a robe.

They combed her eyebrows.

They bombarded her with powder puffs.

They wrestled her into silk tights and ruffled pantaloons and a fluff of petticoats. Lady Puddingbilge, an especially muscular damsel, hefted a wire dome over Anastasia's head.

"Is that a cage?" Anastasia yelped.

"No, you dolt. It's a crinoline," Ludowiga said.

Lady Puddingbilge yanked the contraption down and cinched its top around Anastasia's waist.

BLLLLLLLLLT!

Anastasia froze. Ludowiga froze. *Everyone* froze, with the exception of the Maid of the Royal Nose. This quick-witted hero leapt to pinch Ludowiga's nostrils shut.

"Princess!" Ludowiga quacked. "Was that *a fart*?"

Anastasia crimsoned. "The crinoline squeezed it out."

"That's no excuse." Ludowiga unfurled her fan and flapped it wildly. "Princesses *never* toot."

"But, Aunt, *everyone* toots!"

"*We* do not," Ludowiga intoned. "A royal's bottom must be three things: proper, prudent, unimpeachable. Otherwise, our subjects get nervous. If we can't control our flatus, they lose all confidence that we can control a queendom!"

As the maids at last fastened the final clasp on Anastasia's new pink gown, she wriggled from their clutches to grab her galoshes. "Thanks for the help!" she called over her shoulder, dashing from her cavern. Pippistrella squeaked after her.

"Anastasia!" Ludowiga shrilled. "We're not done here!"

"You may not be, but *I* am," Anastasia muttered. "Come on, Pippistrella. Let's get breakfast."

"Gadzooks! Good morning, fancy pants!" Baldwin whooped as Anastasia hustled into the dining hall. "What a vision!"

"You're both pretty fancy, too." Anastasia smothered a giggle. She was accustomed to seeing Penny in cardigans and penny loafers, but her aunt now wore a midnight-blue frock trimmed with a gold braid and twinkling with brass buttons and foaming with lace at the cuffs and collar. She looked *swashbuckling,* like some sort of librarian-pirate-adventuress. If Penny hadn't been sipping her tea so very primly and smiling so very sweetly, Anastasia could have imagined her aunt hollering, "Avast, ye scurvy swine, and use yer library voices!"

Baldwin also wore a gold-studded coat and a vest shot through with shiny thread. Every gilded stitch and glinting nub underscored his usual dapper magnificence.

"What's that?" Anastasia eyed the necktie jutting beneath her uncle's manly chin.

"A cravat." He sawed into his stack of pancakes. "A cravat should be crisp, Anastasia. Folded *just so,* like origami."

Anastasia squashed into a chair, her crinoline bulging around her thighs. She pulled on her galoshes, noticing that the bottoms of her silk stockings were black with cave dust.

"Princess Anastasia!" Ludowiga stamped through the door. "Galoshes are *not* suitable cave wear."

"On the contrary, Loodie," Baldwin said, "galoshes are *perfectly* suited for stomping around the Cavelands. I'm wearing boots, myself."

Ludowiga stared daggers at him. "Fine. But the princess *will* need wigs, you realize. I've already sent a courier to Sir Marvelmop, telling him to gird his hairbrushes."

"Sir Marvelmop?" Baldwin said. "That crazy old goon?"

"Sir Marvelmop is an *artist*," Ludowiga retorted. "A creative genius. The Michelangelo of wigs!"

"He's barmy as a bedbug!" Baldwin said.

"Anastasia, are you hungry?" Penny cut in. "Look at all these pancakes! And *your* breakfast is ready, too, Pippistrella."

Two footmen scampered from the alcoves. The first lifted the lid on his platter to reveal a single jar, and the second picked up this jar and unscrewed the lid, releasing a dark flurry.

MOTHS!

Before she could think twice about it—before she could consider that, perhaps, princesses did not scramble atop tables, toppling glasses and trampling bacon—Anastasia found herself crouched amidst the flapjacks, cramming a moth into her mouth.

"ABOMINATION!" Ludowiga screamed, and then she keeled over. A cloud of alarmed bats rocketed from her wig.

"Royal down!" bawled a servant. "Fetch the smelling salts!"

An attendant dived from the corner and stuck a little bottle beneath Ludowiga's nostrils. The princess sputtered and sat bolt upright.

"Clearly," she smoldered, "we have much work ahead of us. Your first finishing lesson, Anastasia, is at one o'clock this afternoon. *By order of the queen.*" She glared at the coterie of gawking servants. "Well? Lift me, you fools!"

Two butler types hoisted Ludowiga up by her armpits. She straightened her wig, and then she stalked from the dining hall, bats in tow.

"Bosphorous!" Baldwin muttered. "No wonder Dewey Loondorfer spends so much time 'away on business.' With a wife like Ludowiga, I'd find myself a job at a space station!"

Anastasia backed off the table and plopped into her chair, her cheeks burning.

"My dear child!" Penny said. "Have you eaten moths before?"

Anastasia winced. "At the asylum. I was just so hungry—"

"Why!" Penny thrilled. "That's *wonderful*!"

"And such quick reflexes!" Baldwin declared. "You know what this means, don't you?"

"That we can save on pancake bills?"

"No! That you're going to metamorphose soon! And it seems you're going to be a *bat*!" Penny beamed.

"Oh, you lucky child," Baldwin said. "You're going to *fly*!"

Anastasia gazed at them in wonderment. Up until that moment, her penchant for moths had been her shameful secret. She had considered it a nasty habit, like picking one's nose or digging in one's ears. But, she realized now, it was a harbinger of incredible things to come.

"It's completely natural," Penny reassured her. "Some Morflings run around gobbling moths, and others crave cheese—"

"Like your auntie here," Baldwin said. "And *I* started howling uncontrollably."

"He did it abovecaves once," Penny said.

"Fortunately, it was during the Dinkledorf Annual Yodeling Competition, so nobody took notice," Baldwin said.

"Oh, but they did!" Penny said. "You won first place!"

Baldwin patted his mustache, reflecting pleasurably upon this triumph.

"What about Dad?" Anastasia asked. "Did he do anything strange?"

"He gnawed on sticks," Baldwin said. "Constantly."

Anastasia pondered this. "Muffy does that, too. The vet said it keeps her front teeth from growing too long." Her thoughts moseyed to the conversation she had overheard the night before. "Do you think Dad might be hiding as a guinea pig somewhere? Maybe he's in a cage at the Mooselick Pet Shop."

Penny flinched. "Er—that's a possibility, dear."

"Do you think *anyone* can find him?" Anastasia persisted. She ached to ask about the mysterious, missing Nicodemus—whoever he was—and his wonderful compass, but she also knew from following Francie Dewdrop's sleuthing adventures that good eavesdroppers didn't admit to listening at doorways. Not if they could help it, anyway. It would put the kibosh on future snoopery. If people start worrying about being overheard, you see, they clam up. They whisper. They close doors before spilling the beans.

But maybe she could nudge her aunt and uncle into mentioning the mystery man.

"Anyone?" Anastasia repeated.

Baldwin lowered his fork. "The Crown has a specialized Counter-CRUD unit, Anastasia. Our best spies are scouring the United States for any trace of your father. If anyone can track Fred, they'll do it."

"I want to look for him, too," Anastasia said, her voice growing loud and wobbly. "I don't want to waste my time squishing into crinolines and trying on wigs. Not while my dad is missing."

"We know, dear." Penny reached across the table and covered Anastasia's hand with her own. "But you simply cannot go abovecaves right now."

"I'm sure CRUD already has your mug shot plastered on every single Most Wanted Morfolk poster from here to

Mooselick," Baldwin said. "Listen, there's nothing you could do that our spies aren't already doing. I know you're brave and clever and resourceful—you escaped two CRUD Watchers, for Pete's sake! But our spies have been doing this stuff for *years.* A few of our agents are sometime-wolves, you know. They'll *sniff* your dad out. Literally."

Anastasia nodded, but the gears in her mind whizzed. Maybe, for now, she couldn't do anything *abovecaves.* But if Nicodemus Last-Name-Unknown-for-Now was in the Cavelands, perhaps she could find him. And if Wiggy was right about his compass, it would lead them straight to Fred.

"Your dad wouldn't want you to worry and mope, Anastasia," Baldwin said. "Leave the worrying to us. Your aunt here is a virtuoso worrier."

Penny nodded. "You have enough to think about, with moving to a brand-new home and meeting a brand-new family and adjusting to royal life."

Anastasia frowned. "Do those maids have to help me get dressed and take a bath every morning? It was *mortifying.*"

"Peep!" Pippistrella complained from the chandelier.

Penny sighed. "I'll talk to Ludowiga."

"I don't need a bath every day," Anastasia haggled. "Once a week, tops. And do I really have to wear a wig?"

"Well, I'm afraid *that* is a must," Penny said. "At school, anyway. It's part of the Pettifog uniform."

"Pettifog?"

"Pettifog Academy for Impressionable Young Minds," Penny clarified. "Today is the last day of winter break, so you'll be starting tomorrow."

Anastasia groaned. "Really?"

"I know it seems rushed, but you've already missed two months of school," Penny said. "Besides, I'm sure you'll make all sorts of lovely new friends."

"I just want my *old* friends," Anastasia said quietly.

"Perhaps you'll see the Drybread brothers at Pettifog Academy," Penny suggested. "Quentin did say he would meet us again in Nowhere Special."

"Speaking of Nowhere Special," Baldwin said, "we're taking you on the Grand Tour today, my girl. So finish those pancakes, posthaste—merriment awaits!"

7

Nowhere Special

"THE LAGOON IS very mopey today," Belfry announced. "Woebegone, one might say."

"Booohooooo."

Anastasia peered over the edge of the gondola, watching the reflections of candle flames skate across the lake's silver skin. Thoughts rattled her brain like the candy innards of a tortured piñata. What would Pettifog Academy be like? Would she ever learn how to loo in a crinoline? Would she learn to speak Echolalia? On the other hand, perhaps she didn't really need to converse with her bat-in-waiting. Pippistrella was sound asleep again, snoring beneath one of Anastasia's braids.

"How much do bats sleep?" she whispered.

"It depends," Penny said. "Pippistrella is a little brown

bat, and I think they can sleep up to nineteen hours a day."

Belfry guided the gondola into a tunnel.

"Why didn't Grandwiggy eat breakfast with us?" Anastasia asked.

"Wiggy usually rises very early," Penny said. "She eats in her chambers and then goes to work."

"Work? But she's the queen!" Anastasia envisioned her grandmother, in stiff lace collar and crystal crown, demonstrating vacuum cleaners cave to cave. "I thought queens just sat around and drank tea."

"The queen has a lot of responsibilities, Anastasia," Penny said. "She spends most of her time reviewing laws and meeting with Congress and diplomats."

"What about Saskia? She wasn't at breakfast, either."

"Ludowiga has been taking her meals in her private suite for centuries. I imagine Saskia dines with her."

Baldwin harrumphed.

"While we're on the subject of private quarters," Penny said, "there are places in Cavepearl Palace where you shouldn't wander, dear. Wiggy's office is strictly off-limits, of course, and so are her chambers."

"But the palace is *your* home, too," Baldwin said. "We want you to feel comfortable there."

"How long *will* it be my home, exactly?" Anastasia asked. "Am I ever going back to Mooselick?"

"Oh, Anastasia. I don't know." Penny plucked nervously at one of her buttons. "I'm not sure what the future holds. For now you're safe in Nowhere Special. CRUD has no idea about the Cavelands—thank goodness."

The canal widened. Glass globes flickered over gondolas moored by doorways, and burning chandeliers made windows wink. Wrought-iron balconies scrolled along the tunnel walls, and ladies in fancy dresses munched cinnamon buns and watched them pass.

"This is the Upper East Side of Nowhere Special," Penny said.

"Posh," Baldwin added. "Lots of Ludowiga's ritzy friends live in this neighborhood."

The conduit spat them into a large cave. Across the dome, the lagoon lapped at the edges of a wide plaza swarming with people.

"Dark-o'-the-Moon Common," Belfry announced, angling them toward a dock clustered with gondolas. The boatmen all wore white wigs. Some of them were singing, and several were smoking pipes and chatting.

"The black boats are private gondolas, and the green ones are water taxis," Penny said. "As you've already seen, much of

the Cavelands is connected by the canal system. There are pedestrian tunnels, of course, and some bridges, but there are also places you can only get to by boat."

"Can't people just turn into bats and fly?"

"Ah, but what about clothes?" Baldwin said. "You couldn't very well flap off to tea and arrive in your birthday suit!"

"Besides, not all Morfolk shift into bats," Penny added, boosting Anastasia up to the pier.

The plaza's damp cobblestones gleamed beneath its old-fashioned lamps, and murky puddles mirrored the dark shapes of bats whirring above. Hundreds of people crowded the common, clutching shopping bags and pushing baby buggies and perusing the windows of little shop caves. Many of them carried umbrellas to protect their wigs from the droplets sprinkling from the plaza's snaggle-toothed vault.

Anastasia had worried about looking silly in her fancy gown, but the crowd frothed with crinolines and lace collars. "Does everyone dress funny in Nowhere Special?"

"You have to remember, dear, Morfolk live for centuries," Penny said. "Fashions don't change very swiftly in the Cavelands."

"We're still wearing eighteenth-century duds down here." Baldwin tugged the edges of his cravat.

"Look!" Anastasia cried, hopscotching toward a cylinder

of stones. "A wishing well!" She leaned over its curve, hoping to spot the glimmer of wished-upon coins down below, but the mossy stones pitched into gloom.

"Careful." Baldwin crooked his forefinger under Anastasia's collar and tugged her back. "I'm not sure how sturdy that old thing is."

Two wooden joists extended from the well's sides to support a little roof, and a bucket dangled on a rope coiled around a central rod. Anastasia twisted the crank, lowering the bucket a few feet. "Can I have a penny to throw?"

"How about your aunt Penny?" Baldwin quipped.

"We don't have pennies down here," Penny said, ignoring him. "We have lunamarks, queenlies, quartzes, and pinklies."

"Besides," Baldwin said, "you wouldn't want to send a coin down *this* well, anyway." He pulled her to the far side of the well and tapped a bronze sign bolted to the roof.

BE-CAREFUL-WHAT-YOU-WISH-FOR WELL

"Nobody wishes on this well anymore," he said. "The wishes haven't been coming out right for centuries. The last person to make a wish here was Ralph Dundermooth, the poor sod."

"What happened to him?" Anastasia asked.

"He wished he never had to hear another whoopee cushion. He tested whoopee cushions at a factory, you see," Penny added hastily. "And he was getting tired of it."

"Baffling," Baldwin said. "How anyone could tire of that job, I will never understand."

"Anyway, a few days after Ralph tossed his lunamark down the well, his wish came true: he went deaf. He didn't hear *anything* after that."

"A real shame, because he was a brilliant composer in his spare time," Baldwin said. "And then there was Countess Pewter-Pimple. Remember that, Penny? She wished for a man to sweep her off her feet, and that very night a mugger knocked her down and stole her necklace! Broke her wrist, too."

"Do you really think the *well* made those things happen?" Anastasia contemplated the pile of mossy stones. "Those things might have happened anyway."

"Maybe," Baldwin allowed. "But *I* wouldn't risk it."

"Maggots here! Get your piping-hot maggots here!" called a man by a steel cart that resembled a hot dog stand. "Delicious, hot maggots, three quartzes and a smile!"

Pippistrella rustled against Anastasia's braid and chirped.

"But you just had breakfast," Penny said.

"Squeak prrrp!"

"Oh, all right." Penny rummaged in her purse. The maggot man winked and handed a little paper sack to Anastasia.

She wrinkled her nose. "They look a little like popcorn."

"Peepity-peep!"

Anastasia plucked out a maggot puff and gave it to Pippistrella, who began crunching by her ear.

"The wig shop is down Crescent Way," Penny said, leading them to a narrow corridor twisting off the plaza. They passed a haberdashery (hat store, that is) and a beauty parlor and a watchmaker's before halting by a window bristling with masses of hair. A model ship topped a lofty pompadour, a swarm of silk butterflies garnished a bouffant, and a complete twenty-three-piece tea set nested within the squiggles of a stonking great coiffure.

"The uppercrusters all try to outclass each other with bigger and better wigs," Baldwin said. "They decorate them like birthday cakes. They trim them like Christmas trees." He shuddered. "They bear an uncanny resemblance to poodles, don't they? You ladies will have to soldier on without me. I'll be at the limericker's across the lane."

"Coward!" Penny called after him. "Oh well. Come along, Anastasia; let's get your wig."

8

Sir Marvelmop

A BLAST OF SICKLY-SWEET air twitched Anastasia's sinuses into a tremendous sneeze, shivering a cloud of face powder from her cheeks.

"Ah! A sneezer, have we?" a tiny man shouted, dashing from behind his counter. "My nostril wigs will cure that!"

Anastasia coughed. "It's just the perfume."

"It isn't perfume," he chuckled. "It's hair spray. We use it by the gallon here. Aphrodite's Cement, we call it."

"Oh," Anastasia said, her eyes watering.

Sir Marvelmop grasped her hand. "Many people cry upon beholding my beautiful hairpieces. Don't be ashamed, my dear! Let the tears flow. Now, what can I get for you? I have wigs for every need!"

"But does anyone really *need* a wig?" Anastasia asked.

Sir Marvelmop burst into another round of laughter. "How droll! Oh you jest!"

"Sir Marvelmop," Penny spoke up, "this is the Princess Anastasia. Did you get the message we were coming?"

Sir Marvelmop jumped. "Princess Penelope! I didn't see you standing there! And this . . . *this* is the Princess Anastasia?"

Anastasia nodded.

"Dear me!" He eyeballed her. "You're *sure*?"

"Quite sure," Penny said. "And she needs a wig for school."

"I suppose . . . well . . . we'll see what I can do. If anything," Sir Marvelmop ruminated.

"I thought you were the Michelangelo of wigs," Anastasia said.

Sir Marvelmop drew himself up. "Michelangelo used the finest materials for his sculptures. Marble from Carrara, pure and unblemished. You, my dear"—he grimaced—"are rather freckled."

"There's nothing wrong with freckles," Penny protested. "And what do freckles have to do with a school wig, anyway?"

"I was merely commenting upon artistic media," Sir Marvelmop sniffed. "Well, Princess Anastasia, sit down. I call this the Miracle Seat. Upon this hallowed tuffet, I have united countless pates with wigs."

Anastasia perched on the ruffled ottoman, glumly regarding her reflections in the vanity's angled triple mirror. Sir Marvelmop rested his fingertips on her shoulders. "Choosing your wig is a matter of the greatest importance," he rhapsodized. "But we should hardly call it a choice, really. It's more like destiny."

"Maybe it's my destiny not to wear a wig," Anastasia suggested.

"Don't be absurd!" Sir Marvelmop pulled a tape measure from his waistcoat pocket and cinched it across her temples. "Hmmm. All righty. Gigi! Fetch me Washington, Ben Franklin, and Little Bo Peep's Missing Sheep!"

"Yes, Sir Marvelmop," warbled a voice from the depths of the shop.

"Marm Pettifog has strict rules about her students' hairpieces: small, white, and curled," Sir Marvelmop said. "Very traditional. Ah, thank you, Gigi."

The shop assistant staggered forth, clutching several round cartons. Sir Marvelmop eased the lid from the top box, rustled aside the tissue paper, and lifted out a curly white wig. He lowered it onto Anastasia's coconut with all the solemnity of an archbishop crowning a queen.

Anastasia blinked at her reflection.

"No!" Sir Marvelmop yanked the wig from her head and flung it at Gigi. "Give me the Washington!"

"Yes, sir!"

Marvelmop crammed the Washington over Anastasia's brow, regarded it with a frown, and chucked it aside. "No! The Petite-Marie!"

Anastasia scalp prickled as Sir Marvelmop squashed wig after wig over her ears.

"Terrible! Bring me the Corkscrew!"

"*Monstrous!* Gigi! The Bo Peep!"

"Yes, Sir Marvelmop!"

"Intolerable!" Sir Marvelmop snatched the Bo Peep from Anastasia's head. "Gigi! Roll out Rapunzel's Terror!"

"Sir Marvelmop!" Gigi blanched. *"No!"*

"Get it, and quickly!"

Gigi scurried off.

"Rapunzel's Terror?" Anastasia said nervously. "That's a strange name for a wig."

"It's not a wig, Princess," Sir Marvelmop said. "It's a—"

"A *guillotine*?" Anastasia peered past him at the contraption Gigi now wheeled from a dark corner.

"Precisely." Sir Marvelmop flung the Bo Peep upon its chopping block. "Prepare for *le Grand Thwack,* you mediocrity!" He yanked a cord on Rapunzel's Terror, and its blade shot down. *KRRR-WHOMP!* A tangle of squiggles lolled to the floor.

"There," Sir Marvelmop panted. "I feel better now."

Gigi bowed her head, tears drizzling her cheeks.

"Why," the wiggier cried, spying a jumble of curls on the vanity, "what's this? Let's try this one on you, my dear." He eased the wig over Anastasia's noodle, and then he clasped his hands together and danced in delight. "Brilliant! Sublime! Oh, this is *the one*!"

"Isn't this the Ben Franklin?" Anastasia asked.

"So it is," Sir Marvelmop beamed. "And I deem it perfect for you! Gigi, box it up! Now, Princess, you simply *must* see my brand-new armpit wigs," he went on. "They're all the rage—"

The bell on the shop door jangled as a man scuttled in, pulling a skinny child behind him. Anastasia contemplated this boy in wonderment, astonished that someone her age would wear a wig outside of Pettifog Academy. The wig looked like it had tangled with a blender and the blender had won.

"Princess Penelope!" the man cried. "I haven't seen you for—well, it must be over a decade now. Angus, mind your manners! Say hello to the princess!"

The boy stared at his feet. "Hi."

"Anastasia, this is Mr. Wata," Penny said.

"Princess Anastasia!" Mr. Wata exclaimed. "We read all

about your arrival in the Cavelands in this morning's edition of the *Nowhere Special Echo*."

"What?" Anastasia gasped.

"There was a two-page spread detailing your glorious escape from CRUD! Angus and I clipped the article and pasted it into our scrapbook right after we finished our cornflakes."

"But how did the *Echo* get the story so soon?" Penny asked.

"Those reporters are intrepid indeed," Mr. Wata declared. "And it makes a *gripping* story. The *Echo* said you had to use a chamber pot for two months, Princess. What an ordeal!"

Anastasia wilted within her petticoats, envisioning the citizens of Nowhere Special hashing out her bathroom woes over their coffee and donuts.

"Speaking of ordeals," Mr. Wata said, "we're here to get Angus another wig. This is his third one this month!"

"Angus Wata!" Sir Marvelmop wailed. "Your wig is a *wreck*! Did those wayward serpents of yours get hold of it again?"

"Serpents?" Anastasia asked.

The boy's shoulders sank. "Yeah," he mumbled, pulling his wig off to reveal, sprouting from his dark tufty hair, *a den of striped green snakes.*

"Don't worry," Penny murmured in Anastasia's ear. "He's a *boy* gorgon. Harmless."

"Harmless!" Sir Marvelmop sputtered. "Just *look* at my wig! Those serpents have no appreciation for art."

"They've been coughing up hairballs all morning," Mr. Wata said. "Sick tummies, poor things."

"I thought they looked sort of—er—flopsy," Anastasia said.

"They're always like this," Angus muttered. "They're apathetic."

"Now, son," Mr. Wata coaxed, "don't say things like that. I'm sure your snakes will perk up one of these days! Perhaps when you blossom into a young man! Speaking of puberty, shall we get you some deodorant while we're out? I know you have that powder to keep your feet from smelling, but what about your armpits?"

"Dad!" Angus protested.

"Sir Marvelmop has armpit wigs," Anastasia piped up. "I don't know if they help with sweating, though."

"My armpits are fine!"

"We'll see about that," Sir Marvelmop huffed. "Angus, get thee to the Miracle Seat!"

"More like the Tuffet of Shame," Angus whispered.

Anastasia sneaked him a sympathetic smile. "It was nice to meet you."

"Nice bat, by the way." Angus slunk to the tuffet, and Anastasia and Penny escaped the wiggy lair.

They found Baldwin deep in debate at Ye Olde Limerick Shoppe, a pothole packed with books and parchment rolls and inkwells.

"I say it *exists*! We just haven't found it!" Baldwin thumped a writing desk with his fist.

"You're off your nutter!" the limericker retorted. "Everyone knows: there is no rhyme for *orange*!"

"Baldy," Penny called, "we got the wig."

"Peebles, we'll resume this conversation later." Baldwin stomped back out to Crescent Way. "How was your wig expedition?"

"We ran into Mercurio Wata and his son," Penny said. "Anastasia got her first glimpse of a gorgon."

"Well, well!" Baldwin chuckled. "Just thank your lucky stars you glimpsed a *boy* gorgon!"

"Why?" Anastasia asked. "What's wrong with girl gorgons?"

"A lady gorgon is a dangerous creature indeed," Baldwin explained. "If you look at one's face—whammo! You turn into stone! And there's no cure for it. That's it. You're done. Lawn decoration. Glorified hat rack. And"—he lowered his voice—"for those unfortunate folks short on looks: *gargoyle*."

"Male gorgons can't petrify anyone," Penny said. "I expect it's rather sad for them."

"Why would anyone *want* to turn people into stone?" Anastasia demanded.

"It comes in rather handy at times," Baldwin said. "I wouldn't, for example, mind turning Prim and Prude Snodgrass into two nasty little lawn gnomes. I'd put them on a dock somewhere abovecaves."

"Why a dock?" Penny asked.

"Seagulls." Baldwin smiled meaningfully.

"Angus's dad isn't a gorgon," Anastasia puzzled.

"His mother is," Penny said. "She's that opera singer we mentioned—Bellagorgon."

"But how does Mr. Wata look at her?"

"He doesn't. Apparently he walks around the house blindfolded, or she wears a bag over her head."

"I heard Mercurio was covered with snakebites for the first year of their marriage," Baldwin said. "Such a romantic story."

"It doesn't sound romantic to me," Anastasia said. "It sounds painful."

"Speaking of painful . . ." Baldwin pulled his pocket watch from his waistcoat. "It's almost time for your first finishing lesson with dear old Loodie. We'd better head back to the palace."

9

The Great Banana Catastrophe

"ET. I. QUETTE."

Ludowiga spat each syllable as though it were a pebble aimed at Anastasia's forehead. "Etiquette is essential. Etiquette separates us from the hoi polloi."

"The . . . what?" Anastasia glanced at Saskia. Her cousin perched on a frilly chair across Ludowiga's sitting room, nibbling from a bowl of raspberries and cream. "The . . . *who poo*?"

"You're a princess, Anastasia, as bizarre as that seems to both you and me," Ludowiga went on. "And you're going to learn to act like one."

Anastasia squirmed, trying to ignore the pantaloons wedgie bedeviling her behind.

"First we shall address your walk and posture." Ludowiga sipped from a teacup. "When you came in here, you hunched along like a sloth with gout. Have you not noticed how Wiggy and Saskia and I *glide*? Saskia, demonstrate for your cousin the bearing befitting a royal."

"Yes, Mumsy." Saskia put down her raspberries, stood up, and waltzed across the parlor.

"Note the proud carriage of her swanlike neck!" Ludowiga said.

Saskia pirouetted and returned to her chair.

"Of course, Saskia has a natural talent for walking," Ludowiga said. "But fortunately for you, Anastasia, there are ways to train the weak of ankle and lubberly of foot. Sampson!" She snapped her fingers. "Bananas!"

A footman hustled forth, bearing a cluster of bananas. Ludowiga expertly shucked two. She then tossed the fruit into a nearby fireplace and flung the peels at Anastasia. "Remove those beastly galoshes and stand on these, slippery side down."

Eyeing her aunt's talons, Anastasia did as told.

"Shoulders back! Nose up! Clench your derriere! Now: *glide!*"

Anastasia shambled on her banana slippers, wondering whether she resembled a swan.

"Why is your head bobbling like that?" Ludowiga demanded. "Sampson! *Books!*"

"Yes, Your Highness." Sampson fetched several encyclopedias from a shelf and began stacking them on Anastasia's pate. Her neck wobbled.

"Walk without letting them fall," Ludowiga said. "This will strengthen your sinews."

"But, Aunt—" The heavy tomes seesawed. Anastasia reeled, trying to center the weight.

As you may already know, erudite Reader, the great physicist Sir Wally Bracegirdle calculated the slipperiness of banana peels in his great experiment of 1795, "Banana Skins: The Coefficient of Friction Thereof." After years of study (and countless sprained ankles), the dauntless Bracegirdle determined "Banana skins = *slippery as heck.*"

Anastasia was to arrive at this conclusion much more swiftly. The peels skidded under her feet and she careened into her aunt with the cataclysmic impact of a meteorite crashing into a china shop. Ludowiga's fanciful chair capsized and both princesses tumbled to the floor in a panic of screeching bats and splashing tea and thudding books and ripping silk.

"My goodness!" said Sampson. "My gracious!"

"My *wig*!" Ludowiga screamed. "Give it back, you imbecile!"

Anastasia stared at the mass of curls latched, like an enormous clinging opossum, to the buttons fastening her jacket. Then she raised her gaze to Ludowiga. "Aunt! You're *bald*!"

"Of course I'm bald!" Ludowiga flared. "I want my wigs to fit properly, don't I? I shave my scalp every week."

Anastasia scrambled to untangle the hairpiece. "Sorry."

Ludowiga crammed the mop back over her ears and hopped to her feet. "De-wigging a royal is tantamount to *treason*, Princess! Sampson! My Slappers!"

Sampson brandished a platter loaded with dozens of slim white gloves. Ludowiga's manicured claw hovered above the tray for a moment before snatching a heavy velvet number. "When we royalty are offended, we must respond accordingly. Bring your freckled snoot over here."

"But I didn't mean to—"

"Stand up!" Ludowiga seethed.

Anastasia stood, flinching. Clutching the glove, Ludowiga wound her arm back as though preparing to pitch a baseball. Then she cracked her wrist forward, expertly walloping the mitt across Anastasia's nose.

"Ow!"

"Excellent hit, Your Majesty!" Sampson praised.

"Well done, Mumsy!" Saskia cheered.

"That *was* a good one," Ludowiga agreed, looking pleased.

"It feels like a bee stung me!" Anastasia moaned.

"There's an entire art around glove-slappery," Ludowiga said. "I've perfected my technique for centuries."

"I'm rather good at it, too, Mumsy," Saskia chimed in.

"Yes, cherub, you are. I'll never forget your first slap—with a mitten, it was. Only two years old and you whacked Nanny's sniffer red as a cherry!"

"She learned not to boss me," Saskia said smugly.

"But—but that's *mean*!" Anastasia stammered.

Ludowiga pinched her lips. "How else do you expect to command respect, Princess? If you let the underlings get too comfortable, they'll forget what's what."

"Besides," Saskia giggled, "I like to see their noses turn red."

Anastasia snuffled and touched her own throbbing proboscis.

"You'll learn the virtues of slappery in due time," Ludowiga said. "But today's lesson is officially over. Now, kindly remove yourself from what's left of my parlor, and *do* try not to destroy anything on your way out." She kicked one of the banana peels into the wreckage of china slivers and puddled tea.

"Um. Right." Anastasia nabbed her galoshes and backed toward the door.

"Bye, cousin." Saskia popped a raspberry into her mouth. "See you at school tomorrow."

10
Pettifog Academy for Impressionable Young Minds

AFTER THE MANIFOLD indignities Anastasia had suffered at the hands of Ludowiga and Sir Marvelmop, she was almost glad to escape to Pettifog Academy.

Almost.

She canvassed the students gaggled outside the academy entrance, scouring the sea of blue Pettifog uniforms for any trace of Ollie or Quentin. However, she spotted neither hide nor hair of the Drybread brothers. *Crumbs.* Anastasia tightened her arms around her notebooks. She wouldn't know a single soul at Pettifog Academy except Saskia, and Saskia, Anastasia decided, didn't count. Her cousin had sailed to school in a separate gondola, and now whispered at the center of a bewigged clique. The coterie burst into a chorus of giggles and turned their heads to peek at Anastasia.

"You'll have a grand time," Baldwin reassured her. "Grand!" He thumped Anastasia on the back, sending her notebooks leapfrogging from her arms to splash in the canal. The papers fanned across the murky green water, and then an eel clamped down on the edge of a purple binder and spirited it away.

"Oops," Baldwin said.

Anastasia swiveled her gaze back to her future classmates. "They're *staring.*"

"Well, of course they are," Penny said. "You're the new Cavelands princess. Everyone's going to be very curious about you!"

A brittle woman in a blue dress emerged from the academy entrance. She produced a hand bell from her skirts, held it over her white-wigged head, and swung her arm maniacally. *DING DING DING DING DING!* The schoolchildren groaned and turned to file inside.

"All right, my darling," Penny coaxed, "off you go!"

"If Saskia gives you any trouble, just bite back," Baldwin advised.

"I'll remember that." Anastasia hopped from the gondola and dragged her feet to the school door, where the woman in blue waited.

"You must be Princess Anastasia," she said. "I'm Marm Pettifog. I will be your teacher for the remainder of the school year. I also happen to be the founder and headmistress of this fine educational institution. You'll soon learn that I have a reputation for being a bit of a tyrant."

"Oh," Anastasia croaked.

"It's a reputation for which I worked very hard," Marm Pettifog went on. "*It is better to be feared than loved, if you cannot be both.* Machiavelli said that, and he knew a thing or two about running a tight ship. Now, tell me: are you a weeper?"

"I—I don't think so," Anastasia pondered. "I mean, sometimes I cry—"

"I get it. So you're a hard nut to crack, eh? We'll see about that." Marm Pettifog smiled confidently. "Now, don't think I'm going to give you any special treatment because you're a princess, because I won't. Here at Pettifog Academy, all students are equally lowly."

Anastasia gulped and nodded.

Marm Pettifog consulted her watch again, then rang the bell in Anastasia's ear. Pippistrella jolted awake and burrowed under the Ben Franklin in terror.

"You're late!" the schoolmarm barked. "Get to class."

Anastasia straggled behind Marm Pettifog into a cavernous lobby paneled in dark mahogany and overgrown with a veritable forest of carved spiral staircases. They hiked up one of the dizzying flights to the second story and squeezed through a narrow arch into a craggy, candlelit classroom.

"This is your new schoolmate, Anastasia Merrymoon," Marm Pettifog announced. "Anastasia, you may take the chair beside your cousin."

Crumbs again. Anastasia sidled between the desks. Either her galosh caught on Saskia's frilled ankle, or Saskia's frilled ankle caught on her galosh; either way, Anastasia executed a superb nosedive right into a diorama, crushing a model castle crafted from tongue depressors.

"My history project!" wailed one of the Morflings. Anastasia cringed. It was the gorgon boy from Sir Marvelmop's wig shop. She jumbled the sticks back into the diorama, noting that she had also smashed its label: CAVEPEARL PALACE: ARCHITECTURAL MARVEL.

"Sorry," she mouthed.

"Anastasia, off the floor," Marm Pettifog said. "We don't have nap time at Pettifog Academy."

The children giggled as Anastasia peeled herself from the science project and crept to her seat.

"All right, class," Marm Pettifog said. "Open your

Echolalia primers to chapter forty-five. I hope you all studied hard over the winter holiday."

Anastasia rummaged in her satchel for the thick purple textbook and flipped to "Squeak! A Bat in the City." Vocabulary words mottled the page, bedecked in squiggles and dots and all sorts of symbols:

◇◇◇◇◇◇◇◇◇◇◇◇◇◇◇◇◇◇◇◇◇◇◇◇◇◇◇◇◇

Apothecary . . . . Squeœk
Canal. . . . . Prppßk
Church . . . . Crrcrrk
Cinema. . . . . Eeërree
City. . . . . Prrprrprr
Gondola . . . . Eepseëp
Inn . . . . Eçeeåp

◇◇◇◇◇◇◇◇◇◇◇◇◇◇◇◇◇◇◇◇◇◇◇◇◇◇◇◇◇

And so forth.

"Turn to lesson two. We'll go down the row. Parveen, number one."

"Peep-quee-crIIIck!"

"Correct. Jasper, number two."

"Squee-peeEEEp-squee!"

"Good. Did you practice over break?"

"Yes, Marm Pettifog."

As the interrogation snaked around the room toward Anastasia, her palms began to sweat. Perhaps, scholarly Reader, you have suffered nightmares in which you find yourself at the end of a school semester, in a class you can't remember, on the precipice of an important test for which you are utterly unprepared. Perhaps, in these terrible dreams, you find yourself clad in underpants only. While Anastasia's pantaloons were firmly in place, she otherwise felt she had been transplanted into one of these dark night terrors.

"Saskia, number ten."

"Peep-peep CREEeeee squeak!"

"Excellent. Excellent pronunciation," Marm Pettifog declared. "You would all do well to follow Saskia's example. Listen to the *EE* in her *CREEeeee*. Perfect."

Saskia fluttered her eyelashes.

"Anastasia: eleven."

Anastasia stared at the hieroglyphics scrawling the page. "Um."

"Well?"

"Peep squeeee!" Pippistrella chirped in her ear.

"Peep squeee?" Anastasia ventured.

"Princess!" Marm Pettifog glared over her spectacles. "Accepting help from your bat is cheating. Did you just cheat?"

"I—I was just—" Anastasia floundered.

"Cheating is not tolerated in this school. That's detention for you, and your little bat, too. Now, go to twelve."

Anastasia swallowed. A grandfather clock loomed in the corner, clucking its golden tongue. *Tsk. Tsk. Tsk.*

"Marm Pettifog, I don't speak Echolalia. At all."

The schoolchildren rustled, and a few twisted back in their seats to stare at Anastasia.

"Excuse me," Marm Pettifog said. "I don't think I heard you correctly. Did you just say that *you don't speak Echolalia*?"

Anastasia juddered her chin, scrooching down in her chair.

"This is unheard of," Marm Pettifog said. "A Morfolk child—a *princess,* no less—who doesn't speak a peep of Echolalia? How do you communicate with bats?"

"I *don't,*" Anastasia said. "I've only been down in the Cavelands for two days, Marm Pettifog. Pippistrella and I—"

"Have at least worked out a way to cheat at lessons. Well, I shall certainly speak to your parents about this."

"She doesn't have parents." Saskia's voice was syrupy with fake sympathy. "Nobody knows anything about her *human* mom, and her dad disappeared months ago."

Anastasia's jaw dropped.

There are many inventive insults that one may hurl in times of distress. Anastasia might have called Saskia a louse, or a meanie, or told her to "make like a tree and leave." But Anastasia didn't say any of these things. She instead flared:

"Shut up, you . . . you . . . you witch!"

Kablooey! Shocked exclamations erupted across the classroom like detonating cherry bombs, and Marm Pettifog leapt as though a grenade had exploded within her petticoats.

"*Anastasia!* You will join me in my office *now.*"

11

The Dastardly Deed

OVER THE CENTURIES, tyrants have devised many creative instruments of torture. Despots have shackled their captives to special racks designed to twist and crack bones. They have forced their enemies to sit atop porcupines, which is very painful for victim and porcupine both. There is even a sort of frightful upright casket called an iron maiden, studded inside with hundreds of sharp nails pointing inward, into which particularly unfortunate wretches have been locked.

Marm Pettifog's office didn't feature any of these gruesome doohickeys, but it was no less terrifying to Anastasia than would have been a torture chamber in the cruelest overlord's dungeon.

"Contemptible," Marm Pettifog uttered. "Unforgivable. *Just plain nasty.*"

Anastasia pulled her ears down into her shoulders, hoping to disappear entirely.

"Well?" Marm Pettifog's tone was low and dangerous. "Do you agree with me? Do you think those adjectives fit this situation?"

"I—I shouldn't have told Saskia to shut up," Anastasia faltered.

"That's true," the schoolmistress said. "Here at Pettifog Academy, I'm the only one who gets to tell anyone to shut it. But I think we both know that's not why you're sitting here."

"It isn't?"

Marm Pettifog studied her for a long, hard moment. "It is unforgivable to call Saskia, of all children, what you called her."

"Because she's a princess?"

"Because of *who her grandfather is,*" Marm Pettifog said. "Of course, he's *your* grandfather, too. And that's what makes your behavior so dreadfully shocking. So utterly rotten! And with the anniversary of the Dastardly Deed this very week!"

Anastasia gawped at her. "My grandfather? The Dastardly Deed?"

"Don't play the fool with me, Princess. Every Morfling schoolchild knows that tragedy." Marm Pettifog stood. "Suffice it to say that I will be watching you closely during your matriculation at Pettifog Academy, however brief that may, in fact, prove to be." She shrilled at her bat, and it rocketed from her shoulder and darted out one of the holes windowing the office.

"Since you claim not to speak Echolalia, I'll translate for you," Marm Pettifog said. "I just sent Napoleon to the castle with the message you'll be staying after school today for detention. Now, let's get back to class; you've already wasted enough of your schoolmates' time."

If you have ever started at a brand-new school, then you already appreciate that entering a lunchroom alone is a daunting task indeed. Clenching her lunch box, Anastasia sized up the crowd of children milling in the caveteria, hoping against hope that some kindly soul would halloo, "Over here! You can sit with us!"

Sadly, no one called out any such greeting. The Morflings eyed her, but no one waved her a welcome. Not a single child even smiled at her, with the exception of her cousin. And Saskia's smirk, Reader, could not be described as friendly. It was the evil grin of a crackerjack bully watching her victim suffer.

Anastasia shot Saskia a dirty look and galoshed to the far side of the caveteria, plunking down at the deserted end of one of the long dining tables. As she flicked back the latches on her lunch box, murmurs tickled her ears:

"The Halfling princess thinks she's too good to sit with anyone else."

"*Princess?* That's the new princess? She doesn't *look* like it."

"Did you hear? She can't even speak Echolalia!"

"My little brother is in Pettifog's class, and he said Anastasia called Saskia a *you-know-what.*"

Anastasia pulled a jar from her pail and unscrewed the lid, releasing a flitter of moths. "This is for you, Peeps."

"Squee!" Pippistrella launched herself off Anastasia's head, knocking the Ben Franklin to the floor. Watching her royal companion loop-the-loop amongst the stalactites, Anastasia wondered when *she* might make the magnificent shift from ordinary girl to fuzzy aeronaut. She dug in her pocket and clutched Miss Viola's silver watch, willing her palm to tingle.

It didn't.

Crumbs. Still, she drew a glimmer of comfort from the timepiece. The villainess's clock, looted from a secret turret in the course of Anastasia's asylum snoopery, was proof positive that she wasn't just some scolded schoolchild and social outcast; she was also an accomplished sleuth.

"Um, Princess?"

Anastasia turned.

"You dropped this." The gorgon boy held out the wig.

"Thanks." Anastasia grabbed the hairpiece and jammed it into her satchel.

"Is it okay if I sit here?" Angus asked. "Are these seats saved, Princess?"

"Yes! I mean, no—I mean, *no,* the seats aren't saved, and *yes,* you can sit here. And you don't have to call me Princess. In fact, please don't."

"Okay." The boy looked puzzled. He slouched down opposite her.

"It's Angus, right?"

"Nobody calls me Angus except Pettifog and my parents. I'm just plain Gus to everyone else." He placed his lunch box gently on the table as Pippistrella plunged from the stalactites and crash-bombed Anastasia's sandwich.

"Hi," Gus saluted her. "We met the other day, but you were asleep."

"Peep!"

"I'm sorry I broke your castle model," Anastasia said. "I'll help you fix it, if you want."

"Oh, that's all right." Gus shrugged. "I was thinking about rebuilding it anyway. I realized I left off a few towers, and I want it to be *perfect.*" He paused and then added sheepishly, "I've never seen the castle in person, of course—Stardust Cavern is off-limits to subjects unless they have special clearance—but I read three books about it for my project. It must be pretty neat to live there."

Anastasia's cheeks burned. She wondered whether Gus

deemed her too ordinary to bunk at the phantasmagorical Cavepearl Palace. "Um. How are your snakes?"

"They're okay. They finally stopped coughing up wig fluff."

"Can I meet them?"

Gus grimaced. "Why would you want to meet them?"

"I love animals," Anastasia said. "When I grow up, I'm going to be a detective-veterinarian-artist."

"My snakes aren't very interesting," the gorgon stalled. "They're not venomous or anything. And they hardly ever bite."

"You should be *glad*," Anastasia said. "My guinea pig once bit me and it hurt for two weeks."

"Well . . . okay." He peeled his wig off. The snakes wriggled, and a few of them blinked sleepily.

"This one is Hamish, and this one is Daisy . . . Boris . . . Elmo and Lilybelle . . . and this is Pete."

Anastasia greeted each and every snake. She even stretched her index finger to touch the tip of Daisy's green nose. Daisy's little tongue flicked out in reply.

"Oooh, that's ticklish!"

"She's smelling you," Gus said. "Snakes smell with their tongues."

"Is Boris *snoring*?"

"They've been napping all morning." Gus rolled his eyes. "They're pretty lazy."

"Pippistrella sleeps a lot, too," Anastasia confided. "So, what do you have for lunch?"

Gus cracked the lid of his pail. *Squeak! Squeak!*

"Is your lunch—*squeaking*?" Anastasia asked.

"No." He slammed the lid shut. Something scrabbled against the tin.

"Is there a *bat* in there?"

"Nope. I'm just not hungry." Gus hugged the lunch pail. "So, the newspaper said you flew across the Atlantic in a hot-air balloon? What was that like?"

Anastasia told him. She told him how silky smooth the

takeoff was, like satin gliding through a sky of black cream. She told him about toasting s'mores in the propane burner and spying whales through telescopes. When she told him about navigating by the stars, his eyes widened.

"Stars!" he thrilled. "I saw stars once."

"Once?" Anastasia echoed.

"I can't really go abovecaves," Gus said. "Not with these snakes. I can't blend with humans the way other Morfolk can."

"Your wig hides them pretty well," Anastasia pointed out.

"Nobody wears wigs like these abovecaves except English barristers."

"What about a big hat?"

Gus shook his head. "My dad wouldn't let me abovecaves again in a million years anyway. He was furious when he found out my grandpa took me up! But it was worth it. We went at midnight and hid in the woods outside Dinkledorf. The sky was the most wonderful thing I've ever seen! It was *alive.* Bursting with moonlight and star-magic."

"Star-magic?" Anastasia asked. She knew moonlight piped Morfolk brimful of vigor and vim, but this was the first she'd heard about stars.

Gus hesitated. "My grandpa Baba says we Watas have

starlight in our blood." He spoke shyly and cautiously, like someone repeating a fairy tale without knowing whether the listener would scoff. "He was an astronomer, and so was my great-grandfather, and my great-great-grandfather. In Timbuktu. He's told me all kinds of things about stars. . . ." He sighed. "But Dad thinks it's too dangerous abovecaves. I never get to go *anywhere*."

"Well," Anastasia ventured, "I know it isn't the same as seeing the sky, but you could come over to see Cavepearl Palace. Maybe it would help you with your history project."

"Really? I'd *love* to!" He beamed at her. "How about tomorrow? I'll ask my dad tonight."

"Okay." A friendly little glow pepped Anastasia's heart.

"I can't wait to tell Grandpa Baba," Gus said. "He worked with me on the first model."

Anastasia thought about her own grandfather. What had Marm Pettifog said? *Every Morfling schoolchild knows that tragedy.*

"Gus, have you ever heard of—er—the Dastardly Deed?"

His eyelids stuttered. "Sure," he said slowly. "Everyone has."

"*I* haven't," Anastasia said. "Marm Pettifog mentioned it when I was in her office. She said it had something to do with my grandfather. Something bad."

Gus stared at her. "You don't *know*?"

Anastasia bristled. "The first I ever heard of my Merrymoon family was last week."

"Sorry. It's just—cripes. The Dastardly Deed—"

DINGALINGALINGALING!

The students popped from their seats, clanging their pails shut. Lunch was over.

"The Dastardly Deed?" Anastasia urged.

Gus bit his lip. "We have two minutes to get back to class, and the Dastardly Deed is a long story. Listen, it's all in your *Cavelands History* textbook. Chapter thirteen."

Detention.

"With this piece of chalk," Marm Pettifog said, "you'll atone for this morning's crimes." She placed the dusty chunk on Anastasia's palm. "Now, write this one hundred times: *I will not slander other students.*"

"Slander?" Anastasia asked.

"Sully someone's reputation," Marm Pettifog said. "Spread rumors and lies."

"I did all that?"

"You called your cousin a *witch,*" Marm Pettifog said severely. "That is a very serious charge. You could ruin someone's life with a lie like that!"

"I wasn't really saying that she . . . um . . . rides around on a broom or anything."

"I'm glad to hear it. Now, get writing, and I shall watch you."

Anastasia turned to the chalkboard. *I will not,* she scratched, *slandur other students.*

"It's S-L-A-N-D-E-R," Marm Pettifog admonished. "And your cursive is scandalous."

I will not—

"Marm Pettifog!" A plump woman burst into the cavern. "I need your help! Calamity! Oh, calamity of the worst variety!"

"Miss Ramachandra, your wig is askew," Marm Pettifog snapped. "And your hands are covered in purple paint. Pettifog faculty are supposed to be neat and clean."

Miss Ramachandra grabbed two handfuls of curls and wrenched the wig sideways, leaving the sideburns bright purple. "It's another glue emergency," she panted. "Little Susie Oliphant is glued to Tommy Bucket. She's absolutely howling—"

Marm Pettifog clicked her tongue. "Princess, you keep at your punishment. I'll return as soon as I've cleaned up Miss Ramachandra's mess. *Art teachers,*" she grumbled, stalking from the cave.

Anastasia nipped over to her desk and flung back the lid. "Thirteen," she whispered, cracking open her heavy *Cavelands History* text and breezing past the first twelve sections.

Nicodemus Merrymoon & the Dastardly Deed

Nicodemus! She peered at the color plate below the chapter heading. A ginger-mustachioed man, sitting at a desk in a gentlemanly study, smiled out from the page. The feather of a quill pen tufted from his grasp. Anastasia drew her nose even closer to the book. A golden design gloved Nicodemus's hand: three concentric circles of stars and numbers, ringing a sickle moon. And hugged within the moon's golden arms, wrought in teensy, fanciful letters, gleamed one word: *Fredmund.*

Anastasia's instincts buzzed. *Fredmund,* as in *Fred McCrumpet*?

Who was Nicodemus Merrymoon? And why was her father's name inscribed on his hand?

She read:

In the early eighteenth century, tensions continued to escalate between Morfolk and witches. (Witches? Anastasia boggled.) *Morfolk Congress passed a number of bills attempting to regulate dangerous magic, but the rebellious witches scorned to obey any new laws. Finally, an act of outrageous witch aggression on January 2, 1756, now known as the Dastardly Deed, sparked the Perpetual War.*

January 2! Anastasia squinted at the classroom calendar. Just four days away!

The infamous Calixto Swift, a skilled and crafty warlock, created a magical silver trunk into which he locked Nicodemus Merrymoon. Swift enchanted the chest to vanish, along with the Silver Hammer used to seal (and required to open) it, and neither these silver instruments nor Nicodemus has ever been found. Such a plight would torment any Morfo, but for a Shadowman such as Nicodemus, the suffering would be particularly terrible.

Morfolk anger erupted in response to this Dastardly Deed, and Wigfreda Merrymoon declared a Perpetual War on all witches, driving them from the Cavelands forevermore.

Anastasia's mouth gaped. The mysterious missing Nicodemus was her *grandfather*? And he'd been locked in a trunk by *witches*?

12

The Perpetual War

HEARING FOOTSTEPS APPROACH the classroom, Anastasia slammed the history tome shut and dashed back to the blackboard. *Slander*—she jumped as Baldwin stomped through the door, his face red behind his mustache. Anastasia had never seen him so furious, and it was a frightening sight indeed. She plastered herself against the wall, Pippistrella clinging to her collar.

"In the name of Great Caesar's ghost," he thundered, "what's this baloney about trouble at school?"

"Baldy, keep your temper," Penny urged behind him, but a frown crimped her lips, and her eyes flashed dangerously.

Anastasia ducked her head. "I'm sorry. I'm really sorry."

"*You're* sorry?" Baldwin roared. "Put down that chalk

right now, Anastasia. In fact, throw it to the floor and stomp it to bits!"

"Baldwin!" Penny cried. "I know you're upset, but *violence against chalk*?"

Anastasia replaced the chalk on the blackboard ledge just as Marm Pettifog reappeared. "Ah. If it isn't Penelope and Baldwin Merrymoon. We have much to discuss."

"Indeed we do!" Penny said. "Your courier bat reported that Anastasia *cheated* and *slandered*? I cannot believe either of those accusations."

"She accepted unauthorized help from her bat during Echolalia lessons," Marm Pettifog said coldly. "And then she called Princess Saskia a . . . er . . . the word that begins with *W*."

"I'm sure Saskia deserved that and more," Baldwin retorted. "Have you actually *met* her?"

"I'm not going to comment upon what Saskia does or doesn't deserve," Penny said. "But I will say that Anastasia is new to the Cavelands, and she knows almost nothing of Morfolk history. Abovecaves, it isn't particularly *polite* to call someone a witch, but it's no grave offense."

"It is a grave offense in *my* classroom," Marm Pettifog rejoined.

Penny clenched her jaw. "And as I informed your secretary in my letter of registration, Anastasia never even heard a peep of Echolalia before last weekend. She'll need some extra time before she can participate."

"And how long will that take, Penelope?" Marm Pettifog sneered. "Perhaps we should demote Anastasia to fourth—or third—grade."

"Codswallop!" Baldwin hollered.

"Don't you howl in my school, Prince," Marm Pettifog said. "This isn't the Dinkledorf yodeling competition."

Penny took a deep breath. "Marm Pettifog, why don't you and I step outside for a moment and discuss this?"

Once the two educators disappeared into the corridor, Baldwin snugged Anastasia into a hug. "What a horrible start to your Morfolk school days."

"Marm Pettifog thinks *I'm* horrible," Anastasia sniffled.

"Ah, she does, does she?" A smile twitched Baldwin's mustache. "Don't you worry about that. It may interest you, Anastasia, to know that I have my own sinister record at Pettifog Academy."

"Really?"

"Oh yes." He chortled. "Although, unlike you, I was willfully naughty. Oh, the havoc I wreaked beneath these hallowed stalactites! Suffice it to say that I spent many an afternoon writing *I will not*s on this very blackboard."

Anastasia wiped her eye and grinned.

Marm Pettifog clicked back into the classroom, followed

by Penny. "You are released from today's detention, Princess," the schoolmarm said. "I shall accept (*for now*) that you didn't mean to cheat (even though you *did*), and that you didn't deliberately invoke witches."

"Oh," Anastasia mumbled. "Thank you."

"Your aunt has promised to help you catch up with your classmates," Marm Pettifog said. "But you're going to have to work hard. You're on academic probation, Morfling. Do you understand what that means?"

Anastasia shook her head.

"It means that you have the next few months to prove you're a capable fifth grader. If your grades are sufficient, then you may enter sixth grade with the rest of your classmates at the end of this term. And if your grades are poor"—Marm Pettifog smiled ghoulishly—"then you'll repeat fifth grade with me."

Anastasia shuddered.

"Good day to you all." Marm Pettifog pulled a gruesome red pen from her pocket and sat down at her desk. "I have essays to grade."

Baldwin hustled Anastasia from the room. "You've officially survived your first brush with Marm Pettifog, my girl. This calls for ice cream."

Anastasia heaved a sigh of contentment as she climbed atop one of the stools lining the long marble counter at the Soda Straw. Stalactites spiked the ceilings, but the cavern otherwise looked much like the old-fashioned ice cream parlors portrayed in TV shows from the 1950s. The floors were checkered black and white, and stained-glass lamps beamed jewel-toned candlelight atop lacy iron tables. Of course, soda shops abovecaves didn't have fruit bats dangling from low-hanging dripstone, lapping smoothies from crystal goblets. And soda shops abovecaves didn't normally count wolves amongst their clientele.

"Hey, Roger!" Baldwin greeted a waggy-tailed customer hunkered over a banana split. *"Awoo!"*

Roger lifted his ice-cream-frosted muzzle. "Awoo!"

A white-haired man emerged from a nook behind the counter, wiping his palms on his apron. "Well, hello, Princess Penny—*Baldy!* You old rapscallion! I read in the *Echo* you got back three days ago, and it's taken this long for you to visit?"

Baldwin chuckled. "Anastasia, may I present Hoshi Yukimori, the world's greatest ice creamer, and also one of my greatest friends?"

"Anastasia!" Mr. Yukimori's face lit up. "Anastasia the Brave? I've heard all about you, my dear! Good for you, escaping those poisonous kidnappers!"

Anastasia blushed. "Thanks."

"Now, what strikes your fancy?" Mr. Yukimori handed her a menu.

Anastasia studied the photographs of Guzzlylicious Soda Fizzers, Chocolate-Covered Moths, and Moon-Over-My-Mango Smoothies. "Fermented Fruit Parfait?" Anastasia asked.

"It's like booze for bats," Baldwin explained. "Gets 'em potted."

"Electric Eel Ice Cream?"

"Zaps your taste buds. That's what *I'm* getting," Baldwin said.

"I'll just have a chocolate sundae," Anastasia decided. "And a jar of moths for Pippistrella, please."

"And one Limburger Milk Shake for me," Penny said.

"Coming right up!" Mr. Yukimori bustled behind the counter.

Baldwin snared Anastasia into a friendly noogie. "A sundae will help you forget your troubles."

"I'm terribly sorry, Anastasia," Penny apologized. "We should have prepared you a little better before you started school. We should have told you about—about—"

"About *witches*?" Anastasia pressed.

"Let's go somewhere a bit more private." Penny slid from her stool and led them to a booth squidged into an alcove.

"So witches are *real*?" Anastasia asked, scooching across the vinyl seat. "They actually *exist*? And they do *magic*?"

Even in a secret, subterranean ice cream parlor, with Pippistrella swinging from the lamp and a wolf licking ice cream from a crystal dish, Anastasia found it hard to imagine.

"Yes." Penny fiddled with one of her buttons. "And many, many years ago, Morfolk and witches lived together in harmony."

"Sort of," Baldwin said.

"Sort of," Penny agreed. "After the witch hunts of the fifteenth through seventeenth centuries, we all moved down to the Cavelands. Morfolk weren't working magic, of course, but if a human saw one of us changing into a bat or wolf or shadow, you can guess what they'd think. Quite a few Morfolk were executed as witches back then."

"So we all came to the Cavelands in the 1700s, and things were okay for a little while," Baldwin said. "But then the witches started brewing deadly dangerous spells. Very worrisome to us Morfolk."

"I read about that in my history textbook," Anastasia said.

"How very resourceful!" Penny praised. "The first step in the path to knowledge is very simple: *open a book.*"

Anastasia nodded. Penny had festooned the Mooselick Library with posters bearing that and other inspiring quotes. "But what I don't understand," Anastasia said, "is that Morfolk seem pretty magical, too."

Penny smiled. "We can do some remarkable things, but we aren't magic."

"Changing into wolves and bats and mice *is* magic!"

"Anastasia," Penny said, "other creatures in the animal kingdom metamorphose, too. Like butterflies and moths. They only do it once, but they're much simpler organisms."

"Order up," Mr. Yukimori announced, unloading confections from his tray.

"Ah, Hoshi!" Baldwin saluted. "You're a gentleman and a peach and a peer of the realm."

Mr. Yukimori winked and departed.

"Go on, Aunt Penny," Anastasia prompted, plucking a moth from the jar and handing it up to Pippistrella.

"Now, there are magical items all over the Cavelands from when the witches lived here," Penny said, "but, in general, Morfolk do not use magic. We don't have the—the same *talent* for it."

"Talent!" Baldwin scoffed.

"Some of the things those witches did were marvelous, Baldy." A flush crept into Penny's cheeks. "I feel the same way about witches as you do, but you have to admit they created wonderful things."

"Hmph."

"A wizard made Cavepearl Palace," Penny pointed out.

Anastasia jolted. *"Really?"*

"Yes." Penny shifted uneasily. "Calixto Swift, one of the greatest sorcerers who ever lived."

"We live in *Calixto Swift's* old house?" Anastasia gasped.

"Well . . . yes." Penny sipped her milk shake. "But I'm getting away from the original point, which is that Morfolk tried to outlaw certain spells. Dangerous spells. The witches said no."

THE SODA STRAW
Milk Shakes
odas
e Cream
moothies
ICE CREAM
flavors
Electric Eel
Limburger Cheese
Fermented Fruit
Mango

"Cheeky blighters," Baldwin grumbled.

"So there was a lot of friction."

"It wasn't just the magic problems," Baldwin said. "It also had a lot to do with the silver mines."

"Yes," Penny agreed. "There used to be a silver mine near Nowhere Special, controlled by the witches. They use silver in their magic, you see."

"And silver is, as you already know," Baldwin said, "deadly poisonous to Morfolk." He took a whopping great lick from his triple-scoop cone. "*Ouch!* Just like swallowing a sparkler! . . . *Mmm,* this is a good batch!"

"So Morfolk and witches started quarreling, and hostility just festered in the Cavelands," Penny said. "Screaming in Congress."

"Bar brawls," Baldwin said.

"General nastiness. And then . . ." Penny's voice trailed off.

"And then Calixto Swift locked Nicodemus in a magic trunk," Anastasia said. "The Dastardly Deed."

"Right," Baldwin gruffed. "The villain."

"My book said being locked in a trunk was somehow worse for Nicodemus, because he's a Shadowman," Anastasia said. "Why?"

"Shadowfolk don't need to eat or breathe," Penny replied shakily.

Anastasia's eyebrows drew together. "But Ollie's a Shadowboy, and he's *always* hungry!"

"Sure," Baldwin said. "Shadowfolk like sweets and snacks like everybody else. But they don't need food to *survive*."

"Anyone else trapped in the Silver Chest would have starved or smothered by now," Penny said. "It would be awful, but it would *end*. Poppa will go on suffering. . . ."

Baldwin's mustache bristled. "He's been stuck in that lousy box since 1756."

"I was only sixteen when all that happened," Penny said softly.

"And I was thirteen," Baldwin said. "But it feels like it was yesterday. Oh, Anastasia, how I wish you could meet Poppa. You two would be closer than biscuits and butter." He sniffled.

Anastasia squeezed Baldwin's forearm, lapsing into silence. She was no stranger to the worry and woe linked to a lost father. And, she now realized, both her dad *and* her gramps were missing. She pondered the way Gus Wata's eyes lit up whenever he mentioned Grandpa Baba. Gus and *his* grandpa, she reckoned, were closer than biscuits and butter. It would be nice to know Nicodemus—the *real* Nicodemus, not just stories about a long-lost noble. He certainly looked friendly in his portrait.

"There's a picture of Nicodemus in my textbook."

Anastasia watched her aunt and uncle closely. "I noticed a drawing on his hand. It looks like a compass . . . with *Fredmund* written in the middle."

"Poppa got tattoos of compasses with all our names," Baldwin said. "So he could always find us."

"But how could a tattoo work like a compass? Compass pointers *move.* Tattoos stay still."

"Ah, not Poppa's tattoos," Baldwin said. "The ink was enchanted by . . . well, by Calixto Swift, of all people. He and Pops were great pals before the Dastardly Deed."

"That's why it was so very shocking," Penny said. "Calixto was like an uncle to us before—before all that. He put on the most wonderful puppet show for my eleventh birthday. He even gave me one of the puppets—he made them himself."

Anastasia, herself almost eleven, did not think a puppet show sounded particularly wonderful. The only puppet show she remembered had starred a gaggle of cotton athletic socks with googly eyes. She hoped Penny did not plan a similar spectacle for her upcoming birthday.

"Have you ever seen anyone get a tattoo, Anastasia?" Baldwin asked.

"Of course she hasn't!" Penny said. "Why on earth would she have been to a tattoo parlor?"

Baldwin shrugged. "School field trip?"

Penny gave him a withering look.

"The tattoo artist puts a little ink on his needle, and he

sticks it into the skin," Baldwin explained. "He does it over and over. The design is actually a zillion of those little dots added up. And every time the needle pricks the ink into the skin, a drop of blood comes out."

Anastasia wrinkled her nose.

"So Pops's tattoos were inscribed not only with enchanted ink, but also *father's blood,*" Baldwin said. "Very powerful stuff. Those compasses will always point to Fred, and Penny and me, and"—he made a face—"Loodie."

"So Nicodemus could find my dad now," Anastasia pressed, her heart thumpity-thumping.

"Sure," Baldwin allowed. "Except no one knows where Pops is, either."

"Good heavens, those fruit bats are getting rowdy." Penny frowned across the cavern. "They're going to—oh, I *knew* it."

A crystal goblet toppled from the bat party's table, spattering bits of rotten banana and mango across the marble floor. Mr. Yukimori stalked across the soda shop clutching a broom and dustpan.

"They've been at the fermented fruit," Baldwin said. "Those bats are *sozzled.*"

Pippistrella peeped primly, as if to say, "Disgraceful!"

"After the Dastardly Deed, we drove the witches from the Cavelands," Penny went on.

"What happened to Calixto Swift?" Anastasia asked.

"Dead," Baldwin said. "The first witch to die."

"Maybe he told someone where he hid the chest," Anastasia suggested. "Maybe it's a big Swift family secret and his great-great-great-whatever-grandchildren know about it. We *have* to ask them! They could tell us where Nicodemus is, and then Nicodemus can find Dad."

Penny twiddled her button. "I don't think so, dear. Wiggy interrogated Swift's relatives—the ones we could catch before they fled—back in the eighteenth century. And they wouldn't tell us *anything*."

Anastasia's mind whizzed like a detecting machine oiled with dozens of Francie Dewdrop mysteries. Francie knew how to squeeze information from people. She squeezed so expertly that her suspects didn't even realize they were leaking clues. It made sense, Anastasia mused, that a bunch of witch prisoners in the midst of a war wouldn't blab secrets to the Morfolk queen. But mightn't a witch descendant, feeling cozy over a cup of tea (Francie *always* ferreted out juicy clues during teatime), gossip about their great family secret?

"Maybe someone would tell us something *now*," Anastasia persisted. "Maybe, if we invited some Swift witches over for tea—or s'mores—"

Penny shook her head. "Morfolk and witches don't associate. We've been mortal enemies for over two hundred and fifty years."

"Witches are *bad*, Anastasia," Baldwin stressed. "They're

magic-hoarding, silver-mining murderers. You've never been through war, so you can't understand. We've lost family . . . comrades. . . ."

"Like Klaus," Penny whispered. "My cheesemonger friend."

Baldwin slammed his fist on the table, rattling the dishes. "Those scoundrels used all kinds of awful magic on us. That's how Wiggy lost her eyelids, you know—burned off with a silver spell. And she had them replaced with glass, so she can always watch for the return of the witches even as she sleeps."

"We will never reconcile," Penny said.

"Ever," Baldwin swore.

"But what if—" Anastasia protested.

"No *what-ifs,*" Baldwin decreed. "I know you want to find Fred, but put any thought of finding him with Poppa's tattoo right out of your noodle. Upon my mustache, I wish we could—you have no idea how I wish it! But believe me, plenty of brave and able Morfolk have died looking for the Silver Hammer and Chest. Tangling with witches and their magic only brings death and destruction."

"Baldwin's right, dear," Penny fretted. "Anastasia, we know how—er—*curious* and *persistent* you can be. But you must promise us not to snoop for clues leading to Nicodemus. Any hunt like that could tangle you up with magic, and magic is *dangerous.*" Tears streaked her cheeks. "We've already lost so much. If anything happened to *you,* it would simply break our hearts."

"Promise us," Baldwin insisted. "No Francie Dewdroppery, girl."

Anastasia's shoulders sagged. "I promise."

"Good." Penny sighed. "Besides, we don't even know where witches live now. They're hiding, you understand."

Anastasia stared into the ice cream puddling at the bottom of her bowl, forefingers on each hand firmly crossed beneath the table. She loved Penny and Baldwin, but she loved her dad, too. *Father's blood is powerful stuff.* Well, so was *daughter's* blood, and the heart and mind this blood fueled. Her own compass—not a scientific gizmo, not a magical tattoo, but something deep and internal and strong, like a goose's instinct to fly south in winter or a humble seed knowing when to make the great leap into flowerhood—now pointed straight to her new mission: tracking down her father through Nicodemus.

13
Know Your Enemy

IT IS A maddening fact of life: while you may have a plan of the absolute top-most importance, a million silly chores pop up as hurdles to your great endeavor. Perhaps you are a great inventor, but your glorious doohickey languishes in your laboratory while you vacuum the carpets for an upcoming visit from Granny. Or perhaps you are a great explorer itching to discover a new island, but first you must see the dentist about getting a cavity filled.

Or maybe, like Anastasia, you are an aspiring detective-veterinarian-artist heck-bent on finding your newly lost father by way of your long-lost grandfather, but a mountain of schoolwork blockades your way.

At least, Anastasia pondered, she had a wonderful study spot. A *magnificent* study spot. The sort of study spot that kindled the special, cozy, open-a-book-and-fall-in region of the bibliophile brain. Cavepearl Library was a big, long cavern with roaring fireplaces and squishy leather chairs and behemoth wooden tables glittering with magnifying glasses and microscopes and all other kinds of neat doodads. Dozens upon dozens of Baldwin's beloved cuckoo clocks roosted on the walls.

And, of course, Cavepearl Library was brimful of books: large, important books with gold letters on their spines, and humble little volumes that peeped out from between them, and magazines and scrolls and scientific journals, and even (and most important, in Anastasia's estimation) a complete set of all the Francie Dewdrop novels ever published. These books lined the cavern walls from stalagmite to stalactite, and rolling ladders ran in tracks along the floor so the intrepid bookworm could scale stories of rungs to retrieve an album from the tippy-top shelves.

Penny, the most intrepid bookworm of them all, now perched at the zenith of one of these ladders. "I'm so pleased that young Angus Wata is interested in astronomy," she called, tugging a volume loose. "I'm going to make a nice research list for you two!"

"Thanks," Anastasia said, but her eyes were on the Francie Dewdrop collection. How might Francie approach the *Mystery of the Missing King*? It was a cold case, which is detective jargon for an old, unsolved mystery. Cold cases are especially tricky, because the clues have moldered or dried up. For example: Nicodemus had disappeared centuries earlier. Time had likely swept away any sort of physical evidence. Calixto Swift was long dead, and his descendants were who knew where.

Anastasia frowned. Francie's investigations percolated with piping-fresh clues, like new footprints to track or a telltale button popped from a villain's cummerbund. Anastasia scanned the Francie Dewdrop titles: *The Case of the Pilfered Waffles . . . Enigma of the Underground Maze . . .* Ah! *The Great Caboose Puzzler.* Anastasia had, of course, read that one, because she had read all of them. In *The Great Caboose Puzzler,* Francie studied old newspaper articles to prove, once and for all, the real culprits behind a Wild West train robbery.

Anastasia's attention now flicked to the other books in the library. She wouldn't learn anything by scouring the ground for footprints and buttons, but perhaps some clues nestled within the pages of the Cavelands history tomes.

Reader, perhaps you are familiar with the military strategies of Sun Tzu, a brilliant general and tactician who lived over two thousand years ago. If so, you will recognize this bit of sage advice: *know your enemy.* That is to say, the more you study your adversary, the better you can calculate their motives and moves. Anastasia resolved to find out as much as she could about Calixto Swift. If she learned what made him tick, perhaps she could deduce where he might hide a hammer and chest and Shadowman. And that would lead her to Fred McCrumpet.

"Anastasia, dear," Penny prompted gently, coming down the ladder. "How is your Echolalia coming along?"

"Fine." Anastasia pantomimed jotting answers on her worksheet as her aunt stacked the astronomy tomes on one of the tables. "Aunt Penny?"

"Yes, dear?"

"Do you have a book on the—er—history of the Dastardly Deed? Marm Pettifog is making us write an essay. And I need to learn about Calixto Swift."

This was a fib. Some nitpickers might even have called it a *lie*. Either way, it fooled Penny, that purehearted librarian. "Why, of course! We have a *splendid* history collection." She scaled the ladder halfway, and then she gave a mighty kick, propelling it and herself across the wall. Anastasia watched closely. She didn't need a book for a Pettifog paper, of course. But she wanted to see where Penny kept the history section, and she couldn't very well tell her the *real* reason.

Nope. For this investigation, Anastasia was a secret agent. She was a dauntless detective posing as a mild-mannered egghead. "I just want to do well in school," she added for good measure.

She may as well have shouted, *Open sesame!* Soon a small treasure trove of books cluttered her study table, bearing promising titles such as: *A Detailed History of the Dastardly Deed, Scoundrels and Silver Miners: Witches in the Eighteenth Century,* and most delectable of all, *Ye Olde Compleat Unauthorized Biography of the Treacherous Villain Calixto Swift.*

"I hope reading about these things won't distress you, child." Penny placed *Calixto Swift's Many-Marveled Inventions (Stinker Though He Was)* atop the pile. "These events affected all Morfolk, but especially our family."

"It's okay." Anastasia shrugged. "Everyone else knows about it. I should, too."

Clockwork ground and Baldwin's giddy tick-tockers all vomited forth their screaming birds. *Cuckoo! Cuckoo! Cuckoo! Cuckoo! Cuckoo! Cuckoo! Cuckoo!*

"Seven o'clock already!" Baldwin roused from his hearthside nap. "Dinnertime! Chef's prepared us a proper fondue dinner, Anastasia. Some yummy molten cheese will fuel your intellect!"

Anastasia wrenched her gaze from the Dastardly annals. "I hope so," she said. She would need every last iota of brainpower to unravel the mystery and secrecy and witchery tangling the string of clues leading to her missing kinsfolk.

14
Sixty Thousand Miles of Pure Joy

DOWN IN THE Cavelands, sealed away from the sky and all the wonderful mischief that its clouds may make, there was no hope for a happy blizzard to snuff out Anastasia's next school day. She quailed as they sailed across Old Crescent Lagoon toward Pettifog Academy and the monstrous schoolmarm lurking therein.

"Baldwin and I have meetings in the Senate Cave all day," Penny said. "We won't be able to pick you up at three, but Belfry will come to fetch you and Angus."

"You think *you* have it bad, Anastasia," Baldwin complained. "Try one Senate session with Caesar Dellacava—pure, utter, absolute *torture*! That popinjay *lives* to bicker."

"Hopefully things will go more smoothly with Marm Pettifog today," Penny fretted.

"And if not, we'll work out a bit of Merrymoon mischief." Baldwin hefted Anastasia up to the dock and winked.

"Anastasia! ANASTASIA!"

She whirled.

Perhaps, dear Reader, you have read the travel accounts of brave desert explorers who, spotting a cool oasis—or perhaps an ice cream truck—stumble forth only to have the beauteous vision dissipate before their disappointed eyes. Such apparitions are called mirages, and they are a trick of a mind under duress.

Presented now with the gladsome sight of two beloved chums galloping across the cobbles of Wax Plaza, grinning and waving and hollering her name, Anastasia wondered whether her anxious brain had cooked up a mirage of its own. But then the boys tackled her in a rib-cracking hug and she knew they were real.

"Ollie! Quentin!"

"The League of Beastly Dreadfuls, reunited at last!" Ollie whispered in Anastasia's ear.

"Peep!" Pippistrella protested from the nape of her wig.

"Hello! Who's this?" Quentin asked.

Anastasia hopscotched through the introductions. "Oh, I *missed* you! When did you get back?"

"Late last night," Quentin said. "After a long and arduous journey by sea. *Arduous.*" He clutched his stomach.

"We were both seasick!" Ollie said. "We had to throw up over the side of a boat! It was disgusting."

"Baldwin threw up over the side of a hot-air balloon," Anastasia said.

"And that's even *worse,* because you don't know where the sick will land," Baldwin piped up from the gondola. "Maybe on someone's new hat."

"Maybe down a chimney," Ollie suggested, just noticing Baldwin and Penny. "Why, it's the Great Mouse Destroyer! And the lady from the Dread Woods!"

"Ollie!" Quentin rolled his eyes. "He's not really a Mouse Destroyer, remember? That was just something he told Prim and Prude to get into the asylum."

"I know," Ollie said. "But I never really knew who he was. Who are you, exactly?"

"I'm Anastasia's uncle," Baldwin said, "and Penny here is her aunt."

"Well, Anastasia!" Ollie cried. "Why didn't you tell us back at St. Agony's?"

"I didn't know until we were in the balloon."

"Well, pleased to meet you," Quentin said. "We're the Drybread brothers."

"Drybread? Are you related to Argyle Drybread, of Drybread and Drybread's Music Box Emporium?" Penny asked.

"He's our dad," Ollie said. "That's where Quentin got his musical talent."

"Anastasia told us you play the saw." Penny pointed at Quentin's violin bow and instrument case.

"A wonderful instrument," Baldwin declared. "The first time I heard the musical saw, I thought a ghost was howling at me."

"Anyway," Anastasia pressed, "you said you sailed here?"

"Part of the way," Quentin said. "Shadowfolk can't do long flits over water. So we had to island-hop from Canada to Greenland to Iceland and finally down to England and then here."

"That sounds like fun," Anastasia said.

"It wasn't," Quentin said. "It was terrible. We had to hide on the boats as Shadows, of course, because we didn't have any clothes or tickets. And Shadows don't handle rough seas too well."

Ollie mimed vomiting.

"You boys were very brave," Penny said. "We didn't have a chance to tell you abovecaves, but we're all very grateful to you for helping Anastasia escape St. Agony's Asylum."

Quentin brushed Penny's praise aside. "*She* helped *us,* too."

"Nonetheless, the royal family is in your debt."

"Royal family?" Ollie echoed.

"Um," Anastasia hedged. "It turns out I'm . . . related to the queen."

"How?" Quentin asked.

"She's . . . er . . . my grandmother."

"Which means *you're* a princess!" Ollie cried. *"You?"*

"I *thought* you looked familiar." Quentin blinked at Baldwin and Penny. "You're Queen Wiggy's children, aren't you? You left Nowhere Special when I was only four, but I've seen your pictures."

"Indeed we are," Baldwin said.

"So Anastasia's related to Fredmund and Ludowiga, too," Quentin concluded.

She nodded. "Fred is my dad."

"And *Saskia Loondorfer* is your *cousin*?" Ollie asked.

Anastasia nodded again, wrinkling her nose.

"Well," Ollie philosophized, "you can't win 'em all. Anastasia, the secret princess! It's like a *fairy tale*!"

"Ye—es," Anastasia agreed. Except instead of discovering she was a princess and living happily ever after, she had to hunker in a cave to hide from CRUD. She was still her freckled, tragically flatulent self. And her father was still missing.

RING RING RING RING RING RING RING!

Their heads swiveled toward the school entrance, where Marm Pettifog brandished her bell. She treated Anastasia to a custom-made glower that communicated, *Greetings, Princess. Prepare to be destroyed!* Then she turned on her heel and stomped into Pettifog Academy.

"She's my teacher this year," Ollie agonized. "I've been dreading it since kindergarten."

"You're in Marm Pettifog's class? Me too!" Anastasia said.

"Oh! Well, that makes it much better." Ollie beamed. He lowered his voice. "If the Beastly Dreadfuls survived St. Agony's Asylum, we can survive half a year with old Pettifog. Besides, look what I have." He tugged his jacket pocket open to reveal a jumble of candy and half a squashed donut. "Prisoners' rations."

"Come on," Quentin said. "You don't want to be late."

Reader, did you know that approximately sixty thousand miles of veins and arteries coil within your circulatory system? If you were to unravel these marvelous blood tunnels and lay them end to end, they would wrap two and a half times around Earth! All sixty thousand miles of Anastasia's circulatory system now thrummed with pure joy. Her friends were back in town, and Ollie was in her class, and school was no longer such a dismal prospect, even if a tyrant ran their classroom.

"Oliver Drybread!" Marm Pettifog bellowed. "You haven't been in school since fourth grade. That's over one hundred absences!"

"I went to school abovecaves, Marm Pettifog," Ollie said. "My family moved to Melancholy Falls, remember? Quentin won a yearlong scholarship to the Conservatory of Melancholy Music. We're actually back in Nowhere Special *early,* because two kidnappers—"

"Spare me your excuses. Go take the empty chair at the front."

Ollie gave Anastasia one last little smile and trotted to his desk. She caught Gus's eye across the room before sliding into her own seat. Saskia tilted her nose and sniffed.

"Before we begin our lessons, I have two important points of business," Marm Pettifog said. "First, to the student or students who released a mischief of mice in the caveteria kitchen yesterday: you are *not* funny, and we *will* catch you."

"Mice!" shrilled a girl in the front row. *"Revolting!"*

"They are *not*!" Anastasia countered.

"They're nasty, filthy *vermin*," the girl sneered, narrowing her eyes at Anastasia. "Just because Princess Penelope shifts into a pack of rats doesn't mean—"

"Oh, stuff it, Ophelia Dellacava!" Ollie bristled. "Mice are *nice*!"

"Silence, *all* of you!" Marm Pettifog barked. "Shut your impertinent yaps so I may finish my announcements!"

Swallowing the retorts stinging her tongue, Anastasia glared at the back of Ophelia Dellacava's wig. Filthy vermin, indeed! *Hooey!*

"Now for my other bit of news," Marm Pettifog said sternly. "The annual Pettifog Academy Science Fair will take place in February. Your projects comprise seventy-five percent of your science grade."

"Seventy-five percent!" Gus cried.

"Not only that," Marm Pettifog went on with sadistic relish, "they also count for *ninety* percent of your public-speaking grade, as you will present them to the entire school."

Anastasia's feet went clammy. A presentation to the *entire school*?

"You should be thinking of your projects and choosing your teams," Marm Pettifog said.

"Are you going to join forces with your gorgon boy-friend?" Saskia razzed from across the aisle. "He certainly fancies himself a great scientist—but don't count on him winning the fair."

"He's *not* my boyfriend," Anastasia retorted. "And I bet he *does* win. He's *smart*." She twisted in her seat, turning her back on Saskia.

"And after last year's disaster with your helium cupcakes, Ollie, baking experiments are absolutely forbidden," Marm Pettifog decreed.

"But it *wasn't* a disaster, Marm Pettifog," Ollie protested. "Even if my cupcakes didn't float, we discovered how silly our voices sound when we eat helium."

"It was *very* silly," Marm Pettifog said darkly. "Unfortunately, the Nowhere Special interschool choir competition was that day. If you'll remember, Pettifog Academy placed last."

Ollie's shoulders slumped.

"Open your Echolalia texts," Marm Pettifog said.

"Anastasia, you'll just listen for now, but I expect you to participate within a few weeks."

A few children buzzed behind her, and Anastasia's neck prickled.

Echolalia: *Peep, squeak, krrrrp.* Geography: maps of subterranean towns with names like Limestone-on-the-Lake and Hollow-'Neath-the-Marsh, of which Anastasia had never heard. Biology: a lecture on bioluminescent mushrooms ("other bioluminescent cave species include twinkle beetles and glow moss"). After the novelty of glowing fungus dwindled, Anastasia's mind wandered back to the biography of Calixto Swift. Hours of late-night secret study beneath her quilts had yielded these tidbits about her ancient enemy:

- He learned his alphabet and nursery rhymes from a witch-nanny named Aggie!
- He wore mittens as a child!
- He developed a fondness for jokes, puzzles, and puppet shows that persisted into adulthood! ("Calixto was to remain *perpetually childish,*" the biographer scorned.)

None of it seemed remarkable, but Anastasia had only read up to Swift's seventh birthday.

"And now, students, remove your wigs," Marm Pettifog said. "It's time for your physical education. To the lagoon!"

In the rumpus down the stairs and to the school doors, Gus darted over to Anastasia and Ollie.

"Hi!"

"Gus!" Ollie cried. "Your snakes are looking *grand*! They've gotten so stripy."

"You know each other?" Anastasia asked.

"Sure," Ollie said. "We've been in the same school since kindergarten."

"Right. So, why are we going down to the lagoon to exercise? Is Marm Pettifog going to make us swim with the electric eels?" Anastasia's bottom tingled at this grim prospect.

"Nope." Ollie pulled a taffy from his pocket. "Look."

A line of pink boats bobbed alongside the dock, PETTIFOG ACADEMY painted in green letters on each of their prows. "Rowing," Gus moped. "Not that I dislike boats, but old Pettifog manages to spoil everything."

Ollie nodded. "She could ruin a pie-eating contest!"

"Collect your oars from the bins," Pettifog squawked. "Get into your quads."

"There's Quentin!" Anastasia said. "Why is he rowing with the fifth graders?"

"Every quad has one ninth-grade coxswain," Gus explained. "That's kind of like a boat guide."

"Q! Wait for us!" Ollie called.

Laughing and shoving, the students scrambled aboard.

Quentin hopped into one of the pink vessels, followed by Gus and Ollie, clutching their oars, and Anastasia plunked in behind them. The boat pitched beneath her galoshes and she toppled onto the bench.

"Princess!" Marm Pettifog stamped to the end of the dock. "What's wrong with your sea legs?"

"I don't have any, Marm Pettifog."

"Well, you'd better find some." Marm Pettifog placed her tiny foot onto the stern and gave the boat a mighty kick. "Stop gabbing and get rowing."

Anastasia fumbled with her oars, clunking the paddles against Gus's.

"Like this, Anastasia," Quentin said. "Angle the blades so they don't splash the water. Perfect! Now try to synchronize your paddles with ours."

"Wow," Anastasia said. "You're good at this."

Quentin shrugged. "Our uncle Zed is a gondolier. He takes me and Ollie out all the time."

"You're lucky," Anastasia said. "That must be fun."

"*We're* lucky?" Ollie said. "*You're* a princess! You live in Cavepearl Palace!"

Anastasia's cheeks burned. "You can come over whenever you want."

"Really?"

"Sure. Gus is coming over today after school. Why don't you come, too?"

"We could talk about the science fair," Gus said. "We could be partners, if you want."

"Angus Wata, are you kidding me?" Ollie groused. "We're going inside Cavepearl Palace for the first time in our lives and all you can think about is *science*?"

"This project is a *huge* part of our grade!" Gus said. "Didn't you hear what Marm Pettifog said? Seventy-five percent of—"

"I try not to listen to Marm Pettifog," Ollie interrupted. "Besides, why are *you* worried? You're the best scientist in our class."

Anastasia cringed. Just talking about grades made her stomach curl on itself like a frightened pill bug. She squelched her fear of flunking fifth grade into the shadowiest corner of her brain box and focused on happier prospects. "Will you come over, too, Quentin?"

"I wish I could, but I have rehearsals for *The Flinging Fledermaus*," Quentin said. "The Nowhere Special Orchestra offered me first chair saw this morning!"

"Q! You've been wanting that for years!" Ollie huzzahed.

"They were kind of desperate," Quentin admitted. "Their first saw quarreled with second saw during practice yesterday, and now they're both in the hospital." He shook his head. "They broke the Saw Musicians' Code of Ethics: *never use your saw for harm*."

"Congratulations anyway," Anastasia said.

"Thanks!" Quentin smiled.

"I wish you were coming with us to the palace, though," Ollie said.

"Well, I could come pick you up after practice," Quentin mused. "I'm sure Zed will let me borrow his gondola."

"Merrymoon! Wata! Drybreads!" Marm Pettifog blasted. "This isn't a Sunday pleasure row! Less chattering, more work!"

The quartet dug their oars into the lagoon. "If your story is a fairy tale, Anastasia," Ollie huffed, "then Marm Pettifog is the *ogre.*"

15
The Éclairs of Doom

Dear Children,

As the great astronomer Egbert Ellery Jollywater discovered in 1884, macaroons are the best snack to eat while reading about stars. Enjoy these cookies, and go forth and Discover!

Love,
P.

"Your aunt is terribly smart," Ollie declared around a mouthful of coconut. "This macaroon *does* inspire me to learn." He beamed, basking in the splendor of Cavepearl Library. "Golly, this place is grand!"

"It's *incredible*," Gus agreed, tracing with his forefinger the engraved golden cheek of a celestial globe. "Look, this shows the constellations. . . ."

"Gus wins second place at the science fair every year," Ollie said. "He's got a real genius for stars and mold and atoms and things like that."

"*Second* place? But, Gus, I thought you were the best scientist in school."

Gus frowned.

"He *is*," Ollie said. "But Saskia always gets first place, because she *cheats*."

"Really?" Anastasia gasped.

Ollie nodded sagely. "Everyone knows that Princess Ludowiga hires a real scientist to do Saskia's entire project."

"Last year, Saskia supposedly came up with a cure for hiccups," Gus muttered.

"And that hiccup syrup *did* work," Ollie said. "But there's no way *Saskia* actually brewed it!"

"Why hasn't Marm Pettifog figured it out?" Anastasia puzzled.

"Oh, I'm sure she knows. But Saskia always get special treatment."

"I thought everyone at Pettifog Academy was equally lowly!" Anastasia protested.

"We are," Ollie said. "Everyone except Saskia."

"My parents said Princess Ludowiga has the school board terrorized," Gus said.

Scowling, Anastasia shucked off her Pettifog wig and threw it on a chair. The more she learned about Pettifog Academy, the less she liked it. All the more reason not to repeat fifth grade, she ruminated, vowing not to linger at Pettifog Academy a single second longer than was necessary. She hefted a stack of texts from her desk and bore them to her fellow scholars. "My aunt found these science books for us. Maybe something in here can help us with our project."

Gus pounced on the top volume. "*The Little Star Who Could (Collapse into a Black Hole, That Is)!* I've been wanting to read this!"

"You know what *I'd* really like to do?" Ollie asked.

Inquisitive and fun-loving Reader: if granted the opportunity to prowl a phantasmagorical underground palace, what would you do first? Would you play hide-and-seek in the armory? Frolic through the painting galleries? Plant your derriere on the throne and issue pretend decrees to invisible courtiers?

Or, like Oliver Drybread, would you insist upon touring the castle kitchens?

"Eight ovens! Eight stoves!" he rhapsodized, clasping his hands together in sheer delight. "Just think of all the bundts you could bake here! And smell! Just *smell*!"

They inhaled the delicious perfume of cupcakes and tea cakes and coffee cakes.

"How many sweets does the royal family eat, anyway?" Gus asked, gauging the racks of cooling pastries. "There's enough cake here to feed an army."

"And even more on the way!" Ollie cracked an oven door to peer at the éclairs plumping within.

"Where do you suppose the chefs are?" Gus asked.

"They're probably taking a little break," Ollie said. "*A watched pot never boils,* you know. *Relax while your crumpets rise*—that's another old bit of bakers' wisdom." He beelined to a counter and started rummaging around the cooking equipment.

"Ollie, what are you doing?" Gus demanded.

"I have a brilliant idea," Ollie replied. "I got it during biology today." He dredged two fistfuls of green-glowing mushrooms from his jacket pockets and plonked them onto the counter.

"Did you steal those from school?" Gus yelped.

"I've been thinking about glow-in-the-dark cupcakes for a while," Ollie said. "But I couldn't figure out how to add the glow. I want to see whether these mushrooms keep their light when they're mashed." He brandished a pestle and set about pulverizing the fungi into luminescent gloop.

"That won't be good in cupcakes!" Gus said. "Have you ever *eaten* a mushroom? It's like licking a snail's armpit."

"Plenty of people *adore* mushrooms," Ollie insisted. "But I'm going to sweeten my gloop." He whisked a blizzard of confectioner's sugar into the paste and then shoveled out a sample nibble. "Delicious! Well, *almost* delicious. It isn't exactly revolting, at least. I'll have to perfect the recipe." He stuck out his tongue and regarded his reflection in the back of a spoon. "But it *works*! My tongue is glowing! Here, you try it."

"In a minute," Anastasia stalled. "Come on, Gus—let's—er—inspect these pudding molds." She pulled him over to a stack of copper tins. "I didn't want to hurt Ollie's feelings, but I don't want to eat mushroom gloop."

"Me neither," Gus agreed. "So, what will we explore next? Does this castle have a dungeon?"

"I don't know," Anastasia admitted. "I've only been here a few days. Is there a dungeon here, Pippistrella?"

"Scree!" the bat replied from beneath Anastasia's braid. "Prrrp-peep-squee!"

"She says yes," Gus translated. "But she doesn't know where the entrance is. Do you think there are any *prisoners* down there?"

"I hope not!" Anastasia said. "I wouldn't like to think—"

"*Who dares encroach into my galley?*"

Anastasia's gaze skidded across the kitchen. A chef crowned with a puffy white hat loomed in the doorway, helming a brigade of cooks. This brigade glowered at Ollie.

The Shadowboy smiled innocently from his place at the counter, twisting his hands behind his back to hide two purloined éclairs. "Hi! I'm—"

"A culinary spy sent by Monty Gribble, no doubt!" the chef accused. "That despicable donut monger's been after my éclair recipe for two hundred years! How did you get in here, you little crook? I can't even take a ten-minute coffee break without worrying about snoops sneaking in!" His fingers twitched toward his apron ties. "Well, the great Sir Singeworth doesn't suffer pastry pirates. *En garde!*" He whipped forth a dueling sword.

Ollie squeaked.

"Stop!" Anastasia bolted to the Shadowboy's side. "He's not a spy. He's my friend."

"And who might you be?" Sir Singeworth spluttered.

She gulped, eyeing the foil's steely tip. "I'm . . . Princess Anastasia."

Sir Singeworth scrutinized her. "Perhaps you are," he conceded. "I *heard* the Halfling princess was rather freckly." He huffed, returning the rapier to his belt. "Well, princess or not, you're still trespassing!"

"Sorry," Anastasia nattered. "I was just giving my friends a tour."

Gus shuffled from behind the jumble of pudding molds.

"This is a *kitchen,* not a playground!" Sir Singeworth exploded. "And *not* a sweetshop, either! Planning to pilfer a few pastries for yourselves, were you?" He seized the éclairs from Ollie. "These are for Princess Ludowiga's tea party. If you want éclairs, you'll have to order them, just like everyone else."

"But—" Ollie said.

"Get out!" Sir Singeworth roared. "All of you! Begone from my galley or I'll tell the queen you're interfering with my work!"

"My gosh, he's crusty," Gus said once they were out in the hall. He frowned at Ollie. "And after all that, you forgot your mushroom paste."

"No, I didn't," Ollie said. "It's inside the éclairs."

Anastasia gawped at him. "How did it get in there?"

"I piped it in with an icing bag," Ollie said. "It's easy: first you poke a hole—"

"And now two éclairs full of glowing gloop are going to Ludowiga's tea party," Anastasia concluded. Her stomach flip-flopped, and Pippistrella let out a horrified squeak.

"Six," Ollie corrected. "I made two for each of us."

"We have to get those éclairs back," Anastasia moaned. "Ludowiga will have a *fit* if her fancy guests eat those disgusting things."

"My éclairs aren't disgusting!" Ollie said. "They're *experimental.*"

They peeped around the doorjamb. The kitchen was now a bustle of activity: cooks whirring by the ovens, and black-frocked servants wheeling trolleys of cakes through a side exit.

Gus stiffened. "The éclairs are already gone!"

"Come on," Anastasia said. "Let's find that tea party!"

"Well, we can't go through the kitchen," Gus said. "I think Sir Singeworth would use any excuse to declare a duel."

They raced down the corridor, spiraled up a stairwell, and hustled to the dining hall. The long glass table, however, lay empty. *"Crumbs!"*

The panicky search sent them zigzagging through the labyrinthine palace, peeking into salons and parlors, each of which proved vacant. Anastasia balled her fists.

"At least we're getting to see plenty of the castle," Gus said.

"Wait! What's that sound?" Ollie cupped his hand around his ear.

Zithery music trickled from an arched entrance at the far end of a passageway.

"In there!"

Trailed by the bat, the trio dashed to the door and sidled in, scampering to crouch behind a massive stalagmite. Anastasia scanned the peculiar cavern. A musician plunked the strings of a golden harp, children in fancy dress played croquet on a course of raked pebbles, and ladies with parasols sipped tea at little tables. From the center of each of these tables loomed a five-tiered cake stand. The bottom tier of each of these stands bore luscious, delectable, perfectly-scrumptious-looking chocolate-frosted éclairs.

"It's too late," Gus hissed.

Ludowiga stood. "Ladies, Saskia and I would like to thank you for joining us to celebrate her triumphant return home after a thrilling semester of study in France."

"*Another* welcome-home party?" Anastasia brooded.

"Why weren't *you* invited, Anastasia? You're her cousin!" Ollie said.

"If anyone should get a party, it's *you*," Gus added. "*You* escaped two nasty kidnappers, and *you* survived a balloon crash."

"Shhh." Anastasia turned back to survey the tea party, but her cheeks burned. She hadn't been invited to a festivity *in her own home.*

"Saskia developed a penchant for éclairs at a famous Parisian bakery," Ludowiga went on. "In honor of my daughter's new dessert of choice, join us now in munching these delicious dainties!"

"Oh, Princess, we simply *couldn't* eat your éclairs!" the guests chorused. "They're too beautiful to eat!"

"Please! I insist!" Ludowiga simpered.

The ladies clapped politely, and footmen began transferring éclairs from the cake stands to the revelers' plates. Anastasia despaired: which of the teatimers would gobble the éclairs of doom?

"Mumsy," Saskia said, "your teeth look funny."

"Oh gadberry," Gus muttered.

"They're *glowing*! Your teeth are *green and glowing*!" Saskia cried.

"Ridiculous!" Ludowiga snorted. "But—upon my word! Saskia, *your* teeth are glowing!"

"Perhaps it's your toothpaste," suggested a duchess seated nearby. "Have you recently switched brands?"

"Have you ever heard of glow-in-the-dark toothpaste?" Ludowiga snapped. "Why—it's in the éclair! It's the cream filling!"

"Mine is glowing, too!" exclaimed another guest.

"And mine!"

"The éclairs are full of radioactive waste!" screamed a woman wearing a wig fashioned of pearls.

"Don't be absurd," Ludowiga sputtered. "Why would Sir Singeworth put radioactive waste in his pastry?"

"Well, *something's* wrong with these cakes!"

"Maybe some twinkle beetles fell into the cream!"

"Impossible," Ludowiga quacked. "Impossible. The palace kitchen has the highest standards of hygiene—" She broke off, wobbling to her feet and gripping her stomach.

Sapient Reader, you may already know that eating mushrooms can be a rather dicey endeavor. Some mushrooms are highly poisonous. There are mushrooms that will knock one dead within minutes and others that produce horrible sickness. Perhaps you have been wondering all along whether the glow mushrooms stuffing Ollie's éclairs were of the noxious variety. I commend you for your intellectual inquisitiveness! And now: allow me to satisfy your curiosity.

Ludowiga opened her mouth and out came the éclair and a flood of tea and probably everything else the princess had eaten that afternoon, right onto the frilly bodice of Saskia's gown.

"Mumsy!" Saskia howled, bursting into tears.

"Good golly," Ollie marveled. *"Glow-in-the-dark vomit!"*

"And lots of it," Gus said. "Uh-oh. Look at the lady in the pink dress!"

"And the one with the pearl wig!" Anastasia agonized.

"Help! Help us!" squalled two of the croquet-playing tots. "Mommy's throwing up *green*!"

Retches ricocheted through the cavern. The harpist strummed wildly, trying to camouflage the din.

"Fetch Dr. Lungwort! We've been poisoned!" Ludowiga panted between rib-rattling volleys. "It's an assassination plot! When I find out who's behind this, *heads will roll*!"

Anastasia seized Ollie's elbow in one hand and Gus's in the other. *"Run!"*

16
A Queenly Secret

AMIDST THE HULLABALOO of screaming and gagging, the young poisoners were able to pussyfoot from the garden cavern without anyone spotting them. They escaped down a side corridor, Ludowiga's shrieks echoing around them.

"Search the palace! FIND THE ASSASSINS!"

"Quick! In here!" Anastasia flung a door open and the criminals tumbled through. Gus slammed the door shut and they sprawled on the floor, panting.

"Do you think Ludowiga and Saskia and those other ladies will *die*?" Ollie quavered.

"All that vomiting might be a *good* thing," Gus suggested. "Maybe they'll get all the poison out of their systems."

"Yes," Anastasia agreed uncertainly. "They'll probably

just be sick, Ollie. *You're* alive, and you ate that gloop before anyone else."

"I only tasted a tiny bit," Ollie said. "Oh, why didn't Marm Pettifog tell us those mushrooms were toxic?"

"She probably didn't think anyone would be crazy enough to eat them!" Gus said.

"Kids eat *paste* all the time," Ollie pointed out.

"Not in fifth grade!"

"Do you think we should be planning our escape?" Ollie asked. "Just in case?"

"Maybe . . ." Gus frowned and scrunched his eyelids. "Where are we, anyway? Is this some kind of office?"

The cavern into which they had belly-flopped was very large and very dark, lit by a single lamp glowing on a big black desk. Behind the desk loomed a tall-backed chair, topped with a carved crescent moon. Anastasia staggered to her feet and crossed to the midnight escritoire, her gaze roving over the items scattered on its top: a sheaf of pale envelopes, several sticks of purplish sealing wax, a heavy ring. Anastasia peered at the golden circlet's flat face. A crescent moon embossed one cheek, a tiny butterfly the other.

"What's that?" Holding his side, Gus limped to her. "Is that a signet ring?"

"I think so. Look." Anastasia touched one of the

envelopes. A gob of smashed wax, bearing the moon and butterfly design, gummed its fold.

"That's the queen's royal seal," Gus said. "This must be her office."

"The queen's office?" Ollie darted beside them. "Do you know how much trouble we're in if we get caught? We're *trespassing*!"

"Not really—Anastasia's the *princess*, you know," Gus reasoned.

"But I'm still not supposed to be in here. Aunt Penny told me it's off-limits." Anastasia shivered, imagining Wiggy's wintry eyes finding her in the forbidden cavern. She had only bumbled into the queen's solemn orbit a few times since arriving in the Cavelands, and those brushes had included neither smile nor hug nor cozy bedtime story. Even when sitting beside the queen at the dinner table, Anastasia felt as though her grandmother were a planet glimpsed through a telescope: appearing close enough to touch but in reality existing great starry leagues away.

"Let's get out of here," she said.

But voices sounded in the hallway. The children eyed each other, trapped.

"Lord Monkfish," Wiggy said, "let's step into my office and I'll give you those papers."

Anastasia's heart leapfrogged into her mouth. "Quick! Under the desk!"

"But what if she sits down?" Gus asked as they crowded underneath.

"There's nowhere else to hide." Anastasia pulled the chair as far toward them as she could. "Pippistrella, stop wriggling! That tickles!"

The door creaked and the queen and her adviser entered. Ollie's fingernails bit into Anastasia's arm as papers rustled atop the desk. "Here's the letter," Wiggy said. "You'll take it to Senator Gibbeous yourself?"

"Of course, Your Wigginess," Lord Monkfish replied.

"Good." Wiggy sighed.

"What is it, My Queen? You seem bothered."

"I am," Wiggy said. "I am always uneasy this time of year."

"The anniversary of the Dastardly Deed, you mean," Monkfish said. "Yes, 'tis a date scorched into memory. But *you* won the war, O-Most-Glorious-Queen."

"But I *lost* my husband."

"Verily," Monkfish assented. "A hard sorrow to bear. You

may at least take solace knowing we served the deed's architects an end both terrible and quick."

"*Too* quick," Wiggy said. "My temper blinded me. I realize now I erred profoundly in those early hours of war. I should have chased answers instead of revenge."

"My Queen, we *had* to retaliate!" Monkfish objected. "A crime of that magnitude cried for blood! Morfolk could not suffer such injuries in silence!"

"You misunderstand me," Wiggy said quietly. "I'm not saying we shouldn't have killed them. Calixto Swift and his apprentice deserved to die, and die horribly. Yet I should have given those warlocks more time to betray the whereabouts of the Silver Hammer and Chest—they can't tell us from the grave, Monkfish. But Calixto was deep in his before telling us anything."

"Calixto was the world's most powerful wizard, My Queen," Monkfish argued. "Had we let him live even a moment longer, he would have injured us all the worse. He would not have surrendered his secrets."

"Perhaps," Wiggy allowed. "But what of his apprentice? All we gleaned from Dagfinn Few was this: the Hammer is the key to finding the Chest. Had we waited longer to draw blood—"

"We would know no more," Monkfish said. "Dagfinn Few was Calixto's flunky, not his confidant. He knew nothing." He spat. "Besides, the witches we *did* interrogate—later, at length and at leisure—told us nil. And we were *most* persuasive."

The queen and her adviser sank into heavy silence.

Sweat beaded Anastasia's armpits. When would this gruesome chat end? Her muscles twitched, and one of Gus's snakes (Lilybelle?) was licking her cheek.

"As you know, Lord Monkfish," Wiggy said slowly, "this castle originally housed no monarch and held no throne. Cavepearl Palace was Calixto's whimsy."

"I do know," Monkfish said.

"There's old magic sleeping in this place. It's hiding here. It's *skulking* here."

"Such is the case all over the Cavelands."

"Yes, but Calixto Swift didn't live all over the Cavelands. He lived *here*. And in his hasty flight from our mortal coil, he left behind some powerful magic."

"Yes . . . ?" Monkfish prompted.

"Have you ever heard of the Cavern of Dreams?" Wiggy asked. "Or of the Moonsilk Canopy?"

"I heard tell of it in the days before the Dastardly Deed," Monkfish said. "Witches gossiped at the pub that Swift devised a magical bed for—for magical dreams. Dreams to guide one, to illuminate the path to any hope or the cure for any woe . . . but everyone dismissed it as empty boasting. No one has ever seen the bed."

"*I* have," Wiggy said. "The Cavern of Dreams is in this castle."

"*What?*" Monkfish said.

"I have thought for centuries that it might hold a clue about the Silver Hammer."

The eavesdroppers squashed beneath the desk held their collective breath.

"Alas," Wiggy lamented, "the Canopy remains an enigma."

"Forgive me, Your Wigginess," Lord Monkfish hazarded. "If you believe the Canopy might lead to the Hammer, then surely we should at least try—"

"I have tried, Senator," Wiggy replied sadly. "Secret attempts, over the course of two and a half centuries, and all without success. Whatever alchemy couches within the Canopy, it failed to gild my dreamers' sleep with any glimmer of the Hammer. I suspect Calixto hexed his bed to prevent Morfolk from dreaming in it." Her voice was now little more than a murmur. "And yet, I do think upon the Canopy whenever the anniversary of the Dastardly Deed draws near, magnifying our tragic memories."

"My Queen, we should have every great Morfo thinker investigate that bed! Secrecy is not serving you."

"Oh, but it is," Wiggy maintained. "Can you imagine the catastrophe if our enemies discovered that the Canopy exists? That the entrance to the Cavern of Dreams is in my room?"

"In your room!" Monkfish cried.

"It is hidden, and hidden well," Wiggy said. "And that is how it must remain. What if tales of the Canopy reached the Dellacavas? They might worm a spy into the palace to sleep in that bed, to dream up a way to seize the throne. You know Dellacava ambition waxes fatter than a full moon, and far darker."

"Their hunger for power knows no satisfaction," Monkfish said. "I think the crumbs of authority we allow them in the Senate Cave merely whets their appetites."

"And then," Wiggy added, "there are . . . *the others.*"

Lord Monkfish gasped. "Surely you don't mean—*witches*?"

"That is *exactly* who I mean. If they knew the Canopy was real—not a fable passed down hundreds of years, but *real* and *here*—would witches spring from their lurking holes to storm the castle? We cannot underestimate the power of that bed, and the dreams dreamt therein. Might the witches return to dream up the way to eradicate Morfolk? Perhaps a witch would know how to loose the Canopy's magic. . . ."

"Witches," Lord Monkfish swore.

Anastasia squirmed against Gus and Ollie, her heart thumping her tonsils. How many more minutes might tick by until Wiggy pulled out her chair and found them crouched under her desk, ears stuffed full of her precious secrets?

"Your Mommyness!" The office door banged open. "Your Mommyness! Poison—attempted murder—éclairs—afoot at the palace—" Ludowiga broke off into retches.

"And worst of all, my party is *ruined*!" Saskia wailed.

"What in Caves—" Wiggy exclaimed.

"Hurry! Follow us to the rock garden!"

Anastasia waited until Ludowiga's yowls had faded from hearing range, and then she crawled from the cramped cranny, followed by her cohorts.

"Gadberry, that was a close call!" Gus said. "Well, at least Ludowiga and Saskia survived Ollie's éclairs."

"Oooooh," Ollie said. "My foot fell asleep."

Anastasia barely heard them. She didn't even realize Pippistrella was nipping her earlobe and peeping. Thoughts wrung her brain like saltwater taffy whirling in a taffy puller. Perhaps you have seen one of these contraptions in an old-fashioned candy shop: a great machine twists and twirls and stretches taffy betwixt two metal levers to make it soft and supple. It felt like Anastasia's mind was going through the same contortions.

Maybe the Moonsilk Canopy was hexed not to work for Morfolk. But Anastasia wasn't a Morfo, not entirely; she was a Halfling.

17

The Dreadfuls' New Mission

UPON THEIR RETURN to Cavepearl Library, the frazzled group found Quentin wrestling an eerie melody from his saw. "Salutations!" he greeted them. "The servant who showed me in said this was the last place anyone had seen you."

"Actually," Ollie confessed, "the last place anyone saw us was the kitchen."

They recounted the Great Éclair Debacle, beginning with Ollie's Not-So-Brilliant Idea and concluding with their Noteworthy Strides in Eavesdropping.

"The Cavern of Dreams!" Quentin breathed. "It sounds most magical!"

"Now it's even more like a fairy tale," Ollie said. "An enchanted bed in a castle . . ."

"But it *isn't* a fairy tale," Anastasia said. "It's *real.* And"—she hesitated—"I'm going to try to find it. That bed is going to help me find the Silver Hammer, and the Hammer will help me find my grandfather. And my *father.*" She told them about Fred McCrumpet vanishing from their Mooselick abode.

The boys stared at her in shocked silence.

"You can't tell anyone," Anastasia said. "Baldwin and Penny made me promise not to try to find Nicodemus. And they would definitely think snooping around the Moonsilk Canopy was too dangerous. Because of the magic. Because of the witches."

"They're right," Quentin said. "Witch magic is—can be—very nasty."

"Besides, Anastasia," Ollie said, "you heard the queen: people have already tried napping in that bed, and nobody's dreamed about the Silver Hammer. The Canopy won't work for anyone."

"For any *Morfolk,*" Anastasia corrected him. "And I'm only half Morfo. My mother was human."

"You're a Halfling?" Ollie cried. "I didn't know that!"

"Neither did I, until a week ago," Anastasia said. "I thought I was—um—one hundred percent human."

"Then perhaps the bed *would* work for you," Gus hypothesized.

"No," Ollie insisted. "You shouldn't mess with magic,

Anastasia. Magic is *dangerous.* For pudding's sake, just look at your own family! Your grandpa is trapped in a *magic* trunk, and some witch burned off your grandma's eyelids *with a magic spell*! You shouldn't sleep in that bed, and you shouldn't even go into the Cavern of Dreams."

"For someone who loves fairy tales so much, you seem awfully scared of magic." Quentin poked Ollie's arm.

"Shut up, Q." Ollie blushed and slapped his brother's hand away. "Magic in a book isn't the same as magic in real life. I read about space explorers, too, but that doesn't mean I'd ever get into a rocket."

"I'm just kidding." Quentin ruffled Ollie's hair. "You're right; magic is perilous."

"Maybe you shouldn't do it, Anastasia," Gus said.

Anastasia closed her eyes. She had spent hours studying Nicodemus's tattoo in the illustration in her textbook, and those hours had engraved the golden rings and stars in her memory. Her memory now projected the compass onto the black insides of her eyelids, pointing the path to her vacuum-cleaning, waffle-griddling, guinea-pig-loving father. She shook her head. "I have to try. What if my dad is locked up in some creepy place like St. Agony's Asylum? And Nicodemus has been stuck in a box for *centuries.*"

Gus shivered. "You're awfully brave."

"No, I'm not," Anastasia said. "But I know how it feels to be trapped. It's horrible."

"I know what it's like to be trapped, too," Ollie said. "Remember how Prim and Prude shut me in their dungeon?"

"I wouldn't exactly call it a *dungeon,*" Anastasia said. "It was just a really awful basement."

"Isn't that what a dungeon is?" Ollie frowned at some greeny glow beneath his fingernails. Then he lifted his eyes to Anastasia's face. "I'll help you," he said. "I'll help you find the Silver Hammer and your missing kin."

"You mean it?" Anastasia cried.

"I do," Ollie said. "Q and I would never have escaped St. Agony's if it weren't for you."

"That's right," Quentin said. "We'll both help."

"I'll help you, too," Gus said. "I mean, if you want my help." He ducked his head shyly.

"Squeak peep prrrip!" Pippistrella added.

"She's in," Quentin said.

A lovely combination of hope and gratitude, warm as sunshine and just as sweet, swelled Anastasia's heart. The feeling crept from her ticker and welled into her eyes, and there it shone. "Thank you," she said.

"So the League of Beastly Dreadfuls has another top-secret mission," Ollie said solemnly. "A Daring Search and Rescue Mission this time."

"League of Beastly Dreadfuls?" Gus asked.

"Prrrp?" Pippistrella quizzed.

Ollie froze. His brown eyes, bright with a question, darted to meet Anastasia's and Quentin's. They nodded.

"It's our secret league," Quentin said. "And I think you two are our newest members."

❧

That night, hugging Mr. Bunster in the safety of her own perfectly nonmagical bed, Anastasia listened to Pippistrella's little peep-snores and considered the obstacles blocking entry into the Cavern of Dreams. The Beastly Dreadfuls had discussed these during their great scheming session in the library (the boys, of course, had to translate Pippistrella's contribution to the conversation).

First of all, the entrance to the Cavern of Dreams was somehow hidden. It was hidden well enough within the queen's chamber that it wouldn't be obvious to courier bats and bats-in-waiting and chambermaids and anyone else who might enter at Wiggy's behest. This all made perfect sense, as Gus pointed out: Calixto Swift would have used all his magical trickery to camouflage the door. But, as he added, Wiggy had somehow discovered it, and so would the Dreadfuls.

That challenge, however, would have to wait until they managed to infiltrate Wiggy's cavern itself, forbidden to anyone lacking a royal summons.

There was, Pippistrella informed them, a Royal Guard

Bat policing the door to Wiggy's chamber. And as everyone living in the Cavelands knew full well, *you couldn't distract a Royal Guard Bat.* They couldn't lure it away with a juicy mango loaded with laxatives. Gus and Ollie couldn't make a ruckus down the hall so Anastasia could slip in behind the guard bat's furry back. They couldn't sweet-talk their way into the queen's cavern, even if Anastasia was a princess. No, none of these tricks would work on one of the capable guard bats.

They couldn't even wait for the guard bat to take a bathroom break. Apparently the guard bat's elite training regimen included *learning to hold it for the entirety of its eight-hour shift.* And as soon as the bat on duty completed its stint, another bat arrived to take its place.

The post of a Royal Guard Bat was *always* covered.

Anastasia kicked at her comforters, her worries shifting now to their science project. It wasn't just about her grades anymore: she wanted to *win* the fair. More specifically, she wanted *Gus* to win the fair. The thought of Marm Pettifog pinning a blue ribbon on Saskia's pilfered hiccup cure made Anastasia's blood boil.

Confident now that Saskia and Ludowiga wouldn't perish from mushroom poisoning (as Dr. Lungwort had assured the royal family), Anastasia let herself stew about the tea party to which she had not received an invitation. Of course, she had no actual desire to sip tea with a passel of snooty duchesses, but the Loondorfers' chilly reception of their long-lost Mooselick relation rankled Anastasia.

She thought of Ludowiga vomiting onto Saskia's dress, and her lips twitched into a little smile.

"So," Gus asked at lunch the next day, "did Ollie's éclairs kill anyone?"

"Nope," Anastasia said. "But now Ludowiga insists a royal food-taster test everything she eats. She's convinced someone's trying to poison her."

"It looks like Saskia has the same idea," Gus observed, gazing across the caveteria. "She's making Taffline Plimsole take a bite of everything in her lunch."

"Do you think Sir Singeworth will tell the queen he caught us in the kitchen?" Ollie pothered.

Anastasia shook her head. "He quit last night. He said he wouldn't tolerate anyone questioning his pastry. And everyone else thinks some twinkle beetles flew into the cream and leaked green glow everywhere."

"Whew." Ollie sagged in relief. "That's good news. Gus, aren't you hungry? You haven't even opened your lunch box."

Gus plastered his palms atop his tin. "I ate a big breakfast. So, I have news, too." He lowered his voice. "I have a secret weapon, ninety-nine percent guaranteed to get us past any guard bat."

"Really?" A thrill zinged through Anastasia. "What is it?"

"I can't tell you about it here," Gus said. "Come over to my house after school and I'll show you. And sorry about my parents."

"What have your parents done?" Anastasia asked.

"Just wait," Gus said darkly.

So it was that the Dreadfuls found themselves on the stoop to the suburban lair of a lady gorgon that afternoon. Of course, for Gus it was just home. Anastasia felt a little twitchy, however. She didn't want to be a glorified hat rack.

"Now, kids," Mr. Wata cautioned, "be ever so careful not to look at Mrs. Wata. We wouldn't want you turning into stone."

"Dad." Gus rolled his eyes. "I'm sure Mom will be wearing her sack."

"Better safe than sorry," Mr. Wata reasoned, swinging the door open.

"DO-RE-MI-FA-SO-LA-TI-DO!" rang a powerful voice from the depths of the cavern. Pippistrella squeaked awake from her afternoon snooze.

"Dearest!" Mr. Wata called. "We're home! Angus brought *friends.* They're here to work on their science project!"

"I-WILL-BE-RIGHT-THERE-MY-DAR-LING!" Mrs. Wata sang back.

"We always have tea after school," Gus said. "But nothing as fancy as Saskia's party." He led them to a small sitting room stuffed with furniture covered in clear, protective plastic. An elderly man, small and dark, with moon-white hair, was sitting in one of the chairs, his hands folded over the golden handle of a slim cane. His eyes crinkled behind his spectacles when he saw Angus.

"Hi, Grandpa Baba," Angus said, kissing the man's cheek. "These are my friends Ollie and Anastasia and Pippistrella."

"I've heard all about you," Grandpa Baba said. "The great scientists!"

"Maybe Gus is a great scientist," Ollie said, "but I just want to be a baker."

"Baking is a science unto itself," Grandpa Baba said. "It's much like a chemist's experiments: adding a bit of nutmeg here, subtracting a bit of vanilla there, until you determine the exact combination of variables to produce, for example, a delicious cupcake."

"I *do* make delicious cupcakes," Ollie preened, apparently forgetting the éclair debacle of the day before.

"Speaking of baking, I'll go get the tea things." Mr. Wata hurried off.

Anastasia spotted a curio cabinet tucked in the corner. "Oh! Your family has a lot of snow globes, too."

"My daughter makes them," Grandpa Baba replied proudly. "You may have heard of Celestina Wata, the great Dinkledorfian glassblower?"

"Aunt Teeny makes all sorts of things," Gus said, "but mostly snow globes."

"She supplies the snow globes for my dad's music boxes," Ollie piped up.

Anastasia startled. "Did she make the snow globes in the castle? My grandmother has an entire hallway filled with them."

"Is that so?" Grandpa Baba asked. "How curious! Celestina never mentioned anything about selling her glasswork to the queen—but I guarantee any snow globe within a hundred miles of Dinkledorf came from my daughter's shop."

"How does she get them to snow all the time?" Anastasia asked.

"What do you mean?" Gus puzzled.

"The globes blizzard even if you don't shake them," Anastasia said. "I've never seen anything like it."

Grandpa Baba's white eyebrows drew together. "I'm sorry, my dear. I'm not quite sure what you're talking about. My Celestina's globes are beautiful things indeed, but they don't—er—*snow perpetually.*" He lifted his cane to point at the cupboard. "As you can see, *those* globes aren't storming on their own."

"Oh." Anastasia crinkled her forehead.

"Speaking of globes, Princess," Grandpa Baba said, "Gus told me about your aunt's celestial sphere. And about your black-frocked servants wheeling trolleys of cakes through a side exit.

Gus stiffened. "The éclairs are already gone!"

"Come on," Anastasia said. "Let's find that tea party!"

"Well, we can't go through the kitchen," Gus said. "I think Sir Singeworth would use any excuse to declare a duel."

They raced down the corridor, spiraled up a stairwell, and hustled to the dining hall. The long glass table, however, lay empty. *"Crumbs!"*

The panicky search sent them zigzagging through the labyrinthine palace, peeking into salons and parlors, each of which proved vacant. Anastasia balled her fists.

"At least we're getting to see plenty of the castle," Gus said.

"Wait! What's that sound?" Ollie cupped his hand around his ear.

Zithery music trickled from an arched entrance at the far end of a passageway.

"In there!"

Trailed by the bat, the trio dashed to the door and sidled in, scampering to crouch behind a massive stalagmite. Anastasia scanned the peculiar cavern. A musician plunked the strings of a golden harp, children in fancy dress played croquet on a course of raked pebbles, and ladies with parasols sipped tea at little tables. From the center of each of these tables loomed a five-tiered cake stand. The bottom tier of each of these stands bore luscious, delectable, perfectly-scrumptious-looking chocolate-frosted éclairs.

"It's too late," Gus hissed.

Ludowiga stood. "Ladies, Saskia and I would like to thank you for joining us to celebrate her triumphant return home after a thrilling semester of study in France."

"*Another* welcome-home party?" Anastasia brooded.

"Why weren't *you* invited, Anastasia? You're her cousin!" Ollie said.

"If anyone should get a party, it's *you*," Gus added. "*You* escaped two nasty kidnappers, and *you* survived a balloon crash."

"Shhh." Anastasia turned back to survey the tea party, but her cheeks burned. She hadn't been invited to a festivity *in her own home.*

"Saskia developed a penchant for éclairs at a famous Parisian bakery," Ludowiga went on. "In honor of my daughter's new dessert of choice, join us now in munching these delicious dainties!"

"Oh, Princess, we simply *couldn't* eat your éclairs!" the guests chorused. "They're too beautiful to eat!"

"Please! I insist!" Ludowiga simpered.

The ladies clapped politely, and footmen began transferring éclairs from the cake stands to the revelers' plates. Anastasia despaired: which of the teatimers would gobble the éclairs of doom?

the carton and plucked forth a mouse.

KNOCK KNOCK KNOCK!

"Oh dear." Mrs. Wata clucked. "That must be the pianist." She returned her teatime victim to its paper prison and stumbled away to answer the door.

"I suppose I should go repair this." Mr. Wata stared at the contents of his dustpan. "Well, children, enjoy those scones." He withdrew to track down superglue.

"Gus," Anastasia urged. "The secret weapon?"

Gus jumped up. "I'll be right back."

"Imagine watching your mom *eat mice* every day," Ollie whispered. "Just *thinking* about it gives me the heebie-jeebies."

"Here comes Gus," Anastasia shushed him.

The gorgon tiptoed back into the parlor with a twinkly gold chain dangling from his hand. "As promised: *one secret weapon!*"

"A necklace?" Doubt scrunched Ollie's forehead.

"Are we going to try to *bribe* the guard bat?" Anastasia asked. "I don't think that will work."

Gus shook his head. He opened his fist to reveal a large

golden locket, overlaid with a coral cameo of a lady's solemn profile.

"How is *this* going to help us?" Ollie demanded.

Gus grinned at them. "It has my mom's photograph in it."

"So?"

"So," Gus said, "we'll show my mom's picture to the Royal Guard Bat!"

Anastasia's eyes widened. "But wouldn't that turn him into stone?" she protested. "We can't do that!"

Pippistrella squeaked angrily.

"It won't hurt him a bit," Gus assured them. "If someone looks *directly* at a lady gorgon, they turn to stone. But if they see a *photo* of a gorgon"—he swung the locket like a hypnotist's pendulum—"it just knocks them out for a few hours."

"Gus!" Ollie exclaimed. "You smart cookie!"

"The bat will just go into a very deep sleep. And he won't remember anything, either," Gus promised, pressing the locket into Anastasia's palm. "Don't tell anyone you have this. It's kind of against the law for gorgons to have their photos taken."

"Just imagine what could happen if a pickpocket got hold of that!" Ollie said.

Anastasia hesitated. "You're *sure* this won't petrify the guard bat?"

"Pinky swear," Gus said. "But you've got to keep it hidden. I'm not even supposed to touch it."

"I won't show it to anybody. Anybody besides the guard bat, I mean." Anastasia shoved the necklace into her satchel, guilt prickling her conscience. It didn't seem right to borrow Mrs. Wata's necklace without permission.

A squeak from the coffee table drew her attention back to the mice. "What about them? Are they just waiting to be eaten?"

Gus cringed. "Isn't it awful? I used to have a hamster named Twinkie, but my mom's snakes ate her. I cried for a week."

"Was that squeaking in your lunch box a bunch of *mice*?" Anastasia asked.

"Yeah."

"And were *you* the one who let the mice loose in the caveteria kitchen?" Ollie gasped.

"It wasn't a joke, like Marm Pettifog thinks," Gus said miserably. "I just couldn't bring them home or Mom would know I wasn't feeding them to my snakes."

"If you're not giving them mice, what *are* you feeding them?" Ollie asked.

Gus shrugged. "Gorgons' snakes don't actually *have* to eat. They absorb nutrients from their host. My mom just spoils hers."

"A gorgon's serpents are her crowning glory," Ollie quoted. *"Keep yours happy."*

Gus rolled his eyes. "Over Christmas vacation, Mom gave me a huge lecture about *nurturing* my snakes. And ever since the semester started, she's been putting mice in my lunch pail! It's mortifying! Can you imagine what everyone at school would say?"

"Ophelia Dellacava would probably scream bloody murder and jump on the table," Ollie speculated. "That might be pretty fun to see, actually."

"I've starved through lunch every day this week, because I was scared to open my pail," Gus went on. "What if a mouse hopped out when I was getting my sandwich?"

Anastasia eyed the box of mice. "Maybe we *should* liberate them."

"You mean, set them free?" Ollie asked.

Anastasia nodded. After her ghastly sojourn at St. Agony's Asylum, she knew what it was like to imagine some terrible creature was planning to devour her. It was one of the worst feelings in the world. It ranked up there with wondering whether her father had fallen into the nefarious clutches of CRUD.

"I *like* mice," Ollie said.

"So do I," Gus said. "But my mom will ask a million questions if they just disappear."

"I know!" Ollie cried. "We can say we need the mice for our science project!"

"Grand!" Gus agreed. "My parents won't complain if they think it's for schoolwork. We can just build a mouse maze or something."

"Or teach them tricks," Anastasia suggested.

"Sure," Gus said. "But you guys better take the mice home with you. Even if Mom thinks I need them for our project, she won't be able to resist eating them."

"Hooray!" Ollie cheered. "Can I have them? I've never had a pet."

And that is how ten little mice escaped becoming a gorgon's snack.

18
The Girl in the Glass

AS I'M SURE you are already well aware, dear Reader, school cancellations can be delicious things indeed: even for children who adore learning, a special day off merits celebration. And for children under the baleful watch of tyrants like Marm Pettifog, any extra morsel of liberty would rank with a round-the-world luxury cruise.

However, no jollification or jubilee would accompany the Cavelands school cancellation that Friday, aka the anniversary of the Dastardly Deed. It was a time for grim remembrance. It was a time for shutting oneself into a trunk. Or a closet.

"Or even a cupboard," Baldwin said. "Any uncomfortable little cubbyhole will do."

"It's to honor Poppa," Penny explained. "It's to give everyone a feeling for what he endures every day."

"Be quiet!" Ludowiga hissed. "Don't you twits know *anything* about solemnity? And for goodness' sake, Anastasia, do *try* to frown." She patted her wig and assumed a tragic expression.

Anastasia blinked around Stardust Cavern. Boats dotted the Gloomy Lagoon, and the Morfolk in these boats gazed in solemn silence at a black chest at the end of the dock. A choir of bats circling above screeched an eerie carol as Wiggy glided down the noble-thronged pier to this chest. She climbed inside and stood there for a moment, statue-still, her glass eyelids winking in the candlelight. Then she folded into the trunk like a deflated jack-in-the-box.

Two senators swung the lid shut and the bats hushed their song. The lord mayor of Nowhere Special scampered forth, bearing a hammer.

"In this somber coffer our queen shall stay until midnight," he proclaimed, pulling a nail from his pocket and positioning it at one corner of the crate. "In darkness dark as the dark wrought by witches, she remembers!" He swung the mallet. "Remember you all—*ouch!* My thumb! I *hit* my *thumb*!"

Saskia giggled.

"Eight nails!" the mayor went on. "As eight silver strikes to a Morfolk heart—ow! Blast it!"

After much howling, the mayor finally tamped the last pin and four dukes hefted the chest into a waiting gondola. The crowd on the pier dispersed to their own boats.

"Belfry will steer Wiggy through the canals of Nowhere Special," Baldwin said, "so all the Morfolk in town can see the procession. And then everyone goes home and shuts themselves into their own nooks and crannies."

"Come along, dear," Penny said. "The royal family rides with Wiggy."

Anastasia watched the Loondorfers boarding the gondola, the gears in her mind cranking.

"Ooo-*ooooh,*" she moaned. "My tummy aches."

If you read the first thrilling installment of the Beastly Dreadfuls' adventures, you will recall that Anastasia's stepmother, Trixie McCrumpet, spent her days snuffling and sniveling in bed when she was actually hale as a horse. Anastasia had not witnessed these shenanigans without learning a few tricks of the crock's trade. She knew how to grabble her stomach. She knew all about slumping her shoulders, quivering, and gulping.

"Why, Anastasia!" Penny said. "You don't look well at all!"

"No . . . I'm okay . . . ," Anastasia mumbled. "I just . . . feel really cold."

"I think you should stay home today," Penny fretted. "Do you want me to stay with you?"

"No," Anastasia wheezed. "I think I just need to sleep."

So Anastasia was "sick in bed with a tummy ache" while the rest of the royal family sailed off on their dismal pageant. "Sick in bed with a tummy ache" means, in this particular paragraph, "crouching behind a limestone pillar and eyeing the guard bat patrolling Wiggy's chamber." As you may already have guessed, perceptive Reader, Anastasia was not ill in the least. She didn't have a tummy ache. She had a fire in the belly to find the Cavern of Dreams, and within it, inklings of the Silver Hammer.

She took a deep breath and crept toward the flying fox. "Hi there."

The bat stared straight ahead, neither twitching toe nor flicking whisker. Anastasia pulled the locket from beneath her collar and cracked the gold oval. She held it before the bat's nose and—Bob's your uncle!—his eyes squeezed shut and his wings curled closed. His armor jingled around little snores.

"Success!" She shoved the necklace back into her shirt and darted furtive glances up and down the corridor. It was empty. How long might the queen's procession last? An hour? Two? Wiggy would stay in the trunk until midnight, but where would the *trunk* be? Would the palace staff drag it to the queen's chambers once the royal family returned from their ride?

"Come on, Peeps," Anastasia said. "We have to be quick."

Purple quartz encrusted the entire cavern, glinting and glittering in the glow from chandelier upon chandelier. An enormous metal ring—large enough to be a hippo's hula hoop—hung from the ceiling, and long curtains of chain mail drooped from this ring to mantle a massive bed. It was a *chain-mail canopy.* Trepidation twiddled Anastasia's guts. Not only did Wiggy have guards, and glass eyelids through which she could watch for intruders even in the depths of sleep, but she was also possessed of an armored bed. Anastasia shivered. Perhaps the Cavelands were safe from CRUD, but would Morfolk ever feel safe from *witches*?

As glamorous and glimmery as was the queen's cavern, there wasn't much in it. Anastasia surveyed the width and length of the cave, spotting, aside from the bed, only a vanity with a tall, splotched mirror. No doors chinked the cavern walls; at least, none that she could see. Of course, from following Francie Dewdrop's adventures in detecting, Anastasia knew that doors could be concealed in manifold manners.

"You fly up and look around the ceiling. Look for anything that could trigger a hidden door," she told Pippistrella. "I'll hunt down here." The bat squeaked and glided up to the stalactites, and Anastasia dropped to her hands and knees and crawled on the marble floors. After several painstaking minutes, she creaked to her feet and combed the crystal-spiked walls.

Nothing.

Pippistrella dived from a chandelier and lit on the dressing table, regarding herself in the mirror.

"Peeps, we don't have time to primp," Anastasia scolded. "We're on a mission."

Pippistrella ignored her, twisting to examine her batty rump in the glass.

"What are you doing?" Anastasia asked. "Is this because Baldy said you looked like you put on some weight? He was joking! You weigh *eight ounces.* Hey!"

Her breath snagged as Pippistrella spun, toppling a perfume bottle. "Watch it!" She hopscotched to the vanity and righted the flask. "You could have broken that, Peeps, and then we'd be in huge trouble."

Pippistrella screaked, battering the mirror with her wings.

"It's a shame you don't speak Echolalia."

"Who said that?" Anastasia whirled, but the cavern lay empty; she dashed to the door, but it was shut fast. The hairs at the nape of her neck prickled like the quills on a spooked porcupine.

"Peeps!" Anastasia scurried back to the vanity. "Did you hear that?"

"Squeee peep! Crr-crreakity prrp!"

"I was saying, it's a shame you don't speak Echolalia, because your clever bat has interesting things to say."

The voice again! Anastasia squinted at the stalactites, panicking. Might Wiggy have stationed a Shadowperson to patrol her chamber's darkest corners? "Where are you? Stop hiding! As—as princess of the Cavelands, I command you to show yourself!"

"Interesting things like: *look right in front of your nose.*"

Breathing hard, Anastasia lowered her gaze to the mirror. Carved in the wooden frame were the words LOOK & YE SHALL FIND, and below these words, her reflection grinned. Trembling, Anastasia raised her fingers to her lips. She definitely was *not* smiling. Her mouth was round as an O.

"Hello," the reflection said. Pippistrella shrilled and zipped from the vanity to cower beneath Anastasia's braid.

Anastasia goggled at the girl smirking from the glass. She cautiously stretched to touch her, but her fingertips just bumped the mirror's silvered flank.

"You can't come in here," the girl informed her, sounding amused.

"This must be witch magic!" Anastasia said. "You *can't* be real!"

Her reflection's grin capsized into a scowl. "Of course I'm real. Why wouldn't I be?"

"I—I don't know. Maybe I'm imagining you."

"Don't be insulting," her mirror-twin retorted. "I have an entire existence outside anything your silly noodle could invent. There's a vast *mirror-world* for me to play in: all the places reflected in all the mirrors of the world. My life doesn't start and end with reflecting *you,* you know." She examined her fingernails. "I'm not stuck watching you blow your nose and count your freckles—not all the time, anyway."

"But I *don't* count my freckles!" Anastasia protested.

"You did back in first grade," the mirror-girl said. "When you finally learned how to count over one hundred."

Anastasia's face grew hot, remembering. She quickly cataloged all her embarrassing performances before a mirror: shining a flashlight up her nostrils in the hopes of glimpsing her brain. Excavating caramel from her molars. Her reflection had seen her get out of the bathtub! She had seen her *buck-raving naked.*

"Don't blush," the mirror-girl said, rubbing her own cheeks. "I hate it when you make us blush."

"S-so," Anastasia stammered, "what do you do when you're not—er—reflecting me?"

"Oh," the mirror-girl said, "I go to quite a few parties."

"Parties?"

"With other reflections." She laughed. Her laugh was like a tinkly glass bell. It didn't sound at all like Anastasia's giggle, which was closer to the yip of a coyote pup. Anastasia appraised her mirror-twin. Even though the girl in the glass looked like Anastasia, she also *didn't* look like her. Not exactly. The mirror girl had mousy-brown hair and mousy-brown eyes, but her expression was frosty and her posture was excellent.

"What's your name? Is it Anastasia, too?"

"Certainly not. It's Aisatsana."

"It sounds pretty close," Anastasia said.

"It's *Anastasia* backward," the girl sighed. "And so am I."

"What do you mean?"

"Well," Aisatsana drawled, "for example, you're obsessed with mystery stories. I can't stand them. They're stupid."

"No, they aren't!"

"And, unlike you, I *like* to brush my teeth." The mirror-girl's tinkly laugh shivered amongst the stalactites.

"Shhh!" Anastasia hissed. "Someone might hear you. We're not supposed to be in here!"

"Correction: *you're* not supposed to be in here." Aisatsana folded her arms across her chest. "In fact, you're trespassing.

So, are you just pretending to be that nosy Francie Dewdrop you so admire? Or do you have a good reason for snooping around the queen's cavern?"

Anastasia hesitated, loath to spill her hush-hush beans. But, she reckoned, a girl from an enchanted mirror-world might know something about the magical chamber. Besides, Aisatsana was *her* reflection; they were practically *twins*! And twins were supposed to share a marvelous, practically magical bond—weren't they?

She decided. "I'm looking for the Cavern of Dreams."

A smile curved Aisatsana's silvery lips. "The Cavern of Dreams," she echoed softly, leaning forward. "I can tell you where it is."

"Where?" Anastasia also leaned forward.

"It's a big secret, you know," Aisatsana whispered. "I really shouldn't tell you."

"Please, Aisatsana," Anastasia begged. "I need to find that door!"

Aisatsana tilted her head. "All right," she finally agreed. "I'll tell you. But you'll have to do something for me, too. Let's make a little deal."

"What?"

"I want you to go to Zero Cavern."

"Zero Cavern?" Anastasia echoed.

"Zero, as in *zero gravity.*"

Anastasia blinked. "What's that?"

"Gravity," Aisatsana said, "is the thing that makes you fall down when you jump. It keeps you from floating up into the air like an escaped helium balloon and flying out into space. It's what makes the moon go round the Earth, and the Earth go round the sun—"

"I know what gravity is," Anastasia bristled.

"Well, in Zero Cavern, there's zero gravity."

Anastasia stared at her. "That's impossible."

Aisatsana flipped one braid over her shoulder, oozing superiority.

"But how do *you* know about it?" Anastasia demanded. "I've never even heard of it!"

"I know lots of things you don't!" Aisatsana huffed. "Other reflections told me about it. *Old* reflections. There used to be a mirror there, but vandals stole it a couple of centuries ago. And now nobody from the mirror-world can visit Zero Cavern. A place has to be reflected for it to exist in the mirror realm, you understand." She lifted her chin. "And I want to have a party there. In case you forgot, it's almost our birthday."

"I didn't forget," Anastasia said hotly. "Penny and Baldwin were talking about *my* party last night."

"Oh, *joy.*" Aisatsana rolled her eyes. "I've been to your so-called birthday parties, and they're dull as ditchwater. *You* might like playing Pin the Tail on the Donkey with your dad while a gerbil watches, but *I* don't." She sniffed. "At least we're in a palace now, so I might expect something a little grander."

Tears needled Anastasia's eyes. "Muffy is a *guinea pig,* not a gerbil. And I'd rather see her and my dad than eat cake in a castle."

Aisatsana shrugged. "Well, I'm having my own party this year anyway. And I'm having it in Zero Cavern, which means you need to go there."

"But what exactly do you want me to do?" Anastasia asked.

"I want you to take a looking glass to Zero Cavern," Aisatsana said. "And you have to let yourself be reflected in it, and then leave it behind. I can't visit anyplace where you haven't been mirrored." She planted her hands on her hips. "Deal?"

Anastasia sighed. "Okay."

"Promise me." Aisatsana eyed her coldly. "And just so you know, breaking a promise to your own reflection would be *very* foolish. Remember, we're connected for your entire life. You can never go past a mirror, or a window, or even a puddle or a shiny spoon, without summoning me. I'm *always* watching you."

Anastasia's stomach wambled. "I promise," she said nervously. "Now, how can I get into the Cavern of Dreams?"

"I'll tell you later," Aisatsana said. "*After* you go to Zero Cavern."

"But—"

"And try to brush your hair for once! I'm tired of going around looking like bats roosted on my head." She looked pointedly at Anastasia's plait, where Pippistrella clung upside down. Then she turned her back to the mirror and plugged her ears with her forefingers.

Anastasia ground her teeth. Really! Her reflection was unbearable!

"Come on, Peeps," she muttered. "Let's go."

19
How to Eat Cake

"I HAVE A special treat for you," Ludowiga announced at that Saturday's etiquette lesson.

Most children, when promised by their aunt a special treat, will clasp their hands in joyful anticipation. However, Anastasia's nerves jangled. What sort of diabolical scheme did Ludowiga have tucked up her frilly sleeve?

"Tonight, Princess, we will learn how to eat petit fours. Have a seat."

"Petit fours?"

"*Cakes,* you simpleton. SAMPSON!"

Sampson scurried in, propelling a cake-laden tea cart into the sitting room and swerving it expertly between all the ormolus and ottomans and whatnots.

Anastasia eyed the tray of pink dainties. A cake-eating

exercise? Was this some sort of trick to ferret out the éclair poisoner? She squirmed.

"Anastasia, dear?" Ludowiga said.

"Yes, Aunt?"

"Would you care for a petit four?"

Anastasia thought. Someone who *didn't* go around poisoning pastries would probably say yes. "Yes."

"No, no, no!" Ludowiga tossed her hands in exasperation. "Never appear *eager*! It is gauche! It is loutish! You don't want to seem *hungry*, do you?"

"But what if I *am* hungry?"

"How you *feel* doesn't matter, you silly girl. Whenever anyone offers you a pastry, be it petit four or common cupcake, you must always decline." She cleared her throat. "From the beginning! Anastasia, would you care for a petit four?"

Anastasia sneaked a sideways peek at the cakes. "No, thank you."

"But I insist," Ludowiga said. "They're simply divine. You must try one! Won't you please have one?"

Her mouth watered, but Anastasia steeled her resolve. "No."

"Wrong again!" Ludowiga shrieked, hopping out of her chair. Pippistrella squeaked and flapped to a higher stalactite. "You *have* to accept the second offer! Do you want to offend me? How *dare* you decline my cakes? Do you fancy yourself too good for my petit fours? Well, I daresay my cakes are too good for *you*!"

"But you told me to say no!"

"I said nothing of the sort." Ludowiga sat back down. "I instructed you to refuse the first offer, but even a complete fool knows you accept the second one! Otherwise you will offend your hostess."

Anastasia fidgeted. "But what if I actually *don't* want cake? I mean, I'm hungry *now*, but what if I just had a tooth pulled, or—"

"IT WOULDN'T MATTER!" Ludowiga screamed. "YOU ALWAYS, INVARIABLY, AND AT ALL TIMES ACCEPT THE SECOND OFFER!" She brought her knobby fist down on the coffee table, making the teapot and creamer and sugar bowl jump. Anastasia jumped as well.

"Now, let's try again! Would you please have a cake, my dear?"

Anastasia cringed. "Yes, please."

Sampson plucked a cake from the tippy-top of the stack. He set the cake on a fragile china saucer and set the saucer in front of Anastasia. She noticed that one corner had already been nibbled off. "Thank you," she mumbled.

"Say it to me, not him," Ludowiga flared. "*I* am the one who ordered the cakes made. *I* am the one who ordered the royal taster to test every one of these lousy crumpets. *I* am the one whom you must thank."

"Thank you for the delicious cake, Aunt Ludowiga."

"You are welcome."

Ludowiga watched closely as Anastasia finished the petit four and delicately brushed a few crumbs from her chest and onto the napkin in her lap.

"Fine," she said. Then she glared at Sampson. "We no longer require these cakes. Dispose of them."

"But I've only had one!" Anastasia cried as Sampson whisked the tray of petit fours away. She stared in open-mouthed horror as he marched straight to the fireplace and chucked them in.

"And one is all you shall have," Ludowiga declared. "You must never eat more than one cake. It would be indelicate. One cake is it. Then the remaining cakes are destroyed. They are stamped beneath feet. They are tossed out the window, or smashed in a vise, or squished beneath pillows. I once knew a duchess who liked to blow up pies with firecrackers. She was a genius!"

"But that's a waste of perfectly good cake!"

Ludowiga sniffed. "My dear girl, I could afford to throw away truckloads of cake! That's the entire *point*! You have to show off your wealth somehow, and only so many diamonds can fit on a necklace. And that," she said, "concludes today's session. You now know how to eat petit fours."

Anastasia's stomach twisted as she noticed Aisatsana's face, tiny and squashed, observing her from a teaspoon's shiny hollow. No doubt the mirror girl was impatient for her freckled twin to visit Zero Cavern. Anastasia glowered. Ludowiga's little lesson constituted not only a waste of cake but also of *time.* Every minute frittered away in teatime talk was a minute lost from the Dreadfuls' great search-and-rescue mission. *Or* . . . Anastasia regarded her aunt thoughtfully. Perhaps Ludowiga *could* teach her something worthwhile, after all.

In Francie Dewdrop's thrilling case *Mystery of the Purloined Doily,* the plucky detective gleaned all kinds of clues from a snobby socialite named Millicent Winterbottom. It wasn't because Mrs. Winterbottom was wise or perceptive. It was because Mrs. Winterbottom liked to gossip. And sometimes, mixed within the prattle and yakety-yak, there rattled a significant nugget.

If Calixto Swift had been like an uncle to Penny and Baldwin, it followed that Ludowiga had known him, too. Anastasia hesitated to mention Calixto to Penny and Baldwin, because they *knew* her. They knew about her love for detection. They knew she wanted to find her father. They might descry, within the web of Anastasia's innocently pitched questions, her plan to track down Nicodemus and Mr. McCrumpet. And then they would halt her great investigation.

But Ludowiga wouldn't suspect anything, because she was oblivious. She knew Anastasia was clumsy and freckled and ate moths. But she didn't really *know* Anastasia. She certainly didn't realize her niece aspired to be a great detective-veterinarian-artist.

Sometimes, Reader, it's advantageous to be underestimated.

"I *said,* we're done for tonight." Ludowiga flicked her hand, as though shooing a particularly dim-witted fly.

"Did Calixto Swift ever come over for cake?" Anastasia asked. "I mean, before the Dastardly Deed? I—I just wondered what his manners were like."

"Calixto Swift was a boor," Ludowiga snapped. "Always blustering about with stupid jokes and making rabbits pop out of hats. Of course, all that buffoonery was just a screen for his *real* nature. It never fooled *me.* But Penny and Baldwin and Fred ate up that nonsense like Hansel and Gretel gobbling witch's gingerbread."

"Penny said Calixto put on a puppet show for her eleventh birthday," Anastasia said. "He even gave her a puppet."

Ludowiga laughed. It was a nasty sound. "A powerful warlock, and he spent his spare time playing with dolls. Ridiculous!"

"Did he ever give *you* a present?"

Ludowiga snorted. "No, he did not. And if he had, I certainly wouldn't have accepted it. I saw that man for what he was: a schemer." She drummed the table with her long fingernails. "I've always been a better judge of character than my siblings and even, if I may say so, than my dear, missing father. Poppa adored that treacherous warlock. Allow me to teach you another valuable lesson tonight, you lucky child: *never trust anyone.*"

Anastasia gulped.

"Did Penny tell you about Calixto Swift's most famous puppet show?" Ludowiga asked.

Anastasia shook her head.

"It was the evening of the Dastardly Deed. Calixto locked Father in the trunk that afternoon and set off to stage *The Mermaid and the Magic Key* in Dark-o'-the-Moon Common not three hours later. Callous! And *arrogant*! Just like a witch." She sighed. "I do regret missing *that* show."

"But I thought you didn't like puppet shows," Anastasia said.

"I don't." Ludowiga smiled. "After we discovered Poppa was missing, a Morfolk mob stormed *The Mermaid.* They said even Swift's puppet screen bled that night, but of course that's poetic exaggeration." She sipped her tea. "It was all Swift's blood. Now, run along, Princess—I have to get ready for a ball."

20

Drybread & Drybread's Music Box Emporium

"OH DEAR." PENNY rustled the Sunday newspaper. "Three Morflings went missing yesterday."

Baldwin stopped marmalading his toast. "CRUD's handiwork, I presume?"

"Quite positively."

Even though Anastasia was safe in the Cavelands, sitting at a perfectly cozy breakfast table between her perfectly protective aunt and uncle, her heart kicked like a caffeinated kangaroo. "*Three?* Were they triplets?"

Penny shook her head. "No, child. CRUD is a global ring, and they're *ambitious.* They snatched one of the children from the beach in Spain, and another from a playground in Peru, and the third one from La-La-Land Amusement Park in Texas—right in the middle of his eleventh birthday party, too! *Rupert disappeared from his seat on the Mind-Scrambler somewhere between the second and fourth loop-the-loop,"* she read aloud. "Goodness me, CRUD is kidnapping children off *roller coasters*? How do you suppose they managed that?"

"Poor kid," Baldwin said sadly. "What a sorry end to his birthday jollifications. I wonder if he even got a piece of cake before CRUD swooped in to spoil things."

Anastasia, whose own eleventh birthday approached at a gallop, nibbled her fingernails. Were Prim and Prude still looking for her? Or had they moved on to a new victim? If she ever wanted to venture abovecaves again, perhaps she should invest in a proper disguise. She touched her upper lip, making a mental note to check whether Sir Marvelmop sold mustache wigs.

"Our counter-CRUD agents will investigate," Penny said. "But it may . . . well, it may be too late." She folded the newspaper and stirred her tea, frowning.

Too late. Anastasia's heart sank. Was it *too late* for Fred McCrumpet? Nobody would utter the words aloud, but that's what her family was *thinking*. Were they right? Was Anastasia foolish to keep hoping to find her father?

In many ways, Reader, hope is like a telescope. In the depths of darkened space, the soul peering through a telescope perceives a star. Perhaps it is far-flung; perhaps it is a mere speck; but it is *there,* and that makes all the difference.

Anastasia lifted her jaw. She wasn't ready to throw down *her* telescope, not by a long shot.

She itched to discuss her first expedition into the queen's cavern with her fellow Dreadfuls, but Gus was stuck at home that weekend, and Quentin had orchestra practice, and Ollie was helping his parents ready Drybread & Drybread's Music Box Emporium for its grand reopening. And, of course, Anastasia couldn't telephone her friends. As you will remember, attentive Reader, neither electric cable nor utile telephone wire hummed within the Cavelands.

School on Monday was even worse. There were Ollie and Gus, just a few desks over, and she couldn't utter a word. Her news would have to wait until after school, when the Dreadfuls would convene at Ollie's house to "work on their science project." (Of course, clever Reader, *you* already know that *science project* was Beastly Dreadful code for *secret mission to track down the Silver Hammer.*)

Anastasia stared at the classroom clock, willing its brassy arms to move faster. Soon it would strike three o'clock and the Dreadfuls could consider her findings.

"After the First Declaration of Perpetual War," Marm Pettifog droned, "all witches and witch-sympathizers were driven from the Cavelands, and the Crown's Inquisitors investigated some non-Morfolk during a period of anti-magic hysteria. Such groups included . . ."

Attention drifting, Anastasia dipped her pen in her inkwell.

". . . The Weird Ones . . ."

She drew a circle of stars on the back of her hand.

". . . a group of fortune-tellers who claimed . . ."

She inked a crescent moon inside the circle.

". . . The Wish Hags, a trio of troglobites skilled in brewing potions, although not themselves witches . . ."

In small letters, Anastasia wrote *F-R-E-D*.

FRED

"Anastasia!" Marm Pettifog wheeled from the chalkboard.

She jumped. "Yes, Marm Pettifog?"

"Of all the students in this class, you know the *least* about Cavelands history. Do you suppose that is because you pay the *least* attention?"

Saskia raised her hand. "Marm Pettifog, I think we princesses have a royal *duty* to know history, because we're the ones who will *make* history."

"It's *everyone's* duty to know history," Marm Pettifog said. "But your cousin is right, Anastasia: no subject wants to think the queendom's crown sits on an empty head. And

I suspect the gap betwixt *your* ears is in dire need of padding. Now quit daydreaming and doodling, and focus on your notes."

"Yes, Marm Pettifog." Ignoring Saskia's titters, Anastasia diligently scribbled in her notepad: *Wish Hags—Troglobites (?)—Brew.*

Jingling and jangling, twirling and twinkling, a caboodle of music boxes caroled a merry cacophony behind the window to Drybread & Drybread's. Little wooden ballerinas spun en pointe, and snow globes glittered in the candlelight. Anastasia pancaked her palms against the glass. "It's beautiful!"

"Thanks," Ollie said. "We spent ages getting everything ready."

"Did your dad make all of these?" Anastasia asked.

"He tunes all the music boxes, and he carves all the figurines," Quentin said. "But the snow globes come from Celestina Wata."

"Gus's *aunt,*" Ollie reminded Anastasia.

"What's she like? I've never met a real artist before," Anastasia said.

"Aunt Teeny's pretty nice." Gus shrugged. "Really quiet, though. And she doesn't visit all that much—she spends every waking minute in her workshop." He pressed his nose to the window. "That mouse music box is so realistic—I can almost see its whiskers twitch!"

"*Mouse* music box?" Ollie peered over his shoulder.

"There are *lots* of mice running around in there," Anastasia said. "I didn't see them at first."

"Dad must have brought them down from our apartment," Ollie said. "We live above the shop, you know."

"Come on." Quentin pushed the shop door open. "I have to be at orchestra practice in half an hour. Hi, Dad!"

"Hello, hello!" Mr. Drybread called from a workbench piled with springs and cylinders and other mechanical bits and bobs. "Now, is this Anastasia?"

"Yep." Ollie beamed.

"I've heard so much about you, dear! Ollie and Quentin told me all about your adventures in that asylum." Mr. Drybread waved a screwdriver. "Got nibbled by a few leeches, didn't you? Well, you showed those kidnappers in the end, by Jove!"

"And this is Gus," Quentin said.

"Oh, I remember Gus!" Mr. Drybread said. "Second place at the Pettifog science fair every year! Speaking of that, Ollie told me you're here to work on your science project?"

"That's right," Gus said.

"Well, I'll leave you to it. Just make sure you don't take your mice in the house, Ollie—your mother almost had a nervous breakdown this morning. From now on, the mice will lodge in the shop." Mr. Drybread returned his attention to a pile of gears.

"Let's go into the listening booth," Ollie whispered. "It's soundproof."

He led them to a small glass cubicle nooked in a corner. Squashing everyone in at once was much like a round of

Telephone Booth, an old game in which high-spirited teenagers struggled to stuff as many of their friends as possible into a calling box.

"Tell us quickly, Anastasia," Gus wheezed.

She told them about the queen's chain-mail bed and the vanity, and then she told them about Aisatsana. "And she wants me to—"

"Wait," Ollie interrupted. "You actually *talked* to your reflection?"

"I *have* to see that mirror," Gus said. "I wonder what my reflection's like?"

"Well," Quentin pondered, "he'll be your opposite. And his name would be *Sugna.*"

Ollie hooted. "That sounds like an old lady's name!"

"I wonder whether Sugna can petrify people?" Gus said.

Ollie's eyes rounded. "You'd better stay away from that mirror, Gus. Who knows—Sugna might turn *you* into stone!"

"I bet your reflection hates cupcakes, Ollie," Anastasia mused.

Ollie shook his head. "Shadowfolk don't have reflections."

"Really?" Anastasia gasped. "I knew you couldn't cross over mirrors, but I didn't know you don't show up in them."

"It's very sad," Ollie said mournfully. "I'd love to have a mirror-twin."

"Believe me, you're not missing out on much," Anastasia reassured him. "Aisatsana is a *pain.* She knows how to get into the Cavern of Dreams, but first she's making me take a mirror to this place called Zero Cavern."

"Zero Cavern!" Quentin said.

"But it's *forbidden*!" Ollie exclaimed. "And besides, hardly anyone knows where it is. Do you know, Q?"

"Nope."

"And I can't ask Penny or Baldy," Anastasia said. "They'd get suspicious."

"Attention," Quentin murmured, hastily cranking a music box. "Here comes Dad."

Ollie cracked the door to the listening booth.

"Enjoying those tunes?" Mr. Drybread asked pleasantly. "But you're not neglecting your project, I hope?"

"Not at all," Gus said. "We've done a lot of work already. We're in the research phase."

"And how is that going?"

"Good," Gus said. "Did you know that some scientists spend their whole lives studying whiskers?"

Mr. Drybread's forehead crinkled. "Like the whiskers on your mice?"

Gus nodded. "Whiskers are really special things. They're super-sensitive, and each one grows out of a special follicle packed with nerves. And when something touches the whisker, it jazzes those nerves and sends a signal to the mouse's brain."

"Fascinating! I had no idea!" Mr. Drybread said. "Well, carry on."

"Quick thinking, Gus," Anastasia said as Mr. Drybread bustled away.

"Did you make up that whisker stuff?" Ollie asked.

"No. It's all true." Gus pulled a book from his backpack and flashed its cover. "I got this in the Pettifog school library."

"The Wonderful World of Whiskers," Ollie read.

"You know that mice have super-acute hearing, right?"

Gus asked. "This book says that whiskers are so keen they pick up sound vibrations. Like antennas on an old radio."

"Maybe they don't like listening to music all day," Anastasia fretted.

"They seem to like it just fine. I think they're having a grand time," Quentin said.

Sure enough, the mice were at that moment gathered round a music box jingling Christmas carols. Anastasia squeezed from the booth to peer at their whiskers. The rodents had them all twitched forward toward the music box, the way clever flowers turn to follow the sun.

She ducked back into the booth.

"Back to Project Zero Cavern," Ollie said. "We have to find out where it is."

"Ahem." Gus cleared his throat. "I've been there."

"You?" Anastasia goggled at him. It was difficult to imagine Gus escaping his overprotective parents' clutches long enough to visit the loo, let alone to sneak into a cavern forbidden to all. It occurred to her that his shy and scholarly demeanor concealed a staggering genius for mischief. He

had devised a way to sneak past the Royal Guard Bat—and now this!

"What's it like?" Ollie asked.

"Well," Gus admitted, "I didn't actually go inside. I peeked in from the door. A couple of gondoliers were in there, floating around like astronauts. They were laughing like crazy." He scrunched his face, remembering. "I think they might have been drunk."

"But the Zero Cavern is *forbidden*!" Ollie cried.

"Why?" Anastasia demanded.

"It's a witch's house! And it's full of bad magic!"

Some of the enthusiasm drained from Gus's face. "*Used* to be a witch's house, back before the Perpetual War. It isn't, you know, *naturally* zero gravity; it's enchanted. Mrs. Honeysop—the old witch who lived there—had arthritis or something, and she cast a spell so she could float around without crunching her knees. And now I guess the magic affects certain Morfolk . . . um . . . badly."

"It warps their bones!" Ollie cried.

"My teacher last year told us that some kinds of magic change over time, the way milk spoils." Now Gus looked nervous. "I guess that's what happened in Mrs. Honeysop's cave."

"Our dad told us about a kid who went in there and came out with his neck stretched like a giraffe's," Quentin said.

"I heard that, too," Gus said. "But maybe it's a story to scare kids from going in."

"If the cavern is forbidden to *everyone,* there must be a reason," Anastasia pointed out.

"Sour magic!" Ollie shuddered.

"Where is Zero Cavern, anyway?" Anastasia asked Gus.

"In Sickle Alley," he said. "It's really close to the Cavepearl Theater, actually. There's a little crawlway off the far corner of the backstage area, and it connects with Sickle Alley."

"The Cavepearl Theater!" Quentin perked up. "Well, that makes everything easy, doesn't it? You can come along with me to orchestra practice and slip away to run your mirror errand."

"But my dad is coming to pick me up soon," Gus said.

"And so is my aunt," Anastasia said.

"Oh." Quentin lapsed into thought. "Well, we'll have to do it *sometime* this week, because Friday is opening night of *The Flinging Fledermaus.* No more practice after that; only performances." He sighed. "I would just go to Zero Cavern myself, Anastasia, except Shadowfolk can't carry mirrors."

"That's all right," Anastasia said. "Aisatsana said *I* have to go, because the mirror has to reflect me. Wait! The opera starts this Friday? We'll all be there, right?"

The Dreadfuls nodded.

"So *that's* when we'll go to Zero Cavern!"

"But how can we sneak off when our families are around?" Ollie asked. "Everyone will be watching."

Quentin leapt as though a red-hot poker had scorched his bottom. "Except for the part when *no one's* watching!"

"Brilliant!" Gus said. "Brilliant, Quentin! I know just what you're thinking!"

"Well, tell us, too," Ollie complained. "We can't all be brilliant, you know."

"Bellagorgon has a big solo at the end of the opera," Quentin explained. "Everyone has to blindfold themselves—so they don't look at her and turn to stone."

"And that's when we'll sneak out." Gus grinned.

It was a daring plan. A downright *dangerous* plan. A bold-as-brass humdinger of epic proportions, no ifs, ands, or buts about it.

Anastasia loved it.

"The Gorgon's Aria lasts nineteen minutes exactly," Quentin said. "It's the longest solo in the history of opera."

"That should give us enough time to get to Zero Cavern and back, if we hurry," Gus calculated.

"I won't be able to join you, because I'll be sawing away in the orchestra pit," Quentin said. "But I can let you in the backstage door at the beginning of the aria. My saw stuff doesn't start until about four minutes in."

Bzzzt! The gears in the musical clocks all shifted and

they launched into a hullabaloo of various tinkling melodies. Quentin squinted through the glass wall. "Four o'clock! I've got to go!" He scrambled from the booth and snatched up his saw case, bumping into Penny as she came through the shop door. The Dreadfuls piled out of the cubicle to greet her.

"Hello, dears!" She kissed Anastasia on the top of her head and scratched the snoozing Pippistrella's chin. Then she withdrew a parcel wrapped in brown paper from her capacious purse. "Ollie, I brought a little present for you."

"Oooooh!" Ollie tore back the wrapping. "Thank you, Princess! I've always wanted a . . . well, what is this, exactly?"

"It's an exercise wheel for your mice," Penny said.

Ollie plonked the wheel onto a counter. "Let's see if they like it. Here, Sprinkles." He lifted a spotty mouse and set her in the metal curve.

Sprinkles took a careful step forward. Then she began walking faster and faster. The wheel whirled on its stand.

"Well done, Sprinkles!" Ollie cheered. "You're a real athlete!"

"Most mice are," Penny said. "How's your project coming along?"

The Dreadfuls smiled.

"It promises," Gus said, "to be a great success."

21
The Gorgon's Aria

"WHO IS RESPONSIBLE FOR THE POOP ON MY TEA TRAY?"

Penny glared at the offending swirl nestled betwixt her teacup and cookies.

"Not me!" Anastasia said.

"Peep!" Pippistrella declared.

"Er." Baldwin cleared his manly throat. "There's a chance it *might* have been me."

"Baldwin!" Penny scolded. "You can't just go around leaving poop all over the place!"

"Of course not." Baldwin hung his head and stared at his shoes. Perhaps he spotted his handsome reflection in their shiny black toes, because he licked his fingers and smoothed his mustache, then winked.

"A specimen like this merits the greatest of care." Pinkies crooked, Penny lifted the lump and contemplated it with frank admiration. "Ah! I could gaze at this for hours!"

"It's a beauty!" Baldwin agreed.

"Magnificent!" Penny said. "One of the finest I've ever seen. I would simply be devastated if anything happened to it." She bustled over to a glass cabinet wedged between the paleofungus and paleozoology bookshelves and carefully placed the blob on a small velvet cushion. "There! And in the future, Baldy, if you take out my poop, please be sure to put it back where you found it!"

Baldwin rolled his eyes. "Your aunt, Anastasia, is perhaps a little too protective of her petrified poop collection."

Penny reached into the paleodungus case and adjusted a squiggle on its pedestal. "These specimens are very rare," she said primly. "The pterodactyl scat you left on the tea tray is seventy million years old!"

"Sorry, Penny," Baldwin said. "I'm just so distracted. I can't wait for *The Flinging Fledermaus*!" He patted his vest and glanced around. "By the way, has anyone seen an errant blueberry scone?"

"Good grief, Baldy! It's in *here*!" Penny excavated a jam-smeared crumpet from the poop cabinet. "Well, at least we know why you left fossilized dung with the tea things—you just mixed them up. Poor Baldy! You *are* distracted." She carefully shut the glass chest. "Anastasia, did you know that you can learn all kinds of things about somebody by examining their poop?"

"Ugh. I don't think I want to know that much about *anyone.*"

"Oh, but it's terribly instructive." Penny's eyes sparkled with scientific zeal. "I knew an archaeologist who discovered the most astonishing thing in an ancient Egyptian chamber pot. . . ."

"Scree—ee—pip!" A courier bat glided into the library.

"Wiggy's ready!" Baldwin cried. "And miracle of miracles, so are the Loondorfers! Let's go!"

The queen's gondola was a splendiferous vessel indeed, gold-painted and limousine-long, with a sort of miniature pointy house sprouting from the center. This fanciful floating pagoda was bigger than the biggest dollhouse you have ever beheld but still rather a pinch for several ladies with massive crinolines, plus Ludowiga's titanic wig. Anastasia squirmed within the puff of skirts, the mirror hidden in her satchel jabbing her ribs.

"You'll remember this night for the rest of your life, Anastasia," Baldwin said. "Oh, the drama! Oh, the intrigue! Laughs and tears and the occasional fart joke—*The Flinging Fledermaus* has it all, and then some!"

"I do hope, Princess, that you'll remember our discussion regarding the proper way to applaud," Ludowiga said.

“Give it a rest, Ludowiga,” Baldwin groaned. “Who made *you* the expert on clapping, anyway?”

“Congress,” Ludowiga snapped. “*They* recognize that I have the finest manners in the Cavelands.”

“Your manners are fine indeed,” Baldwin concurred. “Finer than a frog’s hair—why, I can’t see them at all.”

“Here, Anastasia,” Penny interrupted, pulling a length of silk from her purse. “You’ll need this blindfold for the Gorgon’s Aria. You’ll petrify if you so much as glimpse Bellagorgon’s face.”

Anastasia accepted the blindfold, worry pickling the scones in her belly. What if the Dreadfuls got caught sneaking out of the theater? What if her skeleton warped in Mrs. Honeysop’s soured magic? She shivered.

“Don’t worry, cousin.” Saskia shot her a syrupy smile. “If you turn into stone, we’ll find a use for you. You’d make a *charming* doorstop.”

“Enough.” Wiggy smoothed her skirts. “We’re here.”

Morfolk in fancy dress thronged the theater entrance. Their faces turned in tandem as the gold litter anchored to disgorge its royal passengers.

“There’s the Halfling princess!” Whisper though it was, Anastasia’s spry young eardrums snared the comment. She blushed so hard her freckles sizzled.

“There’s Princess Penelope!”

"Oh, just look at Princess Saskia's gown! She's *so lovely.* Pretty as a picture!"

"Is that a sheep or a wig on Princess Ludowiga's head? Why, it's marvelous!"

"The queen!"

Everyone collapsed into bows as Wiggy glided up the velveteen path spooling from the great arched doors of the theater.

"Come on." Baldwin squeezed Anastasia's hand and pulled her along.

An usher guided them up a staircase and down a narrow corridor, halting respectfully by a pair of curtains. "Your balcony, Your Majesties." Anastasia darted to the edge and fumbled in her satchel for her binoculars. She scraped their magical gaze across the theater dome crowded with hanging bats, the limelights fizzing at the edges of the stage, and the gold-frocked musicians tuning their instruments in the orchestra pit below. "There's Quentin!"

"Doesn't he look fine!" Penny said.

"And there," Ludowiga hissed from behind her opera glasses, "is Janet Dellacava. *And look at her wig.* It's definitely taller than mine!"

"Calm down, Loodie," Baldwin chuckled. "Why, it's a splendid wig."

"Shut it, Baldwin," Ludowiga retorted. "Have you been

twisting pretzels abovecaves so long that you've forgotten the Decree of Wig-Loft?"

"No one may wear a wig taller than a royal's," Saskia cited.

Music trembled from the orchestra pit.

"That impertinent creature is deliberately flouting the rules," Ludowiga huffed. "Your Mommyness, aren't you going to *do* something?"

"I'm preparing to enjoy the opera, Ludowiga, and I suggest you do the same."

"But—"

"Hush, you ninny!" Baldwin said. "It's starting!"

The stage curtains parted to reveal an artificial cavern of papier-mâché stalactites. Two women in fruit bat costumes dangled from trapezes, spreading their arms and screeching to the shrill of violins.

Baldwin leaned forward with a contented sigh, propping his elbows on the balcony's lip.

Were *all* operas terrible? Or just *Morfolk* operas? Either way, *The Flinging Fledermaus* was pure torture. Pretending to fix the curls dangling from her wig, Anastasia poked her ears full of fluff. Better. Pippistrella, still roosting in her pompadour, let out a batty snore as one of the actors began catapulting pineapples into the audience.

"What wit!" Baldwin rejoiced. "What verve!"

Anastasia sneaked Miss Viola's watch from her pocket.

Quentin had said the Gorgon's Aria started about an hour into the performance; that was—*fifty-eight minutes away!* Aisatsana's ghostly mug stared at her from the clock's crystal face, the silver arrows twitching around her nose like the whiskers of an angry cat. Anastasia's jitters tripled and she crammed the timepiece back into her skirts.

The hour crawled by in a phantasmagoria of scene changes: from papier-mâché cavern to nighttime desert; from nighttime desert to Viking ship. Anastasia hoisted her binoculars and trained them on Quentin. He drew one last, wobbling note from his saw, and then he looked straight up at the queen's opera box. He nodded, and Anastasia gulped. *It's go-time.* She nudged Pippistrella awake.

"Get out your blindfold," Penny murmured. "You mustn't take it off until the aria is over."

"It's a doozy," Baldwin said, slapping two pirate patches over his eyes. "Bellagorgon sings for almost twenty minutes straight. Tonsils like a Spartan!"

The theater sibilated with the silky sounds of operagoers cinching their blindfolds. *Shh. Shh. Shhhh.* Anastasia fidgeted in the dark, her muscles tensed like those of a runner poised before a race. She would have to dash from the opera box as soon as the music started.

LAAAAAAAAAAAAA!

Mrs. Wata's cry surged through the theater like a tsunami. It swirled amongst the stalactites, eddied in the audience, and flooded Anastasia's soul with strangeness and beauty. She had never heard anything so wonderful in her life, and for one long, glory-drenched moment she remained transfixed in her seat. Then Pippistrella nipped her hand.

"Right," Anastasia mumbled. She had less than twenty minutes for the round-trip scramble to Zero Cavern. Hurry! Twisting her face from the stage, she unknotted the bow on her blindfold and then, gaze riveted to the floor, she grabbed her satchel and crept from the balcony.

Gus and Ollie were already crouching in the corridor. "Ready?"

"Of course," Anastasia fudged.

She followed them through a maze of tunnels to a door marked CREW ONLY! Mrs. Wata's voice thrilled around them, pricking Anastasia's arms with goose bumps. Pippistrella peeped nervously and latched onto the back of her lady's wig.

The door cracked open and Quentin ushered them through. "Good luck," he whispered. "I've got to get down to the pit." He clambered down a staircase, leaving the Dreadfuls to gape at the whirl of backstage activity: actors struggling with costumes, theater bats zinging to and fro, and stagehands barging hither and thither, lugging props and ladders and tugging on ropes that controlled the stage scenery. Makeup artists huddled around candle-ringed mirrors, teasing wigs and slathering performers with creams and rouge.

"Three of my beauty marks fell off in the second act," grumped a puffy singer. "I *told* you to use airplane glue."

"Come on," Gus urged. The Dreadfuls slunk behind a rack of frothy dresses to huddle behind a jumble of downed chandeliers, and from there they burrowed beneath a heap of fake clouds and then tiptoed behind a painted screen. Dodging and ducking, pussyfooting and prowling, they made their way to a papier-mâché tree propped in a neglected corner.

Behind the tree, squidged between two mounds of cave bacon, gaped the hole leading to Sickle Alley.

"How did you ever find this?" Anastasia marveled.

Gus shrugged. "I've spent a lot of time hanging around the theater. Mom used to bring me to rehearsals. Careful—watch your head." He slipped out.

Anastasia's crinolines wheezed as she wriggled through the chink, but with Gus yanking her arms and Ollie pushing from behind, she finally squished through to Sickle Alley. She blinked. Sooty lanterns trickled muted puddles of light down the tunnel's gloomy gullet, and bits of broken glass barbed the shadows. The Dreadfuls pressed against the slimy cave wall as a man in a flapping black coat slouched past, face hidden behind his pushed-up collar.

"This place is *sinister,*" Ollie said.

"Well, we won't be here long." Gus started running.

The *zzzzz*ither of violins licked their heels as they raced down the crumbling cobblestones, each note winding the Gorgon's Aria closer to its end. A dozen grimy shop windows flashed by before Gus stopped at a narrow gap in the wall.

"It's that way," he panted.

They stared at each other.

"We don't all have to go in," Anastasia said. "Just me, so Aisatsana can visit Mrs. Honeysop's house." She shuffled sideways into the crevice.

"I *want* to go," Gus said. "It looked fun."

"I'm not staying in this awful alley by myself," Ollie said, mashing in behind them.

"I see light ahead," Anastasia reported. "I think we're almost there—" A gasp sucked the words from her throat as an unseen power yanked her up into the unknown. She was *floating*! She kicked her legs amidst her billowed petticoats, surprised delight burbling her tonsils. "Whee!" She arced her arms and swanned through a cloud of twinkle beetles.

"Whoopee!" Ollie and Gus blurted into the cavern.

"Incredible! It's like we're in outer space!" Gus said.

"This is ground control to Major Gus," Anastasia called. "Major Gus: your pants have ripped up the back."

Gus clutched the seat of his trousers. "Darn it! Mom's going to have a fit!"

"How do your bones feel?" Ollie asked, examining his hands. "I don't feel like I'm crinkling up."

"Me neither." Anastasia checked Miss Viola's watch. "We have eleven minutes."

"Which means we need to leave Zero Cavern in *four*," Gus said.

Anastasia rocketed off a tall stalagmite and sailed across the parlor. It hadn't been a witch's home for centuries, but a few relics of its long-gone lodger still wandered the cavern: a broken rocking chair, a raggedy cookbook, a woebegone cuckoo clock trailing two pinecone-shaped weights. One tattered sock clung to the grille caging the parlor's abandoned fireplace. Anastasia's attention hiccupped to the blank spot above the mantel. Had a looking glass lacquered the chimneypiece in days of yore, perhaps reflecting Mrs. Honeysop dozing in her chair? Aisatsana had mentioned a stolen mirror.

Even though Mrs. Honeysop had been a witch, and witches were magic-hoarding, silver-mining murderers, the lonely parlor saddened Anastasia. She snared a roaming candelabrum and lit its tapers with a match from her pocket.

"Look!" she said. "The flames are *round*."

Gus paddled to her side. "Hot air rises," he mused. "That's why flames are long and pointy. But without gravity, it isn't going to rise. So the fire fans out in a ball."

Anastasia bore the strangely flamed candelabrum deeper into the cavern, frogging down the hallway to a dark little cavity. A bed hovered in its center, quilts still tucked firmly beneath the mattress. Why didn't the pallet stray from the frame? She released the candlestick and swam toward the bed, plunging her hands between the mattress and wrought-iron skeleton. Ah! The clever witch had devised a system of ties to secure the feather cushion to the bed slats. As Anastasia wrestled her arms free from the mattress, her fingers brushed against something hard and flat and thin. She pulled it free.

"Anastasia!" Gus called from the parlor.

"Just a minute!" She frowned at the peculiar object plundered from the witch's bunk: some kind of oversized paper doll, trimmed of black paper, shiny and stiff with varnish. Tiny perforations dotted the dark maiden's dress and hair, creating a filigreed design delicate as a shadow cast by lace. Silver rivets gleamed at her joints. Anastasia gingerly plucked one paper wrist between her thumb and forefinger and pivoted the arm, marveling. Why had the old witch kept a paper doll hidden under her bed? Was it some kind of talisman?

Anastasia bit her lip, wondering whether she held a snippet of bad magic. But it was so dainty; a doll hewn from midnight. The artist in Anastasia itched for scissors and paper so she could fashion her own paper doll.

"Anastasia!" Ollie hollered.

She carefully swiveled the paper arms over the paper torso and slid the doll into her satchel. "Coming!"

"Watch!" Ollie cried, twisting upside down and launching from a stalactite to kick-start a crazy spin. "I'm a helicopter!"

"Octuple somersault!" Gus yelled.

"I can do a no-hands handstand!" Anastasia said.

"I see London, I see France; I see Anastasia's pantaloons!"

"Shut up, Ollie!"

"Peeps!" Ollie said. "Your mouth is glowing *green*!"

Pippistrella hiccupped.

"She's been eating twinkle beetles!" Gus cried.

"Or maybe she got into Ollie's éclairs!" Anastasia giggled.

"Shhhh!" Gus stiffened and cupped his hand around his ear. "Listen!"

The Dreadfuls hushed. Faint singing echoed down Sickle Alley and into Mrs. Honeysop's cave.

"Mom's almost at the end of her aria," Gus said hoarsely. "We've got to go!"

"Wait!" Anastasia dredged the mirror from her satchel and made a horrible face at Aisatsana, and then she let it float away. "Mission accomplished."

"Wait till we get back to the theater to say that." Gus pushed her toward the door.

Anastasia yelped as gravity lassoed her back into the vestibule. Ollie wheezed in after her, Gus clinging to his coattails. They hotfooted through the narrow shaft and retraced their steps down Sickle Alley, running pell-mell to the hole leading to the theater backstage. From screen to clouds, from chandelier jumble to gowns, the Dreadfuls darted until finally they burst through the CREW ONLY! door.

"If anyone noticed you were gone, just tell them you were in the loo," Ollie advised.

But Anastasia's family was still blindfolded in the opera box. She collapsed into her seat just as Mrs. Wata belted out the final, triumphant note of her aria. LAAAAAA! They had done it! The League of Beastly Dreadfuls had infiltrated Zero Cavern!

The audience burst into ecstatic applause.

22

Donut Moon

"MIRROR, MIRROR, ON the wall," Ollie intoned, "where-oh-where is the Cavern of Dreams?"

Aisatsana crossed her arms over her chest and scowled. "I *hate* fairy tales."

"Of course you do," Anastasia muttered.

"Aisatsana, did you go to Zero Cavern?" Gus called from behind the chain-mail canopy. He was being careful not to let his reflection glide over the looking glass, just in case Sugna's snakes were, indeed, venomous. "Because *we* did."

Aisatsana yawned. "I know. I saw you there, remember?"

"Wasn't it fun?" Ollie enthused.

"I wasn't impressed," Aisatsana said. "It's just a dingy hole overrun with bugs and floating junk. I've already canceled my party."

"She doesn't like Zero Cavern because you *do,*" Ollie whispered to Anastasia.

"Well, whether you like it or not, I held up my end of the deal," Anastasia informed her reflection. "So show us the door to the Cavern of Dreams. Please."

"I'm not a servant," Aisatsana snapped. "I'm not some maid you can order around."

"I don't order people around!" Anastasia retorted. A comment about bossy mirror-twins hovered at the tip of her tongue, but she clamped her mouth shut. She had to focus on finding the Moonsilk Canopy. Tracking down her father took priority over zinging her snooty reflection.

This, dear Reader, is called *keeping your eyes on the prize.*

Aisatsana plucked a necklace from the mirror image of Wiggy's jewelry box and examined the gems. "I've been thinking about it, and maybe I shouldn't tell you. I could get into big trouble."

Anastasia's jaw dropped, and Pippistrella let out a tiny squeak of rage.

"*You* could get into trouble?" Gus cried. "We had to sneak out of the opera, for Pete's sake!"

"Our bones could have warped!" Ollie added.

Aisatsana buckled the necklace to her freckled throat. "Oh boohoo."

"You *promised,* Aisatsana," Anastasia said. "And

remember, I'll be watching you for the rest of my life, too. It would be very unwise for you to break your promise."

Aisatsana trilled with silvery laughter and pinned a brooch to the lapel of her school uniform. "There isn't anything you could do to me."

"Really?" Anastasia challenged. "I can embarrass you in front of your mirror friends. I'll make faces like this." She flared her nostrils and puffed her cheeks.

"And," Ollie piped up, "she could shave her head. *Your* head."

"You wouldn't like to go around bald, would you?" Gus asked.

"You wouldn't dare," Aisatsana hissed.

"Sure I would," Anastasia lied cheerfully. "It would show off our ears."

"Fine!" Aisatsana unclasped the necklace and flung it onto the reflected vanity. "Not that you do much with our hair anyway." She sidled three steps to the left. "The Cavern of Dreams is right through here."

Glimmering, shimmering, glinting in the far depths of the reflection, a pointed silver door nested between crags of crystal.

Anastasia and Ollie whirled around.

"Where did it go?" Ollie exclaimed, darting to run his hands over the wall.

Anastasia turned back to the looking glass. "There isn't a door *here*. Why is there a door in your room?"

Aisatsana rolled her eyes. "In case you haven't noticed, this is a *magical* mirror. It reflects magical things—things that are usually hidden." She huffed. "Didn't you wonder why I've never spoken to you before? You can shout all you like into the mirror in your loo, but I won't respond. I *can't*. It's just a piece of shiny glass—not a Glimmerglass, like this one. Now, keep looking at the door and walk backward. Shadowboy, get out of the way."

Grumbling, Ollie stepped aside.

Anastasia slowly stepped back, eyes glued to the mirror. Her silver twin mimicked her movements, retreating from the surface of the Glimmerglass and treading into the depths of the reflected room.

"Okay," Aisatsana called, "reach back and grab the knob."

Anastasia stretched her arm toward the wall, gasping as her fingers closed around a smooth metal ball.

"Don't turn around!" Aisatsana warned, also twisting her arm behind her back. "You'll break the spell. Now open it."

Anastasia turned the knob. The hinges sang, and backward she tumbled through the silver door and into, of all things, a wintry forest. Trees hemmed this pocket of magic, and the air smelt of pine and earth and snow and freshness, and the night sky vaulted up, up, up, all the way to the stars.

"Look at the moon!" Ollie breathed.

High in the black yonder, the moon floated like a huge, silvery, beautiful Berliner, which is a sort of holeless donut, and twinkly bits snowed down from it like magical powdered sugar.

"Did we—did we somehow get outside?" Anastasia staggered to her feet.

"It must be some kind of illusion," Gus whispered, joining them. "There's no way that door could lead abovecaves. The palace is miles underground."

"That moon is *real,*" Ollie argued. "I can feel its sizzle!" He closed his eyes and tilted his face to sop up the moonlight.

"It can't be real," Gus countered. "It's some kind of magic." But his eyes were brimful of wonder and the sparkles of far-flung stars.

"Peee-*eeeep*!" Pippistrella squealed, whizzing to the moon-tinseled trees.

"Wait!" Anastasia yelled.

"This is probably her first time abovecaves!" Ollie said. "No wonder she feels like frolicking! I feel like frolicking, too!" He galloped off after Pippistrella, disappearing into the forest.

"Come on." Anastasia grabbed Gus's hand and tugged him into a run. "They'll get lost."

They chased Ollie's whoops through the tree trunks. Laughter bubbled up Anastasia's windpipe. Her lungs thrilled with fresh air, and the smell-molecules of a thousand Christmas trees tingled her nostrils like champagne fizz. Perhaps this place was magic, and perhaps magic was bad, but she felt just peachy.

Gus pulled her to a halt. "Listen."

A giggle died behind her molars. "What? I don't hear anything."

His face was tense. "Exactly. Why did Ollie stop yelling?"

They pressed forward cautiously, easing between a cluster of pine trees and into a clearing.

Ollie stood frozen at the edge of the moonlit dell, staring at the phantasm in its center.

The moon hovered directly overhead, and its fall of twinkling moonbits cascaded down to curtain a vast carved bed piled with cushions and pillows and aglow like a silver candle. If Cavepearl Palace was a marvel, the Moonsilk Canopy was a miracle.

"It's beautiful," Ollie said.

"Look, there are words on the headboard: *good night, sleep tight, don't let the bedbugs bite.*" Anastasia's voice snagged. "My dad always said that when he tucked me in." Of course, Anastasia's bunk in the shabby McCrumpet abode was humble indeed compared to Calixto's magic-sugared masterpiece. Hope pitter-pattered her rib cage: would the Moonsilk Canopy really sprinkle her sleep with clues? And by those twinkling inklings, could she truly chart her course to the Silver Hammer; to Nicodemus; to her father?

Pine needles crinkled beneath their feet as they crept toward the apparition. Anastasia held her hand beneath the avalanche of moon-snow, wondering at the soft zinging breath of each individual flake kissing her palm. *Anastasia,* uttered a faraway voice. *Anastasia.*

She snatched her hand away. "Did you hear that?"

"Hear what?" Gus asked.

"Someone was calling my name."

"I didn't hear anything," Ollie said.

Anastasia, come to bed.

"There it is again!"

Gus frowned. "Are you sure you didn't imagine it?"

"I heard *something.*"

The Dreadfuls dawdled at the edge of the Canopy. "Well," Anastasia finally said, "I suppose I'll try to take a nap."

"I don't think you should," Ollie waffled. "I've read *Goldilocks* enough times to know you shouldn't sleep in a bed that isn't yours. Magic or not." He glanced around. "Do you think there are bears in these woods?"

"Ollie." Gus rolled his eyes.

"If Calixto Swift could cook up a cavern full of sky and moon and forest, don't you think he could add a few bears to guard his precious bed?" Ollie demanded.

"Maybe," Anastasia conceded.

"Don't do it, Anastasia." Ollie grabbed her elbow. "No matter how pretty it is, that bed is full of witch magic."

"But it might give us a hint about the Silver Hammer." The compass tucked in Anastasia's memory twirled, its arrow pointing to the moon-soaked cradle. She shook off Ollie's hand and climbed into the glowing eiderdown.

Anastasia, sang the far, faraway voice. *Anastasia, it's bedtime, dear.*

She jerked. "Did you hear that? Someone keeps calling me!"

"Anastasia, it's some kind of trick," Ollie quavered. "I really don't think you should—"

But her ears were already sinking back to the pillow.

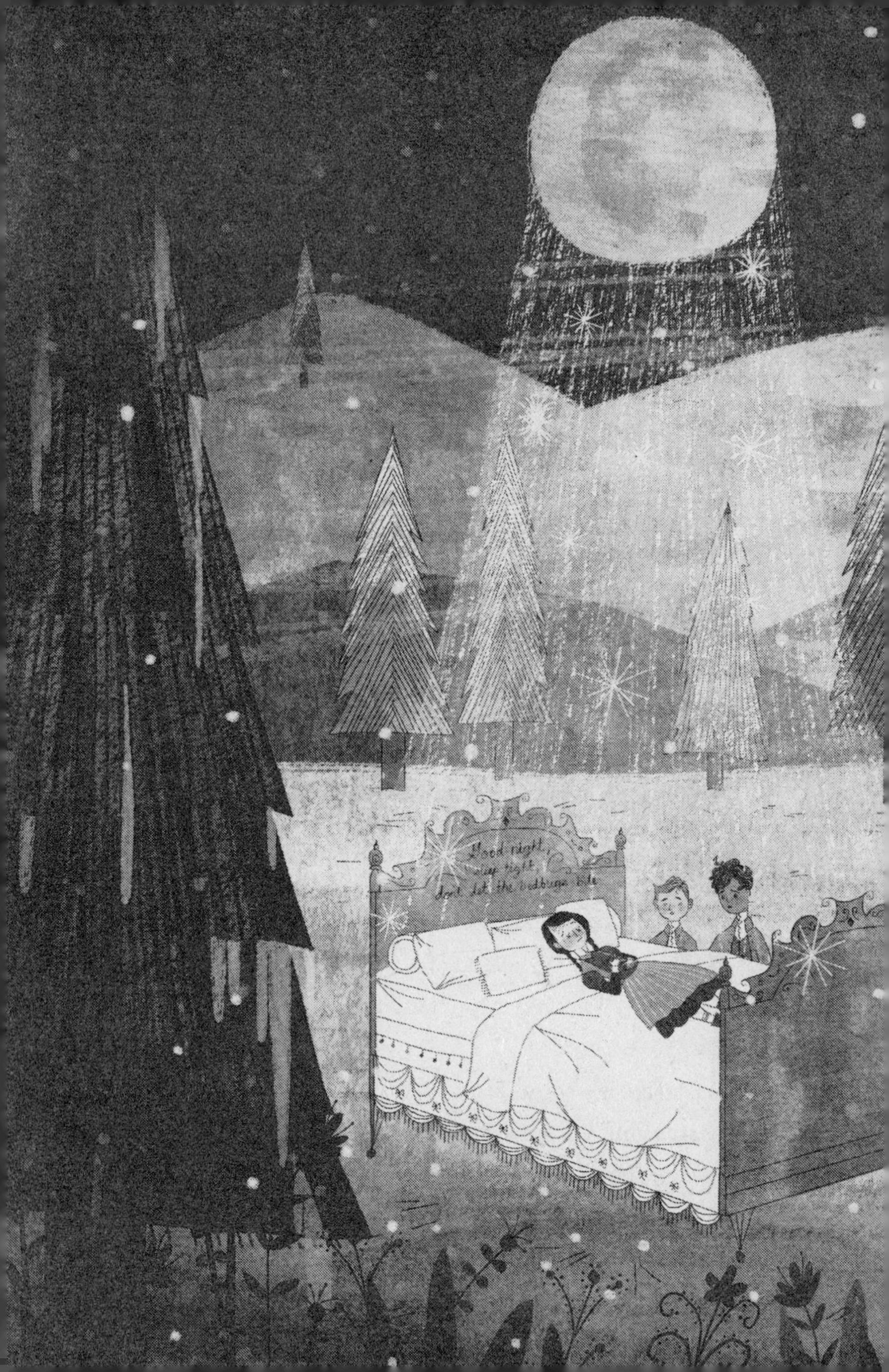
Good night,

23
The Great Mouse Orchestra

ANASTASIA, THE VOICE murmured. It was the lovely lullaby voice of a mermaid singing many fathoms below the sea. *Your dreams long for you almost as much as you long for them.* Tinkling music prickled her eardrums.

When had she ever been so cozy, so comfy? Half-dream thoughts wandered her mind, dancing to the tinkling tune. The music reminded her of the snow globes tintinnabulating in Drybread & Drybread's emporium, which in turn reminded her of their swelling rodent population. Every school day at noon, Gus dispatched a mischief of mice from his lunch box and into Ollie's pockets, so the Dreadfuls now had dozens of subjects for their science project. Their science project! The Pettifog science fair lurked around the corner, and they hadn't done a lick of work. *What can we do about our science project?* Anastasia wondered. *What can we do . . . what . . .*

"Anastasia!" Gus shook her arm.

"Where are we?" She blinked. Why! They were onstage at the Cavepearl Theater! Phonographs jumbled the floorboards. A phonograph, if you don't know, is a sort of old-timey music machine. A round disc called a record swivels atop a table turned by a crank, and the grooves in this record transmit music up a needle and into an enormous horn. However, the phonographs puffing their brassy throats onstage didn't have cranks. And, unlike most phonographs piping music across the globe, a single mouse stood at attention atop the record of each of the music machines Anastasia now beheld.

Ollie trotted forth from the curtains, pulling a conductor's baton from his pocket. Each mouse hunkered down. The Shadowboy swooped the baton.

Tinkle jingle tinkle tinkle . . .

A wild ruckus jangled from the phonographs as the records spun beneath the galloping mice.

Jingle, tinkle, tinkle!

An invisible audience erupted into cheers.

"Bravo!"

"Amazing!"

"SQUEEEAK!"

Anastasia's eyelids stuttered. "Pippistrella?" The last

fanciful figments fizzled from her brain and she sat up, rubbing her peepers.

"She says it's almost dinnertime," Ollie said. "And that your aunt and uncle will come looking for us if we don't show up in the dining hall."

"Did you dream?" Gus asked eagerly.

"Yes. But it wasn't anything about the Silver Hammer. It was about *mice.*"

"Mice?"

"And the opera house, I think. . . ."

"So just a normal dream," Ollie concluded. "A bunch of weird nonsense. Let's go."

Anastasia gazed around Drybread & Drybread's and sighed. The music boxes tinkled toward the ends of their metal melodies, and the Dreadfuls were no closer to finding the Silver Hammer. They were no closer to tracking Nicodemus or his magical tattoo. Anastasia's throat tightened. She calculated: she hadn't snuggled into a cozy dad-hug, or listened to a bedtime story about guinea pig fairies, or eaten a signature Fred McCrumpet waffle for over three months. And perhaps she never would again.

Meanwhile, the days since her unfateful nap in the Canopy had trickled by in classes and quizzes and worry about the upcoming science fair, which loomed the following

Monday. Anastasia dug in her pocket for the note Saskia had flicked to her desk that afternoon:

If your science project stinks as bad as your petticoats, you're going back to third grade.

To be honest, Anastasia *had* issued a silent yet epic flabbergaster not one minute before Saskia scribbled the vexing epistle. Nonetheless, the snipe flooded her with righteous indignation.

She lifted a snow globe from the shelf and shook it, watching the flakes within dance a spritely jig. Then her focus shifted to her reflection, gossamer and ghostly upon the glass sphere's curve. Aisatsana! Would Anastasia *never* escape her evil twin? *Any* slip of glass conjured the contrary girl.

Anastasia huffed an exasperated puff onto the globe, coating her reflection with a patch of steam. *There.* Farewell, Aisatsana! The fog evaporated from the glass in a trice, but not before tickling Anastasia's memory into coughing up a few crumbs from her stint at St. Agony's. Her ponderings flashed to the twinkly pictures her breath had tinseled upon the madhouse's glassy bits and bobs. Had the chilly filigree really been, as Penny and Baldwin assured her, some sort of mirage? Anastasia thought not; she remembered it so *clearly.* If only Ollie or Quentin had witnessed the frosty phenomenon!

Anastasia startled. Perhaps the Shadowboys hadn't

glimpsed the peculiar rime, but someone else *had*—and that someone was now staring her right in the face. In the clammy depths of St. Agony's, Aisatsana had mimed Anastasia's antics in mirrors and darkened windows and the glass breastplates of picture frames. If Anastasia had truly spangled the asylum with frozen designs, *Aisatsana would have seen her do it!* She could simply ask—

"Electric eelmaidens!" Ollie cried, shoving a book under Anastasia's nose.

"What?" She snapped from her reverie.

Ollie tapped the page. "They're like mermaids but with eel tails. And they shoot *electricity* out of their eyes."

Anastasia studied the illustration of a golden-haired eelmaiden. "That can't be real."

"Your aunt lent us this book." Ollie flipped the cover to display the title: *Pliny the Eldest Elder's Compendium of Creatures.* "It's full of all kinds of animals: unicorns and dreameaters—Pliny says they have funny noses to snuffle up dreams, but there isn't a picture. And—"

"I don't think Penny gave us that book for our project, Ollie," Anastasia said. "She knows you like fairy tales. I told you, she misses being an elementary school librarian. Last night I caught her making book lists for *imaginary children.*"

"We don't have time to talk about unicorns and

dreamcatchers," Gus grumped. "We have to decide what we're going to do with these mice."

"We could figure out what kind of cheese they prefer," Ollie suggested. "Our findings could help cheesemongers everywhere!"

Gus shook his head. "That's not much of an experiment. Our parents will expect a Nobel Prize after all the time we've supposedly worked on this project."

"Well, at least we visited the Moonsilk Canopy," Ollie said cheerfully. "Anastasia, tell us about your dream."

Anastasia groaned. "Again?"

"I like the part when the audience cheers."

"We were onstage, and there were a bunch of mice. . . ." Her eyes shifted to a cluster of rodents sitting around a music box tinkling "Edelweiss." "You know, these mice really *do* seem to love music."

"It's probably those super-sensitive whiskers, picking up the sound waves," Gus said.

"Hello, scientists! How are your rodents?" Mr. Drybread said, sidling over to dust a snow globe display. "My goodness! They're getting *pudgy.* Ollie, what have you been feeding them?"

"Well, they get their pellets, and then I also give them crumbs."

"Crumbs?"

"Like cupcake crumbs. And pancake crumbs. And just-plain-cake crumbs."

"Ollie, you can't feed your mice cake!" Mr. Drybread said. "You'll make them sick!"

"But they like it."

"Of course they like cake. Everyone likes cake. But mice don't have the same tummies as we do," Mr. Drybread scolded. "From now on: *pellets only.*"

"Don't they run on their exercise wheel?" Gus asked.

"Nope." Ollie reached out and spun the neglected hoop. "They each gave it a whirl, but I guess the fun ran out."

"Too bad we can't make the wheels play music," Anastasia mused, thinking of the mice in her dream galloping on gramophone records. "I once read about people who hooked their TVs to treadmills so they *had* to exercise to watch their favorite shows."

"Oh," Ollie mourned, "I *miss* TV. I watched it all the time back in Melancholy Falls."

Anastasia picked up a glass music box and turned its crank. The brass cylinder rotated, its freckles plunking the teeth of a musical comb. Her eyes twitched over to the mouse wheel. "Mr. Drybread, how exactly does a music box work?"

He set down his duster. "I'm so glad you asked! The inner workings of a music box are fascinating!"

"Oh bother," Ollie muttered.

"There's a compressed spring inside the box," Mr.

Drybread explained. "When you wind it up, it twists the spring tighter and tighter. And then the spring needs to uncoil, and when it does that, it makes the musical cylinder spin. When the spring uncoils all the way, it stops working the cylinder, and that's why the tune runs out."

"Could you make a music box that didn't have a spring?" Anastasia asked.

"Sure," Mr. Drybread said. "But you'd have to wind the crank constantly if you wanted to listen to music."

"What if you had a big music box with no spring, and you attached the crank to that mouse wheel? Would the music box play when you spun the wheel?"

"I don't see why not," Mr. Drybread said. "It would be pretty easy to fix up."

"That's it!" Anastasia turned to Ollie and Gus. "*We can make a mouse-powered music box* for the science fair!"

"Brilliant!" Gus cried. "We already know the mice love music!"

"And your mice certainly need the exercise," Mr. Drybread said. "I'll go fetch some parts from the back room and you can start building." He disappeared into the depths of the shop.

"Hooray!" Ollie cheered. "Anastasia, it's just like your dream! Mice playing their own music!"

Gus gave a little leap. "Do you think the Canopy *made* you dream about the mouse orchestra to give you the idea for our science project?"

Anastasia's eyes rounded. "I—I don't know." She thought back to her nap in the Moonsilk Canopy. "I was worrying about the science fair before I drowsed off."

"Well, that settles it. You were thinking about it anyway, so of course you dreamed about it," Ollie said.

"Or," Gus whispered, "that's how the Canopy works: you ask it a question before you fall asleep, and then *you dream up the answer.*"

The Dreadfuls stared at each other. Hope throbbed anew in Anastasia's chest.

"We can try again on Saturday," she said. "I was going to invite you over anyway. It's my birthday—"

"Your birthday?" Ollie squealed. "Now you'll be eleven!"

"And we're having a party. Penny said you could come over early and we could play games while everyone else was setting up the palace."

"Oh my golly," Ollie breathed. "Are you going to have a huge, princessy party? With hundreds of guests and a gigantic cake?"

"I guess," Anastasia admitted. "But I don't like . . . you know . . . parading around with people looking at me."

"I wouldn't like it, either." Gus shuddered.

"Anyway, everyone at the palace is going to be running around putting up decorations, which means we"—she wriggled her eyebrows—"will have plenty of time to visit the Moonsilk Canopy again."

24

Birthday Glow

"SQUEAKITY-SCREEEEEE!"

"Just two more minutes, Peeps."

"Squeeee!"

Anastasia rolled over. Pippistrella dangled from the velvet bed curtain, an enormous moth cramming her furry jaws.

"You're already eating breakfast?"

"Peep krr krr sque-eee."

"Wait. Is that moth for me?"

"Kreeee!"

Anastasia sat up, a nice little glow starting in her chest. "Aw, Peeps! Is that a birthday present?"

"Squeeeak!"

"Thanks!" Anastasia plucked the fuzzy bug from

Pippistrella and popped it into her mouth. "Yum. Guess what, Peeps? I'm eleven today."

The glow in her chest was growing and growing. It was a birthday glow. Perhaps you have felt it on *your* birthday. It's your body's way of saying, "Yes, by gum, today we're *officially* special!" You see, dear Reader, your body has a special glow-memory for all the birthday cake candles upon which you have wished. This glow-memory stays quiet and bottled up for the other 364 days of the year, but your birthday uncorks it on the 365th, and all that candle glow flares up and blazes your veins.

And for Anastasia, *this* birthday was particularly momentous. Eleven! Wonderful eleven! Based on everything Penny and Baldwin and the Dreadfuls had told her, turning eleven was like turning a key in a door that led to all sorts of marvelous things.

"Your hearing, for one," Quentin had said. "It's like someone fine-tunes your eardrums."

"And you can see better in the dark," Ollie advised. "That means less bumping around when you get up to use the loo at night."

And, perhaps, she would begin metamorphosing.

"Soon we'll be flying together," Anastasia told Pippistrella. "I hope."

"Prrrp peep!"

Anastasia gasped. "Pippistrella! What did you say?"

"Prrrp peepity kree!"

"Did you just say *something something birthday*?" Anastasia asked.

"Squeak!"

"I understood you!" Anastasia jubilated. "Say it again!"

"Prrrp peep!"

"Birthday!" Anastasia cried. *"Birthday! Prrrp peep!"*

It was beginning! She was shifting into a real Morfo—she was certain! Anastasia shoved Mr. Bunster aside and clambered from bed, hunkering on the floor to rummage through the pockets of her jettisoned school blazer. She extracted Miss Viola's watch from the silk lining and clasped the silver disc between both palms. She scrunched her eyelids. She concentrated. She was eleven now! Surely she would pass the silver rash litmus test of Morfolkiness!

Nothing happened.

"Oh well." She returned the watch to her jacket. "Come on, Peeps! Let's get birthday—I mean, *prrrp peep*—breakfast."

"Well!" Penny said as they entered the dining hall. "You're up early!"

"She has the birthday glow!" Baldwin cried. "Come over here and shine a little of your birthday glow on me!"

Anastasia hugged him, and then she hugged Penny.

"Oh," Penny sighed, "how I wish your father could see you today."

Anastasia's tear ducts twinged. "Me too."

Baldwin squeezed her shoulder. Then he hollered, "Pancakes! We need pancakes to fortify this eleven-year-old!"

"Yes, Your Majesty." A footman hurried off to tell the chef.

"Now that you're eleven, we need to let you soak up some moonlight," Baldwin said. "You'll really feel the moon in your bones and blood now. You'll want to romp and rollick and yodel."

"The Swiss hills are superb for yodeling," Penny chimed in.

"We'll go for moonlight roams in the forest outside Dinkledorf," Baldwin said. "By gadberry, we all need a moonlight ramble! I'm just twitching to go wolf. Ah, here come our pancakes! I'll tell you a little secret, Anastasia. Pancakes are a fair treat any day, but they're especially good on your birthday, and especially *especially* scrummy on your *eleventh* birthday. Eleven years is just the right amount of time for your taste buds to ripen. Go ahead! Try!"

Anastasia poked a forkful of flapjack into her mouth. "Yum."

"This is a present from Wiggy," Penny said, pulling a parcel trussed in gold paper from beneath the table. "It's the queen's privilege to give you your first birthday present of the day, but she's off at a diplomatic meeting in

Limestone-on-the-Lake. She'll be back in time for your party, though."

"We have a heck of a hoopla planned for you tonight," Baldwin said. "I hope that you're in the mood to whoop it up."

Anastasia undid the ribbon and tore back the wrap. "Oil paints!"

Her birthday glow sparkled like a firecracker. Wiggy knew she liked art? Perhaps her queenly grandmother wasn't as remote as she seemed. Anastasia set the paints on the table. "When are the boys getting here?"

"One o'clock–ish," Penny said. "And then you can play games until your party starts at seven."

"We have thousands of balloons to blow up," Baldwin said.

"And cupcakes to frost," Penny said.

"And streamers to stream," Baldwin said.

"And," Penny added, "Baldy and I have a very important, top-secret birthday mission up in Dinkledorf. We'll be gone for a little while, so tell one of the servants if you need anything."

"We'll be fine," Anastasia said hastily. "We're going to play hide-and-seek, so you might not see us all day."

As you already know, perceptive Reader, *play hide-and-seek* was really Dreadful code for *sneak into the Cavern of*

Dreams. But Penny and Baldwin didn't speak Dreadful code, and they just smiled at Anastasia.

"If you get up to any birthday mischief, make sure it's *good.*" Baldwin winked.

"Oh," Anastasia assured him, "I will."

After Gus and the Drybread brothers arrived, and after everyone had traded good-birthday tidings, the Dreadfuls hurried through the network of palace hallways and stairwells, around and up and down, all the way to Wiggy's cavern. Anastasia tugged Mrs. Wata's locket from her collar and flashed it at the guard bat, sending him into a deep snooze, and the Dreadfuls infiltrated the queen's room once more.

"Aisatsana!" Anastasia called, dashing to the Glimmerglass.

"Oh." Her reflection grimaced. "You again."

"Happy birthday, Aisatsana!" Ollie said. He pulled a little parcel wrapped in notebook paper and tied with a string from his jacket pocket and set it on the vanity.

"What's that?" Aisatsana frowned.

"It's a present!" Ollie said. "It's *your* birthday, too, isn't it?"

A funny look flitted over Aisatsana's face. She plucked at the reflected knot, and then she pulled back the paper to reveal a squished cupcake.

"It's my own recipe," Ollie said. "Peanut Butter S'mores Delight. Go ahead! Try it!"

"We—ell," Aisatsana hesitated. "I've never had s'mores."

"Sure you have!" Anastasia said. "I've eaten hundreds of s'mores!"

"Not in front of a mirror," Aisatsana quibbled. She bit into the cupcake. She chewed. "It's good," she muttered. "It's really good. Is this marshmallow in the middle?"

"Yep." Ollie grinned. "But don't expect me to give you the recipe. We pastry chefs guard our secrets *to the grave*."

Aisatsana licked her fingers. "Thank you, Shadowboy. That was delicious." She didn't look, however, like someone who had just devoured a scrumptious treat. She looked sort of *sad*. Faced now with her woebegone reflection, Anastasia harkened back to all the frowns she had shared with Aisatsana in the mirrors at St. Agony's.

"Aisatsana?" she ventured.

"What?"

Anastasia darted a glance at her fellow Dreadfuls, suddenly reluctant to ask about the frost pictures. Pippistrella wouldn't laugh at her, but might Gus and the Shadowboys deem her dilly?

"Um," she faltered. "Happy birthday."

"All right," Gus spoke up from across the room. "Let's get cracking at that bed."

"Aisatsana, we need you to show us the door again," Anastasia said.

The girl in the glass stared at her for a moment, her eyes extra-bright. "I—well, fine." She sidled over, revealing the silver door glimmering in the depths of the reflection. Aisatsana and Anastasia bebopped through a backward bunny hop and then the Dreadfuls were in the Cavern of Dreams once again. Of course, it was Quentin's first venture into the magical hollow.

"The moon!" he cried.

"It's still full!" Ollie exulted.

"Maybe it's *always* full in here," Gus said.

Perhaps it was the full moon, or perhaps it was the birthday glow pepping her body, but an irresistible urge to cavort jazzed Anastasia's feet into a sprint. "Catch me if you can!"

"I'll get you!" Quentin yelled.

"Wait for me!" Ollie howled.

Pippistrella looped and whirled, sing-peeping above them as the Dreadfuls dashed between the pines. She dive-bombed a bough, sending moonflakes avalanching onto Gus's head.

"Hssst!" The snakes uncoiled, snapping at the twinkles.

"They're lively now!" Ollie laughed. He leaned against a tree trunk, panting. "Too bad Aisatsana can't come in here."

"Aisatsana?" Gus exclaimed. "Why would you want to hang out with that pill?"

"I feel sorry for her," Ollie said. "Don't you think she gets lonely?"

"She has her mirror-realm friends," Anastasia said. "Besides, she hates everything I like, remember?"

"She liked that s'mores cupcake," Ollie pointed out. "You like s'mores, too, Anastasia. You're not complete opposites."

"I guess," Anastasia allowed.

"She seemed so sad when we left for the Cavern of Dreams," Quentin pondered. "I think she was about to cry."

"She's just contrary," Anastasia argued, but she lapsed into thought. She had never really considered Aisatsana's wishes or wants before, aside from the mirror-girl's demands to visit Zero Cavern. What would it be like to live in a reflected realm, subject to the whims of a world you could never truly enter?

"Come on," Gus said, dragging Anastasia from her cogitations and down to the moon-plated dell. There the Canopy shimmered, its supernatural bloom illuminating the surrounding trees.

"This time," Gus said, "think about the Silver Hammer before you fall asleep! But don't just ask *where* it is. You might dream of some basement or shed that nobody knows about. Think about *how we'll find it.*"

"Okay." Anastasia shucked off her galoshes and clambered into the bed. The dreamy voice crooned from the pillow as soon as she rested her head. *Anastasia . . . Anastasia . . .*

"She's already falling asleep!" Quentin said.

"Remember," Gus urged, "the Silver Hammer."

Anastasia stretched and tried to focus her fuzzy thoughts. Sleep, warm and sweet as a swallow of hot chocolate, spread through her body. The Canopy was so *soft.* She felt like she was floating. *Was* she floating? Her eyelids flickered. It was dark, and her braids bobbled above her head. Was she underwater? She cricked her gaze upward. Hundreds of tiny lights pinpricked the murk. Stars? Was she deep in a star-dimpled pond? Anastasia frogged toward the glimmer—

"Move over!"

The dream sucked from Anastasia like water guzzled down a drain. She was back in the Canopy, and someone else was with her, elbowing and shoving.

"Saskia?"

25
Bedbugs

"DID YOU EXPECT Prince Charming?" Saskia's porcelain face simpered down at her.

Anastasia sat bolt upright. "Where are Ollie and—"

"Your little playmates are skipping around the woods," Saskia said. "Childish."

"How did you get in here?" Anastasia demanded.

"How do you think? I followed you."

Anastasia's thoughts flitted to the door to the Cavern of Dreams. Had they left it open? She cringed. Yes. Sozzled on moonglow, the Dreadfuls had galloped into the forest with nary a notion of closing the silver hatch.

"Anyway, what are *you* doing in here?" Saskia asked. "Grandwiggy's cavern is off-limits. Strictly forbidden. Death to all who enter, et cetera, et cetera. You'll be in serious trouble if Grandwiggy discovers you've been sneaking in here with your little friends."

Panic clotted Anastasia's tonsils.

"Maybe she'd even banish you abovecaves," Saskia speculated. "Like a witch."

"She wouldn't do that," Anastasia cried. "I'm her granddaughter! Besides, CRUD is still looking for me."

Saskia smiled nastily.

"Wait." Anastasia sat up a little straighter. "*You're* not supposed to be in here, either."

Saskia tossed her hair. "Grandwiggy would never exile *me.* She's known me for years. How long has she known you? A couple of months?"

Anastasia's heart sank.

Saskia tilted her face to catch the falling moonbits. "What a pretty bed this is. Perfect for a princess." Her eyes slewed over to Anastasia. "I said, for a *princess.* So get out. I'm feeling sleepy all of a sudden."

Anastasia climbed from the downy mattress, her hands balled at her sides. "It isn't going to work for you," she said. "It's hexed—"

"Hexed?" Saskia echoed drowsily.

"Anastasia!" Ollie yelped, running into the clearing. "Why is *Saskia* here?"

"She followed us," Anastasia said. "And she woke me up, right when I was starting to dream."

"Well, now *she's* asleep," Quentin said.

Anastasia turned. Saskia's long eyelashes pressed her cheeks, and her chest rose with deep sleep-breaths. Lying in the moonlit Canopy, her silver-blond hair flowing over the pillow, she looked like a storybook illustration. Anastasia's beautiful birthday glow flickered and snuffed out. Saskia was a *real* princess. She had grown up in a castle, and—

"Peep!" Pippistrella squeaked and wheeled, drawing their gazes to the sky.

"What's happening to the moon?" Gus asked.

The magical moon dimmed, its luster going the blackish green of tarnished silver, its fall of glitter turning into ashy bits.

"Is this some kind of eclipse?" Gus asked.

Anastasia bit her lip. "Did that happen before?"

"No," Gus said.

"We should go," Ollie pleaded.

Anastasia shook Saskia's shoulder. "Wake up." But Saskia remained limp as a ragdoll, not even fidgeting to flick away the moonsoot collecting on her lovely face. "Wake up, Saskia!"

"Look at the moonbits!" Quentin gasped. "They're *moving*!"

Anastasia snatched her hand back, boggling at the tiny cinders. First they wriggled, and then they began to dance and dart, to tiddlywink and tic-tac-toe, just like little fleas.

"Those bugs are going into her *ears*!" Ollie said.

"Stop!" Anastasia slapped at the magical mites, but still

they skittered under Saskia's golden-silver locks. The princess finally stirred, letting out a whimper.

"Get her out of that bed!" Gus urged.

The Dreadfuls yanked Saskia's arms, but the comforters cinched her tightly. The peculiar mooncooties continued to snow down and Saskia's mewls pitched into shrieks.

"Why is she still sleeping?" Ollie wailed.

"I don't know," Anastasia said. "Maybe the bed is doing this because she's full Morfo."

"Or maybe the magic just went sour," Ollie said.

"I don't think so." Gus pointed at the carving on the headboard. "I think it's working just like Calixto Swift meant for it to."

Good night, sleep tight, don't let the bedbugs bite!

"Those things are *bedbugs*?" Anastasia said.

"I think so." Gus circled the Moonsilk Canopy, and then he lay on the ground and scooched under the bed.

"What are you doing?" Ollie asked.

"Investigating. Oh, crumbs! Look at *this*!"

Anastasia and the Drybread brothers knelt to peer at the bed's dark underbelly. Carved deep in the planks were the words:

O worm who worms into my bed,
A hundred nightmares blight thy head!
The nightmare bug shall your mind creep
Wi' nightmare-gnawed and wretched sleep.
Your thoughts my bugs shall munch and munch
Until there's nothing left for lunch.
Think not upon a type of cure—
This spell is sealed stronger than steel;
This magic bed shall be thy bier.

"Bier?" Ollie said.

"It's a table for a dead body." Quentin blanched. "Before it goes into a coffin."

Anastasia gasped. Saskia was no paragon of kindly cousinhood, but the prospect of the princess meeting a terrible end in the witch's bed plumbed Anastasia's heart with horror. "We have to get help!"

"I don't know if anyone *can* help." Gus slid from the bed's shadow and stood up, trembling. "Saskia triggered the hex."

"We need a doctor!" Ollie said.

"Do you really think a doctor can cure a—a nightmare bug infestation?" Gus asked. "The poem says there's *no cure.*"

"Then we need an exterminator!" Ollie said.

"We need to do *something,*" Quentin agreed. "Might Princess Penelope and Prince Baldwin have ideas?"

"They went abovecaves, and Wiggy won't be back from her meeting until the party starts." Anastasia pulled Miss Viola's watch from her pocket and checked the time. "And that's hours away." A tear slid down her cheek. "This is all my fault."

"No, it isn't," Quentin said firmly. "*You* didn't invent this loathsome bed. *You* didn't bewitch a swarm of—er—nasty bedbugs to creep into Saskia's ears."

"Do you think they're eating her brain?" Ollie asked.

"Her *thoughts,*" Gus said. "And they'll munch until there aren't any more thoughts left, and then . . . I think Saskia will—will die."

An idea nibbled Anastasia's mind. It was dangerous. It might even be *deadly.*

From the depths of her haunted slumber, Saskia screamed.

Desperate times call for desperate measures, dear Reader.

For example, should the quirks of life one day seal you within a Victorian mansion lacking modern plumbing, you may find yourself stooping to the ghastly last resort of a chamber pot. Anastasia, as you already know, was no stranger to desperate measures. She scrambled into the bed, drawing dismayed shouts from the Dreadfuls.

"What are you doing?" Gus cried.

"Looking for a cure." Anastasia squeezed her eyes shut and grabbed her cousin's icy hand. *How can I save Saskia? How can I save Saskia? How can . . .*

26
Wish-in-a-Bottle

ANASTASIA OPENED HER dream-eyes to the commotion of Dark-o'-the-Moon Common. Morfolk clogged the cobblestones, rushing to work, laughing, shopping, licking electric eel ice cream cones.

"This way, Q!"

Ollie! Anastasia elbowed through the Morfolk, peering over shoulders and past wigs, trying to spot the Shadowboys. There they were, standing by the Be-Careful-What-You-Wish-For Well! Dream-Ollie and Dream-Quentin nodded at each other, and then they umbrated. Their clothes collapsed to the ground in two heaps, and their shadow shapes unfurled to snake up and into the crumbling column.

"Wait!" Anastasia scurried to squint down the murky shaft. Of course, being shadows, the boys were well nigh invisible. "Ollie! Q!" she hollered, but her voice just boomeranged back up the well's throat.

Was she supposed to *wish* for Saskia to wake up? Or was she supposed to follow the Shadowboys down the well? Anastasia eyed the bucket dangling from the pulley. She tugged the frayed rope, wondering whether it would hold her weight. What if she broke her neck? Would it really hurt her? Could an injury from a dream seep into her waking life?

There wasn't time to worry about it.

Anastasia boosted herself onto the edge of the well and grasped the prickly cord with both hands, yanking the bucket down. She stepped on the pail's wooden lip. Then she sucked in a deep breath, like someone tottering on the tippy end of a high-dive board.

She jumped.

WZZZZZZzzzzzzzzzzzzzzzzzz!

The bucket, and Anastasia with it, zinged into the darkness. Before she could think or squeak or scream, the entire kit and caboodle jerked to the end of its tether, jouncing her heart into her throat. She swayed in the gloom, her stomach yo-yoing. How far was she from the bottom?

Crooking one elbow around the rope, she fumbled in her pocket for a match. She pretzeled to strike it against the sole of one galosh. The tip flared with phosphorescent fizz, illuminating the shaft's slimy flanks and, just inches below, water puddling over the shimmer of wish coins. The

Drybreads' silhouettes skulked in the pool like ink jetted from an octopus's rump.

Anastasia hopped to hunker beside them in the shallow splash. Why were the Shadowboys belly-flopped in the puddle? Was there a wish hidden down there? Faint strains of off-key singing tickled her nerves; the strange carol piped from *beneath the coins.* She plunged one hand in the dark puddle and pulled out a fistful of wet queenlies. The gold gleamed on her palm, each disc stamped with Wiggy's solemn profile. Anastasia flung the coins into the bucket and kept digging, plumbing the well for whatever secret its mossy gullet might hide.

Three matches later, she had excavated enough of the queenlies to glimpse what lay below. Was this simply a fantasy door, spun from the dreams cottoning her mind? Or did a hatch exist at the base of the Be-Careful-What-You-Wish-For Well in waking life, too?

She twisted the handle and the door swung down, sluicing coins into the earth's dark belly. This belly, Anastasia saw, was crowded with furniture, rising like shipwreck skeletons adrift a shallow sea brimming with coins and small glass bottles. She knelt, her gaze creeping over the glow-mossed walls. Someone hummed within the shadowy cellar, but a tangle of cobwebs drooping from an unlit chandelier blocked her view. Ollie and Quentin slithered into the secret chamber, and after a moment's hesitation, Anastasia leapt down to the cushion of a soggy chair.

Three scraggy women huddled around a fireplace at the far end of the parlor. Their tangled white hair hid their faces; the skirts of their tattered dresses dragged in the water flooding their strange home. Over their gowns they wore chain-mail tunics, and these tunics jingled dainty accompaniment to their whispers.

"The wolfsbane," muttered one, twisting from the hearth to dig through the jumbled bottles. Anastasia gasped and shrank against the moldy chair even as she realized the old woman couldn't possibly spy her—*for she had no eyes.* She didn't even have empty sockets where her eyes should have been! Her forehead simply slid down into her cheeks, behind the little spectacles perched on her nose. As the other two ladies stooped to claw through the bottles, Anastasia saw that they, too, were eyeless, and she also glimpsed what lay behind them in the fireplace: there, amongst the flames, gleamed a silver cauldron.

Witches.

"Here it is!" The tallest hag held up a vial. She unstopped it and emptied it into the kettle, and the concoction inside sputtered and popped.

"Fizz, my lovely! Fizz, you wonderful stuff!" screeched a hag with bottles braided into her hair. They began chanting:

Gurgling! Gurgling!
Toiling! Boiling!
That is how we ferment wishes!
That is how we help the half-wits!
We love to get them what they covet!
We grant their wish 'cause they deserve it!
Ignore their screams when they receive it!
Will it be nasty? Oh, believe it!

And they shrieked with laughter.

Anastasia struggled to convince herself that she wasn't really in a witch's parlor, that the nasty scene was just a nightmare cooked up by her addled brain. *But what if she never woke up?* What if Calixto's evil bedbugs had swarmed her ears, too, dooming her to hide in a horrible witch lair until she died? She trembled, imagining her life ebbing away without s'mores or waffles, or Penny or Baldwin, or Pippistrella or Gus or the Shadowboys—

The Shadowboys! Anastasia peeled herself from the chair to seek the Drybreads. She found them stooping in a corner, their shadowy hands swiveling the vials to reveal their labels: SNOW DAY (little white crystals); CASTLE IN THE SKY (corked, cottony fluff); UNICORN (a long, silvery horn tucked in a jeweled casket).

A tiny flask bobbed to the surface, glimmering in the murky parlor like a single, bottled star. Anastasia plucked it from the water. The tag dangling from its neck read: COMACURE. The glow inside was lovely and sunny. She pulled the cork and light dazzled her eyeballs as though someone had shoved two sparklers up her nostrils.

"Anastasia!" Gus hauled her from the Canopy in a tight hug. "I wasn't sure whether you'd ever wake up! I've never been so frightened in my life."

"Am I pasty and pale?" she croaked. "Did any bedbugs hop into my ears?"

"No," Ollie said. "You're normal and freckly, and the bedbugs left you alone."

Anastasia shifted to look at her cousin. A diadem of perspiration glittered across the sleeping beauty's lofty coconut: Saskia even *sweated* like a princess.

"You were talking in your sleep," Quentin said. "Something about wishes?"

Anastasia cupped her hands and huffed warm air onto them, and then she told them about the eerie cellar-parlor and the three weird women brewing wishes within it. "I think—I think they were witches."

"Witches!" the Dreadfuls chorused.

"But do witches brew wishes?" Ollie asked.

"It was *something* magical," Anastasia said. "Besides, who else would hole up in a secret room, mixing potions?"

Gus's eyebrows hopped halfway to his snakes. "What about the Wish Hags?"

"Wish Hags?"

"Don't you remember? Marm Pettifog mentioned them in her lecture about 'anti-magic hysteria' after the First Declaration of Perpetual War."

"That's right. . . ." Anastasia strained her memory. "She yelled at me for not paying attention. The hags aren't witches, but they're good at brewing potions, right?"

Gus nodded. "And they're troglobites. *Creatures that live their entire lives in cave darkness.* And lots of troglobites *don't have eyes.*"

"Nobody's seen the Wish Hags for centuries," Quentin said. "Do you really think they're down at the bottom of the well, twisting up wishes?"

Gus pondered. "It makes sense, doesn't it? They disappeared during the eighteenth-century Cavelands 'witch-sympathizer' trials. They're *hiding.*" He turned to Anastasia, perplexed. "But why would you dream about *them*?"

"Well," she said, "there was a bottle." She told them about the Comacure.

"Magic potion to cure a magic coma," Quentin said. "That makes sense."

Saskia let out a scream.

"We have to get that potion," Anastasia cried.

"Maybe we should wait for the queen to get back," Ollie dithered. "Or at least Baldwin and Penny."

Anastasia shook her head. "What if the nightmares scare Saskia into a heart attack?"

"And the bedbugs are supposed to munch her thoughts until they're *gone,*" Quentin said. "We might not have much time. Saskia isn't really a brainy type—no offense."

Anastasia considered. If Saskia's mind were the hourglass measuring the moments to her doom, and her thoughts the sand—well, Quentin was right. They needed to act quickly.

"But how will we get down the well?" Gus demanded. "What if the rope breaks when we ride the bucket down? That pulley system is half-rotted."

"But we have to try," Anastasia said. "Or, at least *I* do. We only monkeyed with Calixto's magic bed to find my dad and grandpa. Besides, I had the dream, so I'll recognize the bottle."

"But how will you get back out?" Gus asked. "What if the Wish Hags chase you? Cranking you back up in the bucket will take forever. And if the rope breaks, you'll be *stuck* down there. With three angry hags."

"Scree-*peep*!" Pippistrella added.

Anastasia swallowed. "But I have to try."

"No, you don't," Quentin spoke up. "Ollie and I will go."

"We *will*?" Ollie squeaked.

"Ollie and I can umbrate and zip down to the bottom

of the well. We'll change back into boy form and open the door. Then we'll sneak into the parlor—"

"In our birthday suits?" Ollie cried.

Quentin sighed. "Gus and Anastasia can throw our underpants down for us."

"Ugh." Anastasia shuddered.

"We nick the Comacure and put it in the bucket, and then we umbrate and flit back up to the top of the well," Quentin concluded. "It shouldn't be too hard."

"That's a magnificent idea!" Gus said.

"I don't really like the bit about wandering into a hag lair in my underpants," Ollie protested.

"Sometimes, Ollie, one must sacrifice for the greater good," Quentin declared. "Now, let's go steal a gondola."

"Are you sure you know how to get to Dark-o'-the-Moon Common?" Crouched in their pirated gondola, Anastasia consulted her pocket watch. Her party started in two hours. She wasn't worried about missing birthday jollifications, of course; she just wanted to rouse Saskia from her deathly slumber before Wiggy returned to the palace.

Quentin unknotted the rope tethering the helm. "Sure. Remember, our uncle Zed is a gondolier. We've been all over the canals." He sat down and grabbed his borrowed paddles. "Ready, all! *Row!*"

They churned their wooden blades. The lagoon let out a sob.

"I know just how you feel," Ollie told it.

"If anyone asks," Gus said, "we'll just tell them you're taking a birthday pleasure row, Anastasia."

"In someone else's boat," Anastasia groaned.

"Harder on starboard," Quentin commanded, and they angled left into one of the tunnels.

"Who knew our rowing lessons would come in so handy?" Gus said.

"Should we sing a sea shanty?" Ollie asked. "I once saw a movie about Vikings, and they sang songs to help them row better."

"No singing, Ollie," Anastasia said. "We don't want anyone to notice us."

"Harder on port!" Quentin charged. "There it is! Dark-o'-the-Moon Common!"

The deserted square appeared at the opposite shore of Dark-o'-the-Moon Lagoon. "Where is everybody?" Anastasia asked.

"It's an official Nowhere Special holiday, silly," Ollie said. "Princess Anastasia's birthday!"

"Oh!"

"That's good for us," Gus said. "Nobody to interfere with Operation Wish Theft."

They pulled in their oars as Quentin docked the gondola,

and then they raced to the well. Anastasia leaned over its edge, straining to see the glint of coins or hear the tweedle of chanting hags, but the well was silent and dark. She swiveled her gaze back to the Shadowboys, standing beside her pale-faced and wide-eyed.

"I can still ride the bucket down," she offered.

"Too risky," Quentin said. "Don't worry about us. Shadowfolk can get in and out of sticky situations."

"Except when I got that sticky toffee pudding in my hair," Ollie said. "Mom had to cut it out with scissors. I had a bald spot for weeks!"

Gus rotated the crank, unspooling the rope and sending the old pail down. When the cord was completely unfurled, he nodded.

"I'll tug on the rope after we put the potion into the bucket," Quentin said. "You start pulling it up."

"All right," Anastasia said. "Pinky clasp for bravery." She extended her hand with the pinky crooked and Gus curled his little finger around hers, and then Quentin's and Ollie's. Pippistrella grasped the salute with her batty thumb.

"May the League of Beastly Dreadfuls triumph again in the face of danger," Ollie intoned. "And don't forget to throw down our underwear."

Then Quentin's and Ollie's pinkies slipped from the clinch and their clothes rustled to the cobblestones.

“Good luck!” Anastasia whispered as the Drybreads’ silhouettes vanished into the well.

“I don’t really fancy touching someone else’s underpants.” Gus stared at the Shadowboys’ discarded clothes. “But I guess we all have to be brave today.” He plucked at the waistbands of the boys’ breeches, extracting two pairs of plaid skivvies, and flung them into the well. Anastasia watched as the undies sailed down to meet their owners.

“I wish *we* could metamorphose,” Gus mumbled. “Then we could go with them. I feel like a real jellyfish staying up here.”

“Jellyfish *sting*,” Anastasia said, but she knew what he meant. The prospect of venturing into the hags’ secret parlor was terrible, but it was far worse to stay behind while Ollie and Quentin sallied forth.

“Do you think they’ve opened the door yet?” Gus asked.

Anastasia bit her lip. “I don’t know.”

“I hope it’s really there.” Gus’s fingers tightened around the rope. “We don’t know how accurate your dream was.”

“If there isn’t a door, then Ollie and Q can come back up and we’ll go home,” Anastasia reasoned.

But the Shadowboys did not reappear to declare the bottom of the well doorless. The minutes ticked by.

“What’s taking them so long?” Gus agonized.

“In my dream, there were hundreds of bottles crammed

in that parlor," Anastasia said. "It would take a while to sort through them."

"What do you think the Wish Hags will do if they catch them?" Gus asked.

"I don't know." Anastasia squirmed.

"I wonder if—" Gus cut off as the rope began to quiver. "They're out!" He seized the crank just as two shadowy forms spilled from the well and onto the cobbles.

"Hurry!" Ollie panted. "They're coming after us!"

"What?" Anastasia cried.

"We knocked over a table on our way out," Quentin said. "A whole tea set went shattering into the mess of bottles."

"Do you think they realized someone was down there with them?" Gus asked, churning the crank like a frenzied organ-grinder. "Maybe they all thought the other one bumped it."

"Well," Quentin admitted, "I *might* have said a bad word."

Shrieking piped up the well. "Thief! THIEF!"

"Sounds like they figured it out," Anastasia said.

"Capture them!"

"Kill them!"

"Boil their bones!"

"Sauté their tonsils!"

"Soufflé their brains!"

"They certainly know a lot about cooking," Ollie noted.

The bucket rattled to the top, a slender vial glowing sunnily in its wooden belly. Anastasia snatched it out and thrust it into her pocket.

"Grab our clothes!" Quentin urged. "Let's make like a trombone and slide out of here!"

"What?" Gus cried.

"FRICASSEE THEIR EYEBALLS!" screamed the hags.

"In simple language," Quentin said, *"run!"*

27
The Dreamdoodle

FOR YOUR SAKE, dear Reader, I hope you will never spend your birthday worrying that you have provoked a trio of Morfolk-guts-hating magical hags. This was how Anastasia passed the journey back to the palace, and very unpleasant it was. While Ollie and Quentin shimmied into their breeches at the back of the gondola, she pondered sautéed tonsils. Amidst the Dreadfuls' terror-stricken row through the tangled canal system, she imagined souffléd eyeballs. Even as they leapt from the hijacked boat and clambered back into the palace and raced through the halls to the darkened Cavern of Dreams, she wondered just how long it might take to properly boil bones.

"The antibiotic!" Ollie crashed into her reverie. "Get the antibiotic!"

"It's *antidote,* you pudding," Quentin corrected him.

Anastasia fumbled for the golden vial. "How do you think it works? Are we supposed to pour it down Saskia's throat or put it in her ears?"

Gus scrutinized the comatose princess. "Well, the bed-bugs are in her ears."

Anastasia pulled out the stopper, and little bits of gold sizzled from the bottle's rim like the twinkles that toot from the rump of a shooting star.

"Ooooooh!" Ollie breathed. "Pretty!"

"Thieves! Grime-livered pirates!"

Anastasia whirled. "Oh, *biscuit crumbs*!"

The sinister Wish Hags hovered at the verge of the dark-ened dream dell. This specter was in itself enough to jellify the giblets of a battle-hardened warlord; and yet behind the hags there loomed something even worse—yes, something more fearsome by far.

"What *is* that?" Gus gasped.

"Meet our little pet, Borg!" the hags shrilled.

"Little?" Quentin echoed.

Borg was anything but little. He was perhaps ten feet tall, with gangling arms and gargantuan hands. The hem of his long black coat now whispered against the forest floor as he paced betwixt the hags, much like an impatient vul-ture. The avian affinity didn't end there: although a wide-brimmed hat shadowed Borg's eyes, the curve of his great, sharp bone-white beak was clearer than a sickle moon at midnight.

Anastasia, who as a rule loved all animals great and small, swiftly made an exception. The sight of this claw-faced man-bird scared her witless.

"Borg doesn't take kindly to nasty, rotten thieves who steal our wish-goop!" the bespectacled hag screaked.

"W-wish-goop?" Anastasia stuttered, corking the vial and closing her hand around it. "What wish-goop?"

"Don't play dumb, Morfling," the tallest hag hissed. "We know some sticky-fingers here took a vial of our special Hag Brew."

"She's got it right now," said the hag with bottles in her hair. "I can hear her crooked little heart beating. Thumpity-bumpity-bump. Are you frightened, little thief? Thumpity-thumpity. A thief's heart always beats like that."

The hags edged closer, chanting, *"Thumpity. Thumpity. Bumpity."*

"Get back, you rotten prunes!" Ollie hollered.

The old women screeched with laughter, their chain mail jingling. The tall hag withdrew a small black bottle from the folds of her dress. "A wish, a wish! I have a wish! A wish to catch a thief therewith!" She lobbed the flasket against the Canopy, where it exploded into cloud of smoke.

One moment Anastasia's galoshes were firmly grounded; the next they flailed several feet above Calixto's bedeviled bed. Her rib cage twanged between Borg's awful meat hooks. How had the monstrous man-bird crossed the vale so swiftly? The hags' powerful brew must have sped him there. Pippistrella squeaked and battered Borg's hat with her wings, but he didn't even seem to notice her.

"Now, Borg: get our goop back!" the hags enjoined.

"Let her go!" Gus shouted, balling his hands into fists and dashing forward.

"Away, away, you thoughtless knave!" A bottle of brew sailed through the air and crashed against his leg. Gus catapulted into the prickly hug of a pine tree, where he lolled like a puppet with snipped strings.

"You *hag*!" Quentin swore. "Ollie! *Umbrate and bite!*"

"Ah, ah, ah!" The closest crone pulled a bottle from her tangled hair and crushed it. A stream of silvery potion drizzled from her bony fist. "Looking glass upon the ground, lock them in a prison round!" The wish-goop zinged across the dell and snaked into a ring around the Shadowboys.

Quentin stopped short at the glinting border. "It's some kind of liquid mirror!"

"We're trapped!" Ollie howled.

Throughout this horrible hullabaloo, Borg gripped Anastasia harder and harder, squooshing the last wafts of oxygen from her hapless lungs. His beak scissored open, revealing rows of jagged teeth.

"Your monster is going to kill her!" Ollie cried. "Please, just let Anastasia go!"

"Not without our brew!" the hags sang.

"Just do it, Anastasia!" Quentin yelled. "Just give the stuff back to them!"

But Anastasia couldn't move. She dangled in Borg's cruel clench, her vision blurring. Her fingers loosened from the vial of Comacure and the glass slipped from her sweaty hand. If she could have said anything, she would have keened,

"No!"

or *"It was all for naught!"*

But Anastasia couldn't make a peep. She couldn't breathe. The bottle plummeted to the ground, the shatter of its sides like a tiny death knoll. The hags moaned, "All gone! All gone!"

"If you can really hear her heart, *listen*!" Quentin implored. "It's going to stop!"

Bump. Bump . . . bump. It was true: Anastasia's ticker was no longer thumping a fearful tattoo.

The bespectacled hag clasped her hands. "Oh, mercy me! Borg, put that stinky little child down right this instant! We don't really want to kill anybody!"

"Borg!"

"Bad Borg! Bad!"

The hags shrilled as Borg lifted Anastasia higher, champing his deadly bill. Her head spun with the flickering faraway magical stars, faster and faster until, at last, everything went black.

Gentle Reader, have you ever fainted? For some people, fainting feels like all the blood is draining from your brain down to your toes. Your head goes light as a helium balloon and your legs get heavy as sacks of wet flour, and then you're in never-never land. Other people have time to gasp and the foresight to swoon onto, for example, a cushy beanbag chair. And other people don't even know it's coming. Out they zonk without a whimper.

In Anastasia's case, she drifted to a quiet place where she was *remembering*. A memory from her early childhood flooded her brain, squeezing out all the pain and fear and confusion. She remembered, with crystalline clarity, the first time she ever tasted cotton candy.

The warm, sweet smell.

The softness. Cloud softness dissolving on her tongue.

Then a prickle of sugar explosions, like each taste bud was a tiny firecracker.

And, finally, the melted sugar seeping down her throat.

Her father's voice: "Yummy, isn't it? Let's give Muffy a nibble, too."

She sighed and smiled.

"Anastasia! Anastasia! There . . . I think she's coming to. Oh, thank goodness."

The sugary taste faded and her eardrums clanged. Anastasia forced her eyelids open. Anxious faces floated above and around her: Gus and Ollie and Quentin and also the three hags, their mouths pulled into fretful frowns . . . and Penny and Baldwin and Wiggy. Wiggy cradled Saskia in her arms.

Crumbs.

"When did *you* get here?" Anastasia mumbled.

"I returned from my meeting and found the door to the Cavern of Dreams ajar, and quite an affray from within," Wiggy said.

"And we got back from abovecaves at about the same time," Penny said, squeezing Anastasia's hand. "Oh, my dear child! We were so worried!"

"Peep!" Pippistrella nuzzled Anastasia's cheek.

"Borg . . . ," she rasped. "Where's Borg?"

"Sound asleep," Baldwin said. "Snoozing over by the Canopy—or what's left of it."

The ringing in her ears dwindled to a painful buzz. Anastasia sat up and rubbed her eyes. "Snoozing?"

"Like a bear in the dark depths of winter," Baldwin said. "Practically hibernating."

"'Twas very odd," said the bespectacled hag. "We all thought Borgie was going to crunch you to bits, but all of a sudden he just dropped you and conked out."

"I'm afraid he fell on your bed," said the tall hag. "Smashed it to smithereens."

"Fortunately, he didn't smash Saskia," Ollie said.

"Listen to him snore!" giggled the hag with bottles in her hair.

They all went silent for a minute, hearkening the funny tootling coming from the Canopy.

"It sounds rather like a flute," Quentin mused. "Or—no; I stand corrected. A *piccolo*."

"It's his nose," explained the tall hag. "Long, you know."

"I *do* know." Anastasia shuddered. "Long and sharp and full of teeth."

"That isn't really how Borg looks," Spectacles said. "We just wished for him to be a frightful creature, to scare you into giving us back our wish-goop. But really, he's just the biggest sweetums!"

"Cute as a button!" Baldwin agreed.

"Cute?" Anastasia staggered to her feet and pushed past the hags to stare at the creature napping atop the smashed Canopy. "Wait. *This* is Borg?"

"Indeed it is!"

Anastasia had never beheld an anteater up close before, but she had the idea that Borg resembled one of these fine animals crossed with a Labradoodle. He had curly fur, flopsy ears, and big, fluffy feet. And as the hags had mentioned, an extra-long fuzzy trunk.

She couldn't help herself. She said, "Awwww."

The Dreadfuls crowded around Borg and started patting and petting him.

"See? A little angel!" one of the hags declared.

"He wasn't such an angel a couple of minutes ago," Penny protested. "He nearly devoured my niece."

"We never meant for Borgie to get quite so feisty," said Bottle Hair. "But, you see, it's been ages since he's had a chance to get out and romp! He just got too excited."

"We've been cramped at the bottom of that well for

centuries," added the tall hag. "Poor Borgie needed to stretch his legs."

"Anyway," concluded Tall One, "don't think for one moment that Borgie would actually have eaten the princess. His diet is very specialized, you see, and children are not on the menu."

"You don't give him souffléd eyeballs and fricasseed brains?" Ollie asked.

"Certainly not!" Spectacles said. "How revolting!"

"What I don't quite understand," mused Bottle Hair, "is why Borg fell asleep right in the middle of the hubbub."

"Maybe he's narcoleptic," Baldwin suggested.

"What does that mean?" Gus asked.

"A narcoleptic falls asleep at odd moments," Penny said. "They can't control it."

Baldwin nodded. "My old friend Bernard was a narcoleptic. He fell asleep two minutes into his routine at the Dinkledorf Ice Skating Championship. Tragic! Woke up to find himself spread-eagled on the pond after everyone else had left." His green eyes grew twinkly with tears. "And you don't even want to hear about his last skydiving attempt."

"That's all very interesting," said Tall One, "but Borg is not narcoleptic."

A golden glimmer amidst the pine needles caught Anastasia's eye and she felt at her collar. "Oh. I think I know what happened." She stooped. Mrs. Wata's locket was butterflied open, facedown on the ground. Anastasia carefully clicked it shut. "Borg saw a gorgon picture."

"Where did that come from?" Penny cried.

"Um . . . we borrowed it from my mom," Gus said. The Beastly Dreadfuls shifted uneasily.

"Does this explain the sleeping guard bat outside my cavern?" Wiggy asked.

Anastasia nodded, her cheeks burning.

"Clever!" Baldwin said.

"And potentially *dangerous,* were the wrong person to get ahold of it," Wiggy said. "I'll take that." She held out her hand.

Worried glances tiddlywinked between the Dreadfuls. "Will Mrs. Wata get into trouble?" Anastasia asked. "She didn't even know that I had it."

"Nonetheless, gorgon portraits are illegal," Wiggy said, pocketing the locket.

"The necklace saved Anastasia's life," Penny pointed out.

"Like we said, Borgie wouldn't really have eaten her," insisted Tall One.

"But he nearly crushed her rib cage!" Penny exclaimed. "For goodness' sake, just look what he did to that *bed*!"

"Sorry about that," said Spectacles.

Anastasia gazed mournfully at the smashed Canopy, the singed moon, and the golden bits of the Comacure bottle twinkling like broken stars on the pillow. The quest to find Nicodemus and Fred had screeched to a sudden, disastrous halt, and Saskia would writhe in a coma until Calixto's bedbugs munched the last of her thoughts.

"We didn't mean for things to get so rough," repeated Spectacles, "but you *did* trespass in our home and you *did* steal our wish-goop."

"I know." Anastasia sighed. "It's because my cousin is in some sort of coma. A magical witch-coma. We were going to"—her voice wobbled—"save her."

"Oh dear," said Tall One.

"Can you brew up more Comacure?" Gus asked.

"We could," said Bottle Hair, "but I'm afraid that won't help your sleeping princess. We brew first-rate goop, but our wishes aren't powerful enough to break a witch's spell."

"Why was your cousin tangling with a witch, anyway?" demanded Tall One. "There aren't any witches in the Cavelands."

"The Moonsilk Canopy is a magical bed, and Saskia tried to nap in it," Wiggy said. "She didn't realize that Calixto Swift had enchanted it."

"Calixto Swift?" cried Spectacles. "Very powerful!"

"Most dangerous!" said Tall One.

"A bunch of creepy nightmare bedbugs hopped into Saskia's ears," Ollie said. "And then she started moaning and shaking."

"How inconvenient," clucked Bottle Hair.

"It's more than *inconvenient*!" Quentin said. "Saskia's stuck in a nightmare until she *dies*!"

"She's just a little girl," Penny agonized.

"What are you crying for?" screeched Tall One. "Our Borgie is a *dreamdoodle,* for bat's sake. Didn't you know that?"

"A *dreamdoodle*?" Anastasia asked. "I thought he was just an anteater—anteaterdoodle."

"No, no, no!" Tall One said. "Borg is a dreamdoodle. A *dreameater,* some might call him."

"Dreameaters!" Ollie exclaimed. "Pliny the Eldest Elder talks about those in his book! See, guys? I told you those creatures were real!"

"Of course Borgie is real," said Bottle Hair. "And he can take care of your princess's ear infestation."

"Really?" Anastasia said.

"Very handy to have a dreamdoodle around when you're in our line of work," said Spectacles. "He'll catch those dream bugs with his wonderful snozzle."

"But I thought you said you couldn't break a witch's spell," Gus said.

"We won't," said Bottle Hair. "Those nightmare bugs will still be nightmare bugs after Borgie gobbles them. We won't change that at all. But they won't be munching the princess's dreams anymore, will they?"

"They might not have much left to munch," Quentin despaired. "What if Borg doesn't wake up in time?"

"That gorgon portrait is more powerful than Dr. Bluster's Patented Sleep Preparation of Most Sleepful Sleep," Ollie agreed. "Borg might nap for *hours*!"

"But we still have a drop of Comacure!" Gus announced, examining the smithereens upon the pillow. One sunny bead of potion glimmered in the crook of a glass shard. "Would this be enough?"

"As we told you, we brew first-rate goop!" Tall One replied indignantly. "That Comacure is *potent*! There were *hundreds* of doses in that vial. If there's even an itty-bitty bit left, it should do the trick. You just have to dribble it in Borg's eye."

With utmost caution, Anastasia picked up the bottle fragment and carried it to Borg. Penny gently nudged the dreamdoodle's fuzzy eyelid, revealing a damp white curve, and Anastasia tilted the piece of glass. The sunshiny droplet fell. *Sploosh!*

Borg stretched his nose and blinked.

"Borgie-pie!" cried Spectacles. "Did you have a nice nappikins?"

Borg yawned. Then he jumped to his feet and pranced over to Anastasia, his tail wagging hello.

"He's happy to see you!" said Ollie.

"Borgie," crooned Tall One, "we have some delicious dream bugs for you to munch! Where's the dream? Where's the dream? Get the dream, Borgie!"

Borgie capered in a circle, pressing his snoot to the pine-needled ground and making excited kazoo-like noises.

"He's got the scent!" Baldwin said.

Borgie followed his nose to Saskia. *Sniff! Sniff!* He snuffed her hair and then applied his wonderful whiffer to her ear. *Sniiiiiiiiifffff!*

"Hear that? He's getting the nightmare bugs out!" said Bottle Hair.

After a minute of delighted snuffling, Borg gave Saskia's cheek a long-tongued lick and then bounded back to his mistresses.

"Good boy! Good Borgie!"

"Now those naughty nightmare bugs are in his tummy," said Tall One.

"And when he poops them out," said Spectacles, "we'll have some magical scat for our brew!"

"That's disgusting!" Ollie said.

"Not at all, Ollie!" Penny declared. "Why, you can learn marvelous things from—"

"Penny." Baldwin shook his head. "Now is not the time."

"Saskia's waking up!" said Quentin.

The princess's eyelashes fluttered and parted. Her glassy gaze swiveled around the cave, taking in the hags and Borgie and finally settling on Anastasia. "You," she croaked. "I thought I smelled rotten eggs."

"Saskia! You're all right!" Penny said.

"And just as rude as ever!" Baldwin added.

"She's probably in shock." Wiggy rocked Saskia. "How do you feel, my dear?"

"I'm so cold." Saskia trembled and pressed her forehead to Wiggy's lace collar. "Oh, I had such awful dreams. . . ."

"She needs rest," Wiggy said. "Rest and perhaps a nice hot bath, Saskia? Tea? Baldwin, will you take her to Ludowiga? You'll have to explain what happened. She'll be most distraught."

"All's well that ends well," Baldwin philosophized. He pulled Saskia from the queen's embrace and swung her over his shoulder. "Upsy-daisy!"

"Careful, you galoot!" Saskia moaned. "I got this dress in Paris!"

"And, Penelope," Wiggy continued, "please show Anastasia's friends to the ballroom. I shall have a word with the Wish Hags, and then, I think, with Anastasia. Anastasia, you'll wait for me in my chamber."

28

The Birthday Cake Wish Bill

BACK IN WIGGY'S chamber, Penny smoothed Anastasia's ragged braids. "Don't worry, dear. Everything will work out."

"We'll see you later." Gus bopped her shoulder with his fist as everyone filed from the queen's room.

"Well, Peeps," Anastasia whispered, "I'm in bog water for sure."

Pippistrella chirruped and clung to her collar.

"What happened in there?" Aisatsana demanded. "You look like you wrestled a bear, and so do *I*!"

"I'll tell you later." Anastasia turned from the mirror-girl and limped over to Wiggy's chain-mail-curtained bed. "What do you think Grandwiggy's going to do?" she whispered to Pippistrella. "Do you think she'll exile me, like Saskia said?"

"Squeak!"

"I can't understand you." Tears trickled down Anastasia's cheeks. "I only speak one word of Echolalia, and I can't metamorphose. I'm a terrible Morfo and a worse princess." She leaned her forehead against the metal filigree. "And now I'll never find the Silver Hammer. I'll never find Nicodemus and my dad. The Canopy is ruined."

"Anastasia."

She whirled. Wiggy was standing by the Glimmerglass, watching her. "You've had quite an exciting birthday, haven't you?"

Anastasia swallowed and stared at her feet.

"What you did today was extremely dangerous."

"I'm sorry." Anastasia wiped her face on her sleeve. Pippistrella's pulse thumped against her neck, and she wondered whether, as her loyal bat-in-waiting, her furry friend would also be banished abovecaves.

"Dangerous and *brave*," Wiggy continued. "You risked your life to save Saskia. I'm very, very proud of you."

"Proud?" Anastasia's head snapped up. "Then you're not mad?"

"Well," Wiggy pondered, "I'm displeased that you sneaked into my private cavern. And it particularly troubles me that you rendered a Royal Guard Bat unconscious to do so. The Royal Guard *must* be on the alert at all times, you understand. We need to watch for . . . certain enemies."

"Witches?"

Wiggy's strange eyes gleamed. "Imagine the disaster if witches returned. The Royal Guard is here to sound the alarm if that should ever occur. You saw what the Wish Hags can do; witch magic is even more powerful."

Anastasia gulped. "I'm sorry."

"I know you are." Wiggy's solemn lips slid into something like a smile. "I think we'll have to order a suit of chain mail for you. You're becoming rather the adventuress, my dear. You remind me of myself when I was young—when I was a warrior queen charging into the Perpetual War."

"Really?"

"In some ways."

Anastasia paused. "Grandwiggy . . . will Gus's mom get into trouble? Honestly, she didn't know we took her locket. And to her it's just jewelry—she wasn't doing anything bad with it."

Wiggy thought. "I won't penalize her, but I can't return the portrait. After the royal jeweler has prized Mrs. Wata's picture from the locket, we'll return the necklace." Perhaps perceiving Anastasia's torment, the queen went on, "I'll ask the court painter to fashion a miniature of Gus to replace the gorgon likeness. Does that seem fair? I'm sure Mrs. Wata would be happy to have a cameo with her son's portrait."

Anastasia heaved a deep breath. "Thank you, Grandwiggy."

Wiggy reached out and stiffly patted Anastasia's sleeve. "All right, Princess. You may go. I believe we still have a birthday to celebrate, don't we?"

"Splendid! Just splendid!" Baldwin beheld the Grand Ballroom with delight. Balloons bumped amidst the chandeliers, their long ribbons twirling down to graze tall wigs sprouting from the crowd of guests. Bats cavorted overhead, flinging confetti down on the partygoers. Pippistrella zoomed by to bomb Anastasia with glitter, then wheeled off into the stalactites. "A birthday marvelment indeed!"

"Have you seen Mr. Yukimori's ice sculpture?" Penny asked.

"It's super!" Gus said. "It looks just like an electric eel!"

"And it *tastes* like a kiwi fizzer," Ollie added.

"This is my favorite song!" Baldwin cried. "Penny, hold my soda! I'm going to ask that fetching Veronica Bunion to foxtrot with me!" He danced off as the musicians struck up a jaunty tune, Quentin's saw warbling like a ghostly canary.

"Soda, my foot." Penny sniffed Baldwin's glass. "There's something much stronger than soda in here."

"When are they going to bring out the cake?" Ollie asked.

"It should be any minute now, dear," Penny said. She

slugged back the remainder of Baldwin's not-soda. "I'm going to fetch your birthday present, Anastasia. Wait right here."

Despite the frolicsome fun around them, gloom steeped the Dreadfuls' faces.

"What are we going to do about our quest?" Gus asked. "I don't think anyone's ever going to dream in the Canopy again."

"I don't think the Canopy really worked anyway," Ollie said. "Anastasia's dream about the Wish Hags was all wrong. That wish-goop didn't help Saskia."

"But it led us to Borg," Gus argued. "It's like the Canopy *knew* the hags would come after us."

"Just how far did you get in your first dream before Saskia woke you up? Did you see the Hammer?" Ollie asked.

"No. I hardly saw anything," Anastasia lamented. "I was swimming, and I saw stars . . . I think. I could breathe underwater. Oh—shh. Here comes my uncle."

"Whew!" Baldwin tottered up to them, dabbing his forehead with a handkerchief. "That Veronica has the stamina of an Olympic jitterbugger! Say, where's my drink?"

"All hail the queen! All hail the queen!" someone cried.

The musicians muzzled their instruments as Wiggy glided into the ballroom. "Good evening. We are all here to celebrate a very special event: my granddaughter's *eleventh* birthday."

A cheer went up. Mr. Yukimori shouted, "Happy birthday, Princess Anastasia!"

"And celebrate it we shall, in just a moment. But now I have an important announcement to make," Wiggy went on. "This evening marks another momentous occasion, for I have just signed a diplomatic treaty with the Wish Hags."

Several people gasped.

"Recent inquiries have revealed that any suspicion surrounding their names in the eighteenth century was entirely unfounded. The Wish Hags were innocent of any witchery or witch-sympathy, and the persecution they suffered was unjust. Hags, please come forth."

The eyeless Wish Hags shuffled through the door, their chain mail chinkling. Tall One raised her shrill voice. "We realize that our wish-granting has been, at best, erratic for the past few centuries. However, we promise to henceforth do our best to grant wishes, within reason, of course. We can't grant *every* wish—that would be impossible, you know—but we will be more generous—"

"Can the chatter, Maude!" cut in Spectacles. "You always did ramble on! Princess Anastasia, we hags shall grant your birthday wish as our first act under the new treaty."

Wiggy twitched her index finger, and two servants wheeled forth a dessert trolley trembling beneath a magnificent cake a-twinkle with eleven candles, plus "one to grow on." The musicians played a note, and the crowd began to sing:

Happy birthday! You're oh so old:
If you were cheese, then you'd have mold!
Hip, hip, hooray, and all that rot;
Now make a wish for what is not!

A hush fell over the ballroom as a third attendant set up a ladder beside the cake. Anastasia climbed the rungs and, once at the top, craned her head toward the glittering candles. She closed her eyes. Her cheeks puffed around the wish percolating her wits. Would it work? *Could* it? Could the hags possibly brew a wish *that* powerful?

WSSSSSHHHHHHH! The flames fizzled into trailing plumes of smoke.

"Out in one breath!" Baldwin reported, and everyone looked at the Wish Hags.

"Well," said Maude, "we think . . ."

"Your wish is strange but fine," said Spectacles.

"And we shall be delighted to grant it!" proclaimed Bottle Hair.

If every single person in the ballroom had a bit of dynamite powder in their soul, then the Wish Hags' words ignited this powder. The crowd erupted into applause.

"But remember," Maude warned, "you mustn't reveal your birthday wish! If you blab it, it won't come true!"

"Birthday wishes must be brewed in an atmosphere of absolute secrecy," said Bottle Hair.

"Article Seventy-six, Clause Two of the Birthday Cake Wish Bill: spilling the beans renders your wish null and void," cited Spectacles.

"Crumbs," Ollie moped as Anastasia tiptoed back to the floor. "I'm dying of curiosity!"

"You'll find out soon," Anastasia promised.

"Here, dear," Penny said. "Here's your present from Baldy and me." She pressed a box riddled with holes into Anastasia's hands.

"This is what you had to go into Dinkledorf for?" Anastasia asked.

Baldwin nodded. "This birthday present is the culmination of weeks of plotting, secret communiqués, and a hush-hush transatlantic voyage for two of our best spies."

"Really?" Gus cried. "Open it, Anastasia!"

She tore off the lid. "MUFFY!"

"Who's Muffy?" Ollie asked.

"My guinea pig." Anastasia pulled the fluffy rodent into a hug. "We had to leave her back in Mooselick when we escaped."

"Our agents had to fetch Muffy with the greatest caution," Penny said. "We knew the minions of CRUD would be watching to see if we came back for her."

"Oh, Muffy! I missed you! Muffy—*ow!*" Anastasia peered at her thumb, prickled with tiny teeth marks.

"She must be fussy after her long trip," Penny hypothesized.

"Muffy's always like this," Anastasia said. "She'll probably poop on my pillow tonight, too. Oh, thank you! Thank you so much!"

Baldwin's eyes glossed with tears. "I just love happy endings. And a happy ending plus a happy birthday is the happiest thing of all."

Anastasia nodded, cradling her guinea pig. But, she thought, if her birthday wish came true, this wasn't an ending at all. It was just the Beginning, and the Beginning of Something Very Big at that.

Early the next Monday morning, Anastasia jolted upright in bed, her head still swimming with dream-shadows. What time was it? She fumbled in the pocket of her pajama pants for Miss Viola's watch and held its face close to the bedside candle. Five o'clock. The science fair was in a mere three hours.

She sank back against her comforters, trying to knit the gossamer shreds of her dream back together. The Wish Hags had granted her birthday wish and delivered it swiftly to the fanciful dream-center of her nighttime mind. If only she could remember . . . She closed her eyes. Shadows. Shadows dancing. Not Ollie and Quentin. Lovely, lacelike shadows . . .

Anastasia's breath caught in her throat. She slid from her bed and padded to her wardrobe and flung back the doors. She rummaged for Calixto Swift's biography, stashed beneath two pairs of unworn silk slippers. She opened the tome to the very middle page and pulled out the witch's paper doll.

But it wasn't a paper doll. Not really. Anastasia returned to her candle and held the paper maiden before the flame. Her delicate silhouette sprang into being on the wall, filigreed tattoos traced in shadow. Anastasia tugged the paper arms, watching the shadow creature dance and wave.

"Pippistrella! Pippistrella, wake up!" she urged. "I need you to deliver a message to the rest of the league!"

29

Look and Ye Shall Find

"CONGRATULATIONS, CHILDREN!" PENNY cheered for the umpteenth time, smiling proudly as she straightened the blue award ribbon festooning Anastasia's lapel. "Winning the Pettifog Academy Science Fair is a tremendous accomplishment!"

"It's a grand achievement," Baldwin agreed. "Just grand!"

"Squeak!" Pippistrella chimed in.

Gus grinned. He grinned so broadly that his smile crept all the way over into Anastasia's face. The good score from their Musical Wheel for Discerning Mice would bump her own class grades into a pretty nice place—she didn't think Marm Pettifog would flunk her for the year.

"And I understand Mrs. Wata has sworn off eating mice," Penny added. "That pleases me to no end!"

Gus nodded. "She said she could never eat another mouse, knowing that they appreciate music."

Ollie beamed, and so did Anastasia. As an aspiring veterinarian-detective-artist, she was happier about Mrs. Wata's dietary switch than snagging a frilly first-place ribbon. Of course, watching Saskia fling her Certificate of Second Place ("For a Decent Effort!") to the floor and storm from the Pettifog auditorium had been plenty satisfying, too. It was the cherry atop an already delectable sundae.

"Was that your birthday wish?" Ollie whispered. "That we'd win the fair?" He glanced at the Dreadfuls' acclaimed invention. One keen-whiskered, nimble-footed rodent jogged within the twirling mouse wheel, cranking the cylinder of the attached music box. *Tinkle bingle tingalingaling!*

Anastasia shook her head. "No. But my wish came true this morning. It didn't take the hags long to brew it."

"We need to celebrate your triumph!" Baldwin said. "How about a trip to the Soda Straw?"

"Actually, Baldy," Ollie said, "I promised my brother that I'd go with him to the Cavepearl Theater. He has—um—"

"A new solo he wants us to hear," Gus interjected. "He's practicing with the Nowhere Special Orchestra this afternoon for the upcoming symphony."

"There he is!" Ollie said, standing on tiptoe to find Quentin amidst the hubbub of young Pettifog scientists packing up their projects. "Q! Q!"

"Can Peeps and I go, too?" Anastasia pleaded.

"Well—" Penny hesitated, no doubt thinking of the Dreadfuls' perilous shenanigans the weekend before.

"How could we deny these triumphant scientists their fun?" Baldwin said. "Run along with your friends, Anastasia, and we'll come pick you up in an hour."

"Thanks!" Anastasia grabbed Gus's and Ollie's hands and pulled them to Quentin before Penny could protest.

"So, what's your big surprise?" Quentin asked as they fled Pettifog Academy to hurry by alley and avenue toward the opera house. "Pippistrella wouldn't tell us much this morning. She just flew over before school and told me what to bring." He jiggled his saw case, rattling its secret contents.

"I think it has something to do with her birthday wish," Ollie said. "What did you wish for, Anastasia? You can tell us. It's already come true."

"I wished to finish the dream I started on my birthday. The one about swimming."

"What happened?" Gus quizzed.

"It was really short," Anastasia said. "I swam into a tunnel, and at the end there was a dancing shadow. A *man's* shadow."

"Was it Nicodemus?" Quentin puzzled. "He's a Shadowman."

"Nope. I'm getting to it. When I woke up and thought about it, I realized that I hadn't been swimming at all,"

Anastasia said. "I'd been *floating*. And the twinkles around me weren't stars—they were twinkle beetles."

"Like in Mrs. Honeysop's cavern?" Gus asked.

"Exactly. And the shadow wasn't a Shadowman. Remember that paper doll I found in the witch's bedroom?" Anastasia slipped the paper maiden from her satchel. "It's not a doll. It's a *shadow puppet*."

"So what?" Ollie said. "So the old witch liked puppets. Why is that important?"

"Calixto Swift made puppets," Anastasia said. "Ludowiga told me a mob killed Calixto at his last puppet show, and that people said 'even the puppet screen bled that night.' I thought she meant the painted scenery at the back of a little puppet stage, but maybe it was the screen of a *shadow puppet* theater. And if Calixto used shadow puppets . . . maybe he made this one and gave it to Mrs. Honeysop."

"I wonder if *Calixto* enchanted that cavern to be zero gravity," Gus pondered. "That would take pretty powerful magic, you know. I don't know if an everyday witch could do it."

"But there aren't any tunnels in Mrs. Honeysop's house," Ollie said.

"No tunnels," Anastasia agreed, "but there *is* a fireplace. And fireplaces have chimneys."

"We *have* been lucky with chimneys," Quentin said. "That's how we escaped St. Agony's Asylum, Gus." He led them through the musician's side entrance and into the theater. "I'm skipping practice to come with you, so we have to be extra-stealthy when we're sneaking out the back."

Fortunately, the backstage area was deserted. The Dreadfuls sidled through the hole in the back corner and into Sickle Alley, and thence ran to Mrs. Honeysop's strange old house.

"Why, this is fun!" Quentin cried, executing a somersault in the parlor. His Pettifog wig levitated off his head and swirled up to the stalactites.

Anastasia, however, had no time for acrobatics. She beelined to the fireplace grille, lacing her fingers through the mesh to keep from drifting away. "See how the gate is bolted down? I thought it was to keep it from sailing off, but maybe it's to hide something that's inside the chimney. Quentin, did you bring your dad's tools?"

"Yep." Quentin opened his saw case. "All in here—oops."

Metal gizmos floated from the trunk and began to wander the parlor. Anastasia grabbed a screwdriver and fiddled with the screen. "One," she muttered as the first rivet blurted from its hole. "Two . . ."

"What do you think is in the chimney?" Ollie asked. "The Silver Hammer?"

"I don't know . . . three . . . four . . ."

After Anastasia had prized loose all the bolts, the Dreadfuls tamped the tips of their screwdrivers in the seam between the grate and the wall. They wriggled and wiggled the steely tips of their tools, cracking the screen from the stone bit by bit until at last it wrenched free. Anastasia shoved the grate aside and stuck her head into the fireplace.

"Tons of twinkle beetles," she reported. "Just like my dream. I'm going up! You stay here in case—well, just in case."

"In case it's some kind of Calixto Swift booby trap?" Ollie faltered.

"Something like that." She pulled herself into the flue, floating up amongst the glittering insects, her petticoats puffing around her kicking legs, Pippistrella clinging to her back like a baby opossum. It was easy to imagine she was traveling through a starry tunnel to outer space. Through the glow she rose, remembering Baldwin murmuring to her in the HMB *Flying Fox: Find your star and follow it, Anastasia. Trust your star over anybody else's idea of where you should go.*

The bugs shining her way may not have been real stars, but she sensed that, for the moment, she was just where she was supposed to be.

"I'm at the top," she called.

"Did you find anything?" Gus asked.

A swarm of twinkle beetles corked the chimney. She brushed them aside, scattering the glow. "Shoo."

"Anastasia!" Quentin hallooed. "What's up there?"

The last bugs glided off, winking their annoyance.

"Anastasia!" Ollie cried.

Craning her neck, Anastasia could now see what lay at the end of the tunnel. Her eyes widened.

"Anastasia!" Quentin bellowed.

"I don't think this was ever really a fireplace." Her voice trickled down the shaft.

"What is it, then?" Gus asked.

"It's a secret passageway. And it leads to a trapdoor."

The click of a doorknob, the squeal of old hinges, and then . . . silence.

"I'm not just going to wait here," Gus muttered, diving into the chimney. Quentin and Ollie followed behind him, and they shimmied up the flue and through the little door at the end.

Anastasia's eyes, big and bright in the glow of a match, turned to meet theirs. She touched the match to the tapers of a candelabrum and shined it around the secret chamber. A massive wooden desk drifted through the cavern like a drowned ship, flurrying a school of little vials. An hourglass cruised by, sand swimming in its fragile bulbs. Thick books hovered in the dust, their yellow pages fanned open.

Gus peered at the silver letters stamped on one tome's spine. *"Codex of Spells!"*

"Witch books are forbidden," Ollie yipped. "They burned them years ago."

"This one's handwritten," Gus said. "*Protection Spell . . . Binding a Looking Glass . . . Curative Spell for Ye Stomack Maladie* . . . oops!"

A flock of shadow puppets fluttered from between the book's folios and meandered into the gloom.

The Dreadfuls stared at each other.

"I think," Quentin murmured, "we've found Calixto Swift's secret study."

"I think you're right." Gus peeled back the pages of *Codex of Spells* to show them a green-inked inscription inside the front cover: FROM THE LIBRARY OF C.S.

There are times in life, dear Reader, when a fierce and sudden certainty will grip every itty-bitty atom of your body, and that certainty is this: *you tremble on the threshold of something momentous.* Something life-changing. Something that shall click the stars of your fate into position like the tumblers of a picked golden lock. Anastasia tottered on that threshold now. Somewhere, she savvied—scrawled in those books, or sealed in a bottle, or locked in the desk—was the next crumb in the magical trail leading to Nicodemus and his Fred-finding compass. *Look and ye shall find.*

She dredged another match from her pocket and lit the tapers of a candelabrum. The glow tangoed with the drifting puppets, festooning the walls with children and butterflies and unicorns and dragons. Anastasia swanned through this shadowy kaleidoscope to a glass-fronted cabinet at the study's far end. The curios inside clinked against its crystalline breast like creatures trying to escape: seashells and blood-red branches of coral, bejeweled boxes, suspiciously bonelike bits and bobs, and *there,* glinting in the darkest corner—

There it was. The slender silver fuse that ignited a Perpetual War. The device of centuries of misery, and perhaps also the instrument for that misery's undoing. It seemed nothing more than a rod capped with a metal wedge, crooking on one side into a double-pronged claw. And yet, Anastasia knew, it was the only tool in the world capable of uprooting the nails binding the Silver Chest, releasing Nicodemus to point the way to her father.

"We found it," she whispered. *"The Silver Hammer."*

You and Your Wig

Greetings . . . and *congratulations*! Your selection of a 100 percent genuine Marvelmop Wig distinguishes you as a person of taste and refinement! As the world's preeminent wiggier since 1703, I have upholstered the pates of monarchs, knights, and other uppercruster types . . . and now YOU!

—*What Is a Wig?*—

I'm so *glad you asked! Certain vulgarians would have you believe that a wig is nothing more than artificial hair slopped upon one's noggin—a sort of hair hat. Piffle! This couldn't be farther from the truth! The wig is an exterior extension of your personality, hopes, and dreams—indeed, your wig is* your soul made manifest (with hair!). *What else can a wig offer you?*

❧ *Elevated Social Status*—A Marvelmop Wig is incontrovertible proof that you are RVII (Really Very Important Indeed). You are fashionable! You know what's what! You are probably very, very rich!

❧ *Companionship—Never Be Lonely Again!* Your wig is your constant companion, escorting you everywhere, sharing in all your joys and worries. You'll find your wig to be an excellent confidant. It won't blab your secrets—it *can't*! One of my royal clients appointed *his* wig chancellor of the realm, and it worked out really well for everyone.

Protection—Your wig will warm and shelter you in *every* situation. Protect your ears and eyebrows from frostbite with my Arctic Explorer wig. Or for those in warmer climes: promenade in the park with confidence! Should a gaggle of incontinent geese or ducks fly overhead, your wig shall shield you from all things fowl.

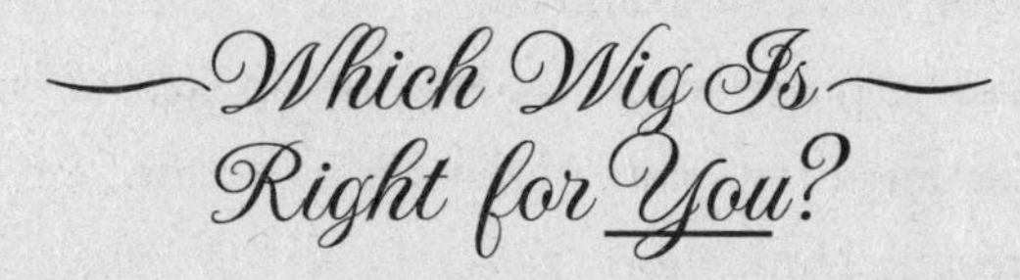

Which Wig Is Right for You?

The choice of your wig is a difficult matter,
It isn't just one of your holiday larks;
You may think at first I'm as mad as a hatter
When I tell you, your wig is part FATE and part ART!

The linking of wig with head is a mystical alchemy of *destiny* and *artistry.* Many wig disciples profess that *they* didn't choose their wig: 'twas a union forged by fortune's stars (and *my* wiggier know-how!). For this reason, the best way to seek your wig is to visit my atelier. Meet me, and meet my wigs. Chat with them and find common interests—or, perhaps, *fall in love at first sight.* However, in the sad event that you cannot grace my shop in person, then I urge you to avail yourself of the attached, convenient wig order form. First, take my Marvelmop Patented Wig Quiz.

Wig Quiz

Set aside an hour or two—don't rush! This is a Matter of Utmost Importance! Consider each question carefully, and circle the appropriate answer.

Your dream vacation would be:

1. A perilous transatlantic hot-air balloon voyage
2. Visiting an all-you-can-eat cheese buffet in picturesque Dinkledorf
3. Getting a pedicure and/or lobotomy at St. Agony's Lunatic Asylum and Bed & Breakfast

If you were a dessert, you would be:

1. A hasty pudding
2. A figgy pudding
3. A figgy pudding that wishes it were a plum pudding

You prefer to spend your free time:

1. Knitting. If not knitting, then crocheting.
2. Reading exciting tales about intrepid children, especially if those tales include a s'mores reference or two
3. Laughing at peasants while munching cake in an opulent palace

What is your favorite color?

1. Magenta
2. Hot pink
3. Fuchsia

With which historical figure do you most identify?

1. A Scrabble-loving monarch
2. A wise diplomat who moonlights as a scullery maid
3. A scullery maid who moonlights as a wise diplomat moonlighting as a scullery maid

Which would you like to receive for your birthday?

1. An elegant cuckoo clock
2. A unicorn
3. A practical gift, like socks or an elegant cuckoo clock

What is the quality you value most in a wig?

1. Comfort
2. Height
3. Loyalty

Which best describes your personal style?

1. A posh hybrid of eighteenth-century luxury and nineteenth-century bustles
2. Ascots, ascots, and more ascots!
3. What's an ascot?

Which is your favorite canine?

1. A beautifully groomed poodle

2. A shaggy-chic sheepdog

3. A Labradoodle in a wig

Please send your results, along with your head measurements (circumference; top of eyebrow to hairline; ear to ear), to Sir Marvelmop, the Michelangelo of Wigs (that is, *me*!), at 729 Crescent Way, Nowhere Special, Under Dinkledorf, Switzerland. Then wait by your mailbox in breathless anticipation. . . . YOUR DESTINY ARRIVES (by parcel post, shipping and handling not included)!

If You Chose Mostly 1s

Your noble coconut is full of Great Thoughts and destined for Great Things! Have you considered a career in politics, law, or cheesemongery? You'll need a wig befitting your dignified vocation—might I suggest Caesar's Toupee (pre-garnished with laurels)? Do you crave a weighty hairpiece to match your mental gravitas? My twenty-pound Philosopher's Mop has festooned the noggins of notable eggheads for centuries! Or if world domination is your cup of tea, my Machiavelli wig is custom-designed to strike fear in the hearts of your enemies. (Caution: it may also inspire *love*!)

If You Chose Mostly 2s

Egads—aren't *you* the daredevil! Whether your next adventure is aboard a roller coaster or at the end of a bungee cord, you require a lionhearted wig that can hang on for the ride! Don my streamlined and chic Whirligig for trapeze tricks, skydiving, and other aerial stunts. (Each Whirligig purchase includes one *free* tube of Bouffant Bond, guaranteed to keep your coiffure in place through even the most hair-raising exploits!) Are you an aquatic explorer? Then the Snorkeler's Delight would be a *perfect* fit: it's waterproof and sharkproof, and it even doubles as a life vest in a pinch (number one bestseller amongst mermaids, octopi, and pirates)! Planning a life-or-death duel? Try the Swashbuckler; Alexander Hamilton sported this gallant wig when he bit the bullet in 1804, and he looked *smashing*!

If You Chose Mostly 3s

Poetical and starry-eyed, you while away your hours in daydreams and fairylands. You'll need a whimsical wig for jaunts to your castle in the sky; might I suggest Rapunzel's Beehive? Or if you're feeling peckish, sample one of my edible cotton-candy toupees—at last you can satisfy your sweet tooth whilst dazzling your imaginary friends! For the truly capricious, my Make-Believe Wig is a must-have: weightless and infinitely versatile, this hairpiece changes to suit your every whim—just add a dollop of your own favorite fancy, and this wig metamorphoses into *whatever you want*!

Were Your Answers Divided Equally Amongst Numbers?

Then you are Admirably Well Rounded—a true Renaissance sort! You'll require wigs from every category—lucky, lucky you!

THE AUTHOR WISHES TO THANK

Her Most Honorable Bee's Knees,
The Right Splendid Agent,
Dame of the Order of Golden-Limned Letters,
Lady
Brianne Johnson

&

Her Most Excellent Editrix,
The Grand Duchess of the Printed Page,
The Baroness of the Ripping Yarn,
Peach of the Realm
Shana Corey

* * * * in addition to * * * *

The Noble Peerage of Joy-Practitioners at
Random House Children's Books

FEELING ADVENTUROUS?

LOOK FOR

THE LEAGUE OF BEASTLY DREADFULS

BOOK 3: The Witch's Glass

Coming Soon!

1
The Marvelous Flop

ANASTASIA WAS DREAMING about her father.

She was back in the McCrumpet house, back on the morning before tragedy had turned her life upside down. Rain spattered the windows, but the kitchen was warm and homey and smelled of waffles. Anastasia had not yet been kidnapped. She was sitting at the table eating marmalade. Mr. McCrumpet had not yet vanished. He was slopping cinnamony batter onto the griddle.

It should have been a cozy dream. And yet somewhere in the depths of her slumbering brainbox, Anastasia was uneasily aware of the grim events that, in reality, had followed this ordinary breakfast. Dream-Anastasia stared at her flour-dusted father, knowing she wouldn't see him again for many months. Perhaps she would never see him again. In fact . . . his face was growing hazy right before her eyes. The harder she looked at Fred McCrumpet, the foggier he became. "Dad!" She blinked—and blinked—

Anastasia blinked awake, her heart thumping a panicked little tattoo. Sleep still fuzzed her peepers; she blinked again. Something felt different. Something felt *wrong*. Her bones ached. Her head throbbed. Green and pink shapes wobbled in her vision. Her eyelids stuttered as she strained to focus, the blurs finally crystallizing into a design of roses and briars pricked out in nimble stitches. It was, she realized, the embroidered canopy on her new bed in her new home, thousands of miles away from the McCrumpet abode. But why did the roses look so *big*, floating above like squashed pink clouds?

Anastasia swallowed and called to her lady-in-waiting: "SQUEEEEEAK!"

If she had been possessed of hands, Anastasia would have covered her mouth in shock. However, she now discovered, *she didn't have hands.* She had great bulky flaps—*wings!*—and these she rustled in alarm.

Anastasia McCrumpet had turned into a bat.

For the first eleven years of her life, Anastasia played the part of an ordinary child to perfection. She played it so well that even she believed she was utterly average. She had mousy-brown hair and mousy-brown eyes and exactly 127 freckles. Were you to bump into her at the ice cream parlor or the post office or the library, you probably wouldn't give her a second glance. Anastasia didn't have what the bigwigs in Hollywood call *star quality.*

But all the time she was brushing her teeth, tripping over her shoelaces, and attending to the thousands of other tiny chores that make up a normal human life, a potpourri of secrets simmered in her blood—secrets so secret that even *she* didn't know them. However, by age ten and three-quarters, these hidden truths had started bubbling up into her daily existence.

I wonder, dear Reader, what sort of secrets might be brewing inside *you.*

Perhaps the biggest, strangest, most shocking secret of all was that Anastasia McCrumpet, despite all outward appearances, was not entirely *human.* But you already knew that. After all, how many humans wake up as fuzzy, pointy-eared, moth-craving bats?

"Squeak! Squeak! Screeee!"

Anastasia tumbled from the bedstead and onto the floor, landing in a tangle of wings. "Peep!" Her mind twirled in a wild carousel of shock and confusion and fear: *It's happened, just as they said it would. . . . Why does everything hurt so much? . . . I'm a bat I'm a bat I'm a bat!*

"Princess Anastasia! We've come for your morning toilette!"

CLUNK! CLUMP! STOMPITY-STUMP! Anastasia swiveled her head to glimpse a herd of monstrous silk slippers, buffalo-big, stomping across the marble floor.

"And I've brought something to—why, where *is* the little twerp?"

Anastasia's sensitive bat eardrums amplified the irritation in her aunt Ludowiga's voice. Even in the midst of her shock and fear, Anastasia cringed. She had two aunts, one good and one bad, and Ludowiga *wasn't* the good one.

"Are you *hiding*, you silly twit?" Ludowiga demanded. "Show yourself, girl! You've already weaseled out of one bath this week—"

"Squeak!" Anastasia cried.

"Well, well. What do we have here?" Ludowiga stooped. Her face (enormous—she was bigger than the Statue of Liberty!) lurched into view. "Look who *finally* metamorphosed."

Anastasia let out an unhappy peep.

"Well?" Ludowiga glowered at her. "Why are you lying on the floor like a senseless banana peel? Get up. *Fly!*"

With great effort, Anastasia wriggled her wings.

Ludowiga gawped, aghast. "Princess! *Can't you fly?*"

But at that moment, in a flash and a twinkling, Anastasia morphed back into a girl.

"Anastasia!" Baldwin Merrymoon exclaimed, his voice warm with admiration. "Just *look* at your mustache!"

Baldwin possessed a beautiful ginger-colored mustache of his own, and he took great joy in its everyday grooming and display. Unlike her uncle, Anastasia had never sported whiskers of any kind. She was, as you will remember, a normal-looking eleven-year-old girl most of the time, and most normal-looking eleven-year-old girls do not have enormous handlebar mustaches sprouting from their upper lips. But this morning, she did.

"Oh my!" Penny Merrymoon cried, staring as Anastasia slunk into the dining hall. Penny was Anastasia's *good* aunt. She was lovely and patient and full of hugs.

Over the previous three months, Anastasia's family tree had plopped forth all kinds of heretofore-unknown relatives. Some of them were sweet peaches, like Aunt Penny, and some of them were bad apples, like Ludowiga. Uncle Baldwin was another of these strange fruits. Fortunately, he was a peach.

"My darling, did you *shift*?" Penny asked.

"Of course she shifted, Penny!" Baldwin said. "Where else would she have gotten that splendid mustache?"

"When you first start morphing, a bit of animal fluff

sometimes sticks to you," Penny explained to Anastasia. "Back when I was your age, I'd keep a few whiskers after shifting into a mischief of mice. Don't worry, dear. That mustache will fall out by the end of the day."

"Pity," Baldwin said. "It's a beauty! If I didn't have such wonderful mustaches myself, I'd be *chartreuse* with envy."

Anastasia groaned, sitting down at the table. "I don't want to go to school with a mustache!"

"There, there," Penny consoled her. "I'm sure your classmates will understand. They're all starting to morph as well, you know."

Anastasia moped. "I've never seen a fifth grader with a mustache. And it's *itchy.*"

"One must suffer for beauty," Baldwin rhapsodized, patting his own cookie-duster.

"I *am* suffering," Anastasia said. "I feel like I have the flu."

"You're going to ache for a few days. It's no small feat, shrinking an eleven-year-old girl into a little six-ounce bat body and back again!" Baldwin beamed. "Ah! Your first morph! It's a landmark event in a Morfo's life!"

"Winthrop." Penny signaled to one of the white-wigged servants stationed in the dining hall. "Would you please bring some of Dr. Lungwort's Miracle Fizz? That will make you feel better, Anastasia." She reached over to squeeze Anastasia's hand. "How I wish your father could be here. He'd be so proud."

After discovering she was a Morfo, Anastasia had dreamed of the glorious day she would shift into another creature. Some Morfolk, like Baldwin, changed into wolves. Some metamorphosed into mice, like Penny. Two of Anastasia's very best friends, Ollie and Quentin Drybread, turned into shadows. However, most Morfolk, like Anastasia, changed into bats. A Morfling's first shift was generally the subject of hugs and hoorays. It was better than a birthday.

Anastasia, however, did not feel like jubilating. She felt as if someone had squished her through an old-fashioned clothes wringer.

Winthrop whisked back into the dining hall, bearing a domed platter. He removed the dome to reveal a goblet of water and two purple tablets on a saucer. Penny dropped the tablets into the goblet. The water started to fizz.

"Oh, the fun you'll have!" Baldwin said. "We'll take you abovecaves for moonlit flits—"

"Ahem." Ludowiga stormed into the dining hall. "Don't make any grand plans yet, Baldy. The princess *can't fly.* I discovered her this morning sprawled on the floor. She lay there and wiggled. And I've seen better wiggling in a worm!"

"We-ell." Penny hesitated. "The first few shifts are always awkward."

"This morning's performance was *beyond* awkward, Penny," Ludowiga snapped. "It was a *disaster.* It was, quite literally, a *flop.* It was a parody of proper metamorphosis."

"Oh, shove it, Loodie," Baldwin retorted. "Your *wig* is a parody of a stupefied poodle."

Ludowiga ignored him. "My Saskia flew *laps* around the palace the first time she metamorphosed. She zigzagged through the corridors like a stunt plane. She did loop-the-loops and barrel rolls and climbing spins and lazy eights. And then she adjourned to her chambers and morphed back into a well-bred girl and put on a charming gabardine gown for the Duchess of Cummerbund's tea party. It was all entirely *dignified.*"

Cheeks flaming, Anastasia slouched lower in her seat. She was now decently clad in her school uniform. However, at the moment of her shift from bat to girl form, she had been buck raving au naturel. She had crouched on the floor in her birthday suit, naked as a jaybird, before Ludowiga and the astonished maids.

Clothing was a cumbersome point of metamorphosis: one's duds didn't morph along with one's body. This irksome little detail yielded endless opportunities for embarrassment. Morfolk learned to control their morphs over time, but young Morflings' blood was unruly and mercurial and triggered shifts with neither rhyme nor reason.

Anastasia suddenly yearned to be one hundred years old. To a Morfo, that was still pretty young. Most Morfolk lived for centuries.

"Yes," Ludowiga said, "Saskia's first morph was a tour de force."

Anastasia winced and slugged down Dr. Lungwort's purple medicine, stifling a belch against the back of her hand. *Saskia.* Was she doomed to constant comparison with her cousin? She hadn't even met Saskia until three months earlier, and yet people constantly measured them against each other like specimens in a science experiment. Saskia had beautiful moon-blond hair (Anastasia's was mouse-brown)! Saskia glided like a swan on a cloud of silk (Anastasia clumped around in galoshes)! Saskia this; Saskia that. It was unbearable.

"I wonder," Ludowiga said, narrowing her eyes, "whether Anastasia will *ever* learn to fly. She is, you will remember, only half Morfo."

"Anastasia will be a proper aeronaut in no time," Baldwin huffed.

"I certainly hope so. It will shame the Crown if she sprawls on the floor like a dazed rat every time she shifts." Ludowiga sniffed. She was a big sniffer, Ludowiga. One whuffle of her pinched nose could express anything from disdain to delight. "You know, my Saskia is to dance the role of Vespertina in the Twinkle Toe Ballet's upcoming production of *Dance of the Sugarplum Bat.*"

"Bully for her," Baldwin said.

"Bully, nothing! Saskia's triumphs bring glory to the royal family. What has *this* one done to honor us lately?" Ludowiga aimed her nostrils at Anastasia. "You'd better shape up, Princess!" With one final, scornful snort, she sailed from the dining room.

Baldwin clapped Anastasia on the shoulder. "Don't let Loodie spoil this momentous occasion. That woman could find fault with *anything,* even a happy event like your first morph. Think of *that,* Anastasia: *you turned into a bat!* That's something *big.*"

"Something *marvelous,*" Penny agreed.

"A marvelous *flop,*" Anastasia said, Ludowiga's scorn still reverberating in her aching ears.

"Pshaw. Don't you start quoting Ludowiga to me! No, my girl, you're becoming a proper Morfo!" Baldwin enthused. "We need to get you abovecaves and into the moonlight. Moonglow is mother's milk to Morfolk. I know—let's go moonlight sledding tomorrow night! The Swiss hills are chock-full of top-notch sledding spots!"

Anastasia perked up. *"Moonlight sledding?"*

"Anastasia can't go gallivanting through the Swiss

hills right now, Baldy!" Penny protested. "CRUD is still hunting her."

Anastasia shivered, her memories scrolling back to her recent brush with the Committee for Rubbing-out Unnatural Dreadfuls. It had all started with a ride in a pink station wagon. You *must,* prudent Reader, keep your eyes peeled for these sinister vehicles! If you happen to see one, peek to see whether a child of perhaps ten or eleven or twelve years of age is sitting in the backseat. Look closely!

The sad statistical truth is that you are probably-most-definitely spotting the victim of a diabolical kid-napping scheme.

Now, if you can: get a glimpse into the front seat. That nice lady driving the car? She's the kidnapper. Even worse, she's a *murderess.* She's one of the most accom-plished and dangerous murderesses you could ever meet.

You are shocked. You are, perhaps, even scandalized. But pink station wagons and sweet-faced murderesses are just one of the thousands of unpleasant facts of life, much like ingrown toenails and tonsillitis and expired milk.

Not every kidnapper drives a pink station wagon. This particular automobile is the preferred mode of transport for the crème de la crème of kidnappers work-ing with CRUD. Have you heard of it? I suspect not, because CRUD is hush-hush. It *needs* to be, because CRUD is a villainous society devoted to abducting Morfolk like Anastasia. In CRUD's perspective, the more Morflings snatched and snuffed, the better. Each kidnapping brings joy to the members' hearts and delight to their souls. The minions of CRUD celebrate squelched children with cake and confetti and cards of congratulations. And CRUD rewards its most successful Watchers with a jolly pink station wagon, the perfect vehicle with which to lure children to their doom.

So, good Reader, I implore you: no matter what anyone tells you—

even if—

especially if—

she's a little old lady with rosy cheeks and a purse full of sugarplums—

NEVER GET INTO A PINK STATION WAGON.

Anastasia had, and all sorts of ghastliness ensued. And even though she had escaped CRUD and moved halfway across the world, she still had to be careful. CRUD was looking for her, and they had agents in every nook and cranny you could spot on globe or map.

Fortunately, Anastasia now lived in a village that showed up on neither globe nor map—at least, not any of the globes or maps CRUD Watchers might have at their disposal. This village was, you see, entirely *underground.*

"Anastasia should stay in Nowhere Special for now," Penny said, a fretful little line creasing her brow. "Especially while she's growing into her morphs. Imagine if she turned into a bat in the middle of Dinkledorf!"

"Anastasia can't stay underground *forever,* you know. That's no kind of life for a child." Mischief twitched Baldwin's mustache. "Besides, the sledding season isn't going to last much longer. Spring looms nigh, Penny! And *I* want to go sledding, too."

Penny bit her lip. "I'm not sure. . . ."

"It's settled," Baldwin proclaimed. "You can bring your friends, Anastasia. When it comes to moonlight sledding, the more, the merrier!"

Penny frowned, her gaze twitching to the stack of cold pancakes on Anastasia's plate. "You haven't touched your breakfast, child. My goodness, you don't look well at *all.* Should you stay home from the academy today?"

Most children would leap at the opportunity for a day off from school, but Anastasia did not make this leap. Despite the collywobbles curdling her tummy and the headache hammering her brain and the mustache bristling upon her upper lip, she was bursting at the seams to get to school. This was not, as you might think, because Anastasia was an especially diligent scholar. She wasn't.

Nope; Anastasia yearned to hightail it to Pettifog Academy for a different reason entirely. She was anxious to see her friends, aka the League of Beastly Dreadfuls. In the grand tradition of all great secret societies, the Dreadfuls had a Matter Most Urgent to discuss. They needed to work out the nitty-gritty of a Secret Mission of Life-and-Death Importance.

"I'm fine," she fibbed. "Dr. Lungwort's Miracle Fizz really helped."

"Oh, good," Penny said.

"Splendid stuff, that fizz," Baldwin declared. "Just a sip peps me full of get-up-and-go."

Anastasia nodded, even though Miracle Fizz had nothing to do with the moxie now propelling her schoolward. Her get-up-and-go issued from something far more potent than any potion or pill: a mixture equal parts love and fear, the powerful combination of which has propelled many brave souls directly into the waiting arms of Doom.

"Ready to go?" Penny asked.

Squaring her shoulders, Anastasia patted her mustache with her napkin. "Ready."